THE COST OF LIBERTY

STEPHEN
BEST OF LUCK
WITH ACADEMY

THE COST OF LIBERTY

MICHAEL SKEEN

BookVenture Publishing LLC
1000 Country Lane Ste 300
Ishpeming MI 49849
www.bookventure.com
Hotline: 1(877) 276-9751
Fax: 1(877) 864-1686

Ordering Information:
Quantity sales. Special discounts are available on quantity purchases by corporations, associations, and others. For details, contact the publisher at the address above.

Printed in the United States of America

Library of Congress Control Number		2016957044
ISBN-13:	Paperback	978-1-945960-05-5
	Hardcover	978-1-945960-06-2
	Pdf	978-1-945960-07-9
	ePub	978-1-945960-08-6
	Kindle	978-1-945960-09-3

Rev. date: 12/08/2016

To Pam and Mike, Angie and Morgan, Michelle and Mike, Tyler and Stacey, Victoria and Brian, Taylor, Madison, Grant, Carter, Mike, Aiden, Alex, Harper, Tristan, and Andy, you are all loved and a source of real pride for me. I pray that the events in this book always remain a figment of my imagination and never come to pass.

NOTE FROM THE AUTHOR

This book is fiction but not science fiction. The weapons and technology talked about in this book do exist.

The book refers to an EMP frequently. For those that do not know, an EMP is an electromagnetic pulse. This can be caused by the detonation of a nuclear weapon dozens of miles above the ground. The explosion would not cause buildings to fall but would send a wave across a large area that would greatly affect our lives. This pulse or wave is invisible and would not necessarily be felt by people that it passes through, however it would destroy all circuits and wiring unless it is specially protected. Few devises have this protection and neither does our electrical grid. The results would be that the computer you were using would simply stop working, as would your television, radio, cell phone, refrigerator, heating and cooling system, electric lights and all electric based appliances. Your cars would suddenly stop working since most newer cars have a computer managed operating system and so would commercial airliners who have computers on board to operate the engines and navigation. Life support systems in hospitals that are operated electrically would no longer work. These problems could be corrected but imagine the time it would take for new wire and circuits to be obtained and to replace in the items that were damaged.

The area of coverage would depend on the altitude of the detonation and the size of the nuclear explosion. In the first book of this series, 'The Cost of Freedom', an EMP occurs in the northeast and the southeast regions of the United States. This is the story of events that follow the EMP.

Michael Skeen

JUNE 4, 2018

MONDAY 9:00 AM

I walked over to a window in the room and looked outside. July fourth was a month away and during my lifetime that was a day of celebration; picnics, parades, and fireworks. Today, as I looked outside at the overcast skies I did not feel like celebrating instead I worried that I might not live till that day. Despite the dirty windows and the debris littering the inside of this room and others in this building, I now recognize the location. This was the embassy of Oman. I had visited here several times while I served as chief of staff to President T. J. Samuels. That seemed like a lifetime ago, before World War III began really going downhill.

I had been told when I arrived that I was brought to this location for debriefing but I was sure that the real reason was for execution. I knew that World War III was a long way from over however, for several weeks now I kept hearing that there have been only minor skirmishes as most hostilities had ended at least temporarily. The status of what was left of the world was reportedly considerably different than it was when I first went to work for President Samuels according to my guards. A host of smaller nations signed treaties with the major powers agreeing to pay fees for their safety. The map looked much different today than it did a few years ago. Russia stretched from the Baltic to China, north into the Arctic and south including France, Italy,

Greece and the surrounding countries. China now controlled Mongolia, much of Southeast Asia and all of the Pacific except the Philippines. The rest of the world including the United States was now part of the Islamic Caliphate, with the exception of Israel which still stood alone. At least this was what I had been told the status of the world was because I only knew what the Islamic guards passed on. Television, when you could find a working one, had been under the control of the caliphate now for about a year. I had heard rumors of fighting in the Midwest and many believed that the west was still free, but information was limited and only those that were able to find an open internet connection had access to information that had not been sanitized by the Islamic leaders. There was also the explosion that I heard after leaving the first detention site. It had been nearly a week now since I had been brought here but I had been treated well.

As I continued gazing out the window a light rain began to fall. The door behind me opened quietly and a man entered and announced that it was time for my interview. He then directed me into the hall and down the staircase to a room that appeared to have been the library. He took me to a table in the northeast corner of the room and instructed me to have a seat.

About fifteen minutes later a short man wearing a dark suit entered the room. After looking around the room he told his assistant something in Arabic and then walked over to where I was seated.

"Good morning, Mr. Ladner. I am Mohammed Ali Saud but you may simply call me sir. Do you understand?"

"Yes, sir."

"Very good. Let me explain what it is we hope to accomplish by bringing you here for this debriefing. I have been assigned the task of writing the official historical record of the events since 2017 that led to this violent and unnecessary war. I pride myself in doing very careful research in all of my assignments and this one will be no different. I know that you most likely have imagined many things in your head about what is going to happen here but let me assure you that no harm will come to you as long as you cooperate with my research. Of course, when I am finished and the official record is released you will be expected to support the document I release regardless of how closely it matches your memory, since I can assure you that my research will be correct. If you agree and comply with these requirements, no harm will come to you from the Islamic Caliphate. Do you understand and agree?"

This was not what I had expected since I arrived here and my mind was racing. What can I answer and if I answer questions am I committing treason? Of course, I believe that the United States officially may no longer exist today, so what am I committing treason against? I looked at Mr. Saud and replied, "Yes, sir."

"Excellent! Praise Allah."

His associate walked back into the room carrying a pitcher of water and two glasses. As he slid them onto the table there was another short conversation in Arabic between Saud and the man.

"Mr. Ladner, would you like something to drink?'

"Yes, please."

Saud then motioned for his associate to pour a glass of water which he then handed to me. I took a long slow drink of the warm water while watching Saud who never seemed to take his eyes off me. I was still uneasy and nervous and I am sure Saud was sizing me up.

"Mr. Ladner, I have studied the official records that we have obtained from the White House. I believe I am quite familiar with the first six months of the administration that you served. My main concern is what happened after that since the records are less helpful. I also want to know the thoughts and reasoning of your President Samuels in all of these actions. I know that you did not debrief his thoughts everyday but through your conversations you must have some insight into his thoughts. But first allow me to tell you what we know about the first six months.

"I know that the Russian President had worked with Mexican drug cartels to send a number of people into your country illegally who had been infected with a weaponized version of the smallpox virus. This became an issue in the first week of President Samuels's term. This was followed almost immediately by the insertion of offensive missiles in Venezuela. Next the Russian government persuaded the Chinese to call a loan and to attempt to take a large section of your country in place of the cash. This was followed by an attempt to insert drugs and terrorist into your country again by the Russian government. At this point your president reacted severely and there was much unnecessary bloodshed. This was followed by an attempted assassination and ultimately the deadly EMP attacks again controlled and instigated by Russia after your president had illegally captured

Vladimir and held him inappropriately. Does this agree with your recollection?"

As he finished he smiled at me and nodded his head affirmatively as if he was attempting to influence my answer.

"Much of what you said is true but there was much more involved and other countries involved in the events."

As I was finishing my sentence Saud's expression changed and he stood up and turned his back on me while walking across the room. Suddenly I felt a massive blow to the left side of my head. The force of the blow knocked me to the ground and before I could react I was being kicked repeatedly in the abdomen by Saud's associate. As I struggled for air the man picked me up off the ground and slammed me against the wall. He repeatedly struck me in the face and I could feel my eyes puffing up and my vision was becoming blurred. I could feel the warmth of my blood running down my face and I continued to struggle to breath. I heard a command in Arabic and the associate released me. I simply collapsed onto the floor.

As I struggled to remain conscious I saw Saud walk over to me and stare down at me. "You were told to agree completely. This is what will happen when you fail to obey my instructions. Be sure you remember this. We will talk again tomorrow."

As Saud left the room the associate and another man picked me up off the floor and took me back to my room. They dropped me onto the floor and at this point I became unconscious.

When I awoke I could see the sun just starting to shine into the window. I got up carefully because I felt as though I had been run over by a truck. I walked into the bathroom connected to the room because I had a real urge to piss but what filled the toilet was a coffee-colored liquid and I realized I needed medical attention. My vision was blurred and I felt warm as if I had a fever. I washed my face and tried to freshen up a little but the pain was still very severe. I walked over to the window and noticed a police car driving down the street in front of the embassy. When I was captured several weeks ago in Baltimore there were no police on the street, only Islamic fighters travelling around in open pickups. I thought how strange it was to see civilian police on the street instead of the sharia police or Islamic fighters, maybe something has changed. My belief that the United States had surrendered was based solely on what my capturers had told me but could that be propaganda? The last news I had received independently had indicated that Islamists had secured much of the northeast and the upper Midwest but that active battles were still raging in Texas and the lower Midwest. I had not seen the president since he boarded Air Force One back in June 2017. It was thought to be better to have him constantly moving to prevent another assassination attempt or his capture but to make sure that worked, I was not told where he was at either. I wasn't sure what to believe now.

One thing I was sure of though was that my interview would be starting soon and I had to make up my mind to cooperate or risk death. I was pretty sure I would not survive many beatings like the one I had yesterday so I was going to have to carefully keep Saud happy or face my death.

A woman, or at least what I believed to be a woman as she was covered with the exception of her eyes, entered my room carrying a tray of food. Without a word she placed the tray on a table near the window and then turned and left the room. I thought about the color of my urine and the way my abdomen felt, I wasn't sure if I should eat or not because I was worried that my physical condition could get worse. Then I looked at the tray; scrambled eggs, a small steak, toast with butter and grape jelly, coffee and orange juice. This was the best meal I had been given since they captured me, I had to eat what I could.

I tried to tell myself to eat slowly but I gulped it down quickly, and surprisingly it was very good. When I finished I just sat and stared out the window wishing to have the freedom to leave and resume my life again. My vision was blurred but it appeared that it was going to be a very nice day out. Birds were fluttering between trees and I even noticed people walking down the sidewalks as if all was good in the world. My senses were telling me that Saud and his gorilla were not being totally honest with me.

After a few minutes I heard Saud's associate walk into the room and as I turned he motioned for me to come with him. I was able to walk with some pain so I followed him down the long hallway and along the carpeted stairway into the library. This time Saud was waiting for me.

"Mr. Landry, we ended yesterday's session on a harsh note but I have to make sure you fully understand what is expected of you. I would like nothing more than to avoid that unfortunate scene in the future. I know that you may have some strong opinions on the details but you are no longer in power and your opinions do not matter. I want enough information from you to make sure my finished product will have something from both sides of this story. You do not have to like what I write but if you wish to continue your life you will have to publicly approve and if you feel you cannot do this then you are of no value to me. If you are of no value to me then I will turn you over to those who deal with government officials that do not cooperate. So, will you make yourself of value to me or should I not waste my time?"

"I will cooperate with you."

"Praise Allah! Now have a seat at the table and let's get started as I have only a limited amount of time to gather the information I need."

MAY 14, 2017

As the president and I entered the situation room the activity level was high. The president walked to his spot at the table and as he sat down Admiral McCain approached and sat down to his right.

"Mr. President, I have a couple of things to pass on to you of interest. First of all, we now have a relatively accurate initial count on casualties from the EMP attack. It appears that we lost 5,750 citizens as a result of the initial attack. Most of those in the northeast region and were the result of airplane crashes and traffic crashes. We now have national guard units providing security in New York, Pennsylvania, and Maryland. The southern region experienced a number of casualties as well but seems to be coping a little better. People in that region seemed to be better prepared and since the residences in that area are a little more separated there have been considerably fewer problems. The second issue is that the hyper-speed weapon is prepared and in the final stages before launch. We simply are awaiting your final order."

The president bowed his head for a moment and appeared to say a prayer. Then he turned to the admiral and said, "You can launch on my authority. The target is Tehran and you are authorized to use a tactical nuclear warhead. Is there anything else you need?"

The admiral indicated there was not and left the table to walk across the room to the communications center where he made the necessary communications with the army launch center in Alaska.

As I watched TJ he was restless and appeared concerned about what he had just authorized. I could see a glistening in his eyes as they watered like he was about to cry. He reached into his jacket pocket and pulled out a small bible. He turned to a specific page and began reading and rereading. I just sat there quietly as we both waited for word of the launch.

Admiral McCain shouted from across the room, "The missile has launched!"

Suddenly there was some commotion around the communications equipment and there was concern on all the faces of the officers working but they were talking in whispers that we could not understand across the room.

Admiral McCain approached the president with a very distressed look on his face. There were no tears in the admiral's eyes but his face showed his concern and left little doubt that something was terribly wrong. "Mr. President, I regret to inform you, sir, that the hyper-speed weapon exploded five seconds after liftoff. We have no idea as to why at this point, however, the fuel tanks on the engines may have malfunctioned causing the explosion. The falling debris injured several people on the ground. The nuclear warhead had not armed yet and fell nearby but should be easily recovered. It will take us a couple of days to get another launch vehicle prepared and that will be the last one we have capable for use. More are being assembled however it could take months before we have additional missiles available."

The president lowered his head and seemed to be carefully studying the top of the table. After about forty-five seconds of dead and very uncomfortable silence he looked up and straight into the eyes of Admiral McCain. "Admiral, I want a complete investigation conducted regarding what happened to that weapon. This is probably not what you expect to hear or want to hear but I have had a change of heart. Our 'eye for an eye' strategy has failed. Each time we retaliate it only leads to another action by the enemy that escalates from the prior one. The Lord says that we need to love our enemies and trust in Him. We haven't been doing that but I think it is time we change our attitude and start following this wisdom."

The admiral looked shocked and confused. He stood with a blank look on his face for about a minute and then replied, "What are my orders, sir?"

The president sat quietly for some time leaving everyone on edge. Finally, after at least two minutes the president turned to face Admiral McCain and stood up.

"Admiral, I want all military personnel currently in England, Germany, Japan, Spain, and Guam returned to the United States as quickly as feasible. You can maintain a small residual force at those locations you deem to be essential. I also want half of our forces in South Korea returned to the States. I want all of those troops then placed in the areas along our southern border and in the areas most recently victimized by the EMP attack. They are to assist in providing security on our border and in the EMP areas and in any other way they are qualified to help in these areas. Do you have any questions, admiral?"

The admiral replied that he had no questions and he returned over to the communications area of the room. The president then stood up and left the room without another word and went straight to his residence for the night. World War III was already underway even if it wasn't official but this decision was going to give the other side a huge advantage.

MAY 17, 2017

OVAL OFFICE

It was about 6:45 AM, when I arrived at the Oval Office to talk to the president about the events of the day. As I entered the outer office I was met by Patrick Simmons, the Secretary of Homeland Security. We knocked and entered the office together. The president was at his desk looking through newspapers from Miami and Chicago, since none of his regular east coast papers had published since the attack.

"Good morning, gentlemen. Have a seat." The president motioned for us both to sit down on the sofa opposite his desk as he moved to an overstuffed chair next to it.

Patrick Simmons didn't waste any time, opening a portfolio he had been carrying and starting at the top of his list. "Mr. President, I have a number of things here to brief you on and to obtain some guidance. First, the border patrol and customs have some serious concerns regarding our border crossings. It seems that the electronic monitoring is all off-line since the attack and they have simply been unable to keep up with the flow. Many of their vehicles were disabled and we have not been able to get many replacements to them yet. The scary part of this is that it is not just the Texas border that we are having problems with but along most of the Gulf Coast and along the border crossings in New York as well. We have large trucks moving across the border without cargo inspections because we haven't got the personnel to keep up. Most frequently officers are being told that the trucks contain emergency supplies but there are so many that inspections would take too long to conduct and without our monitoring equipment we have no way of determining if there is anything dangerous on board. In Louisiana we have ships traveling further north on the Mississippi River than ever before and off-loading onto barges again without inspections. Many of these ships are meeting the barges in remote areas that would not normally see this type of activity."

The president interrupted Patrick at this point. "Do you suspect this cargo is some type of contraband or is this just a matter of taxes not being paid?"

"Sir, it has been three days since the attack and we have had such a large influx in the numbers of ships and trucks entering the country. I think this may have been coordinated with the attack. I know they say emergency supplies but let's face facts, sir, there is no way in the world today that these supplies could have been located, shipped, and arrived in our country in less than seventy-two hours especially when you consider that the manifests show them originating in France, Italy, and Australia. It is just not feasible."

"Okay, I understand. I have recalled a number of military personnel from overseas and as soon as they get in the country I will have as many as possible assigned to assist you with border security. I will also have the navy and the coast guard to intercept and inspect any ships in the Gulf and Atlantic which appear to be headed toward our shores. Will that ease your concern?"

"No, sir, but it will help with the problems. Next, I wanted to let you know that the power companies have been able to work with the grid and have managed to redirect power into Indiana, Southern Michigan, and parts of Ohio. That is unfortunately only half the problem though, now that power is available we need to repair or replace the machinery at the other end that will be using the power. The power companies are moving all the personnel they can into the areas hardest hit to make repairs but parts are running low."

"Do they have any idea as to when we will have the grid completely up and running?"

"If you are asking when our power situation will be like it was on May first, I don't think anyone is quite sure. I do know that the initial estimates range from months to years."

TJ shook his head and said, "That is simply not acceptable. I don't care what it costs or what you have to do I want this country back to normal, power wise of course, in less than six months. I will make whatever I can available to you but you need to get this done."

Patrick looked at me with a shocked look on his face and then turned to the president and said, "Sir, I will do my best but I can't make you any promises. I have noted that you have become much more religious lately, sir, so maybe you should find a power prayer to assist me." Patrick laughed a little nervously and it was obvious he regretted that last statement.

The president looked at him with a cold stare for a few seconds then forced a little smile. "I will work on that for you, Patrick, in the meantime have you got anything else?"

"Yes, sir. Crime is becoming a serious problem in most metropolitan areas. We are working with local departments that were not affected by the EMP and we are obtaining vehicles and handheld radios which are being taken to these areas so the police can do a better job of getting on top of the problem. Once again, however, it will be a month or two before we can make any real headway in this area. We also have some concern regarding the smallpox problem. The vaccine that was being used in the areas of the EMP has been lost due to the inability to keep it refrigerated. The Centers for Disease Control are now saying that it is likely that the smallpox epidemic which seemed to be under control will now bounce back and become a serious problem once again. We have already dispatched medical personnel to these areas and we will monitor how this plays out."

With that Patrick stood up and told TJ that he would get back to him with any updates as he receives them. He turned and shook my hand and then turned to the president to do the same. There was an uncomfortable moment when the president simply looked at Patrick without moving but then shook his hand and patted him on the back. "Patrick, you are doing a good job and I appreciate it, keep it up. And may God bless you."

Patrick thanked him and left the office quickly.

TJ then turned to me and said, "I know that my faith in God has increased over these last few months. I think we need His help to survive what is going on. I don't want to make anyone uncomfortable because of my faith however and I will rely on you to let me know if I start to do that. I will not, however, put up with anyone making jokes about my faith and I want you to get that word around."

"Yes, sir, I will take care of that, but I don't believe Patrick was trying to make a joke, he was simply uncomfortable with everything he just dumped on you and you asked him to accomplish what would be a monumental task."

TJ gave me a little smile and walked back to his desk as we discussed other items in the paper.

MAY 20, 2017

WHITE HOUSE

It was unusual to receive a call on a Saturday morning from Admiral McCain to meet with the president but I immediately set the meeting up. The admiral must have called for the meeting while he was already on his way because he was waiting outside the Oval Office when the president and I arrived.

"Come on inside admiral, you obviously got something important for me."

"Yes, sir."

As we walked into the office the president directed the group to the sitting area opposite his desk. The early morning sunshine penetrating through the spotless windows and reflecting off the white walls of the office caused the room to be full of light. As we settled into the plush furniture the admiral opened his briefcase and pulled out his tablet to recall his notes.

"I apologize for bothering you on a Saturday because I know you have plans for today but I felt I needed to brief you on the plans we have for the troops we are bringing back stateside."

The admiral barely took a breath before he went into a list of the new assignments that he and the service Chiefs of Staff had developed. The president sat patiently listening to information about which brigade and wing and ship was going where but finally asked the admiral for an executive summary.

"Well sir, basically by May twenty-fifth, we will have fifty thousand troops from South Korea, Germany, England, Italy and elsewhere back in the states. About seventy percent of them will be in the northeast working security primarily and about thirty percent in the south working border security and law enforcement in the metropolitan areas. We hope this will be sufficient to accomplish the mission you have in mind. I am very concerned with the removal of any additional troops from South Korea or Germany. I know you are aware that North Korea is very unstable but there is also reason to be concerned with the eastern area of Europe as well."

As the two of them continued to discuss the security of Europe, the phone rang and the president asked me to answer it and find out who needed what now. The tone of his voice reflecting his frustration with the quantity of problems that seemed to be popping up everywhere you looked.

As I picked up the phone I quickly identified myself as the president's Chief of Staff and asked how I could help the caller.

"This is Colonel Schulte from the Huntsville Space Center Mission Control. I need to inform the president that there is a reported accident aboard the International Space Station and that the United States section of the station has been evacuated. We are told that a chemical spill occurred and that it was necessary for the safety of the crew to be moved to the Russian section."

I asked the Colonel to hold and informed the president of the situation. He immediately walked to the desk and took the call and after several minutes hung up and sat down at his desk. He then explained the situation to the Admiral and asked for his opinion about what he thought about this situation. The president added a fact I had not obtained—a Russian supply ship had docked with the station just about twenty minutes prior to this incident.

"Frankly, sir, I don't believe it. I think our current situation with the Russians is fragile to say the least and the fact that we have no ability to send a rescue mission alarms me greatly."

The president nodded and explained that he was in total agreement and was certainly concerned about the present situation. "I think it might be a good idea for me to call President Gryzlovski and thank him for his help just to see if there is some other issue at play here."

It was about a half hour after Admiral McCain left the office when the call to the Kremlin was connected.

"President Gryzlovski, this is President Samuels and I wanted to contact you to thank you for your cosmonauts' assistance with the apparent mishap in the space station earlier today."

As TJ listened on the phone I could see his face change to one of great concern. He flipped a switch and motioned for me to pick up another phone to listen to the call.

"And while we were risking our brave cosmonauts' lives to try to minimize the problems your people were busy committing espionage and sabotage in the Russian section, nearly causing a catastrophe in the process. This cannot be tolerated and we will charge your people with espionage. A trial will be arranged as soon as we can return them to our country."

TJ could barely get a word in and it was obvious that nothing he would say at this point could resolve the situation. It was also obvious that we had no power at this point to minimize this new crisis. The conversation ended very abruptly and TJ just sat at his desk with a blank look on his face.

After contacting the NASA director and discussing the situation with him it became apparent that this was a setup and no espionage had taken place and in fact no accident in the US section of the station had taken place. The supply ship was not scheduled nor was there a necessary delivery to the station expected and that the personnel on board the ship had included officers attached to the KGB. This was obviously a ploy to obtain the release of Vladimir. TJ looked at me and told me to set up an emergency cabinet meeting as soon as possible.

Before I could set up the cabinet meeting the Russian television network in the United States was already broadcasting how Americans had nearly destroyed the International Space Station and reported that the espionage they attempted to carry out was directed by the president himself. The two astronauts reportedly had confessed to their crimes and would be tried in the People's Court upon their return to the Russian Federation. The space station was reportedly safe due to the quick and efficient work of the Russian personnel on board the craft.

The cabinet meeting only lasted a few minutes as the members were briefed and then asked for guidance. Everyone in the room unanimously supported the President and announced that he should do whatever is necessary to obtain the safe release of the American astronauts. TJ was sure this would mean the release of Vladimir.

MAY 21, 2017

NEW YORK PRESBYTERIAN CHURCH

TJ and Angela were attending the Sunday morning service at what has become their home church since they moved to Washington. The president was very attentive and prayerful during the service but just a few minutes before the end of the service a secret service agent approached the president and whispered something in his ear. The president started to get up and tapped Angela on the shoulder motioning her to come with him. As he started out into the aisle he mouthed the words thank you to the pastor who simply nodded and continued with the prayer he was reciting at the time.

I followed them out of the pew as the group quickly moved to the back of the church and out to the limo waiting outside. As we climbed into the car I asked what was going on.

"It didn't take long for the Russians to make their move. Gryzlovski apparently called with an ultimatum regarding the astronauts and talked to Arturo, we need to meet him as soon as possible."

The vice president was in his residence at the Naval Observatory and the motorcade sped straight to that location. We arrived in just a few minutes and we hurried inside where Angela was escorted to a sitting room to meet with Mrs. Sanchez and the president and I walked to a conference room to meet with the vice president.

"Good morning, Arturo. Thank you for contacting me so quickly."

"Yes, sir. Gryzlovski apparently tried the White House and when he was told you were unavailable he asked to be connected to me."

"I understand. What did he have to say?"

"President Gryzlovski informed me that our astronauts will be tried by the People's Court in Moscow for espionage and sabotage on June first. He went on to say that the punishment for these crimes in the Russian Federation was death and that we could make arrangements for their bodies to be returned about June ninth."

"So the trial is simply a farce?"

"Apparently, but that is not what this is all about and we both know that. He indicated that he would make a one-time offer to exchange prisoners. On Tuesday, May twenty-third, if we deliver Vladimir Lenoidivic to Russian officials at Heathrow Airport in London, then they will deliver both of the astronauts to our officials at the same time. We have until midnight tonight to accept this offer or the trials will occur."

The president just sat back in his chair and looked out the window for a couple of minutes while Vice President Sanchez and I looked at each other uncomfortably waiting for what would come next. Then before we received our reply the vice president dropped one more bombshell. "Oh, I almost forgot.

President Gryzlovski also stated that due to this incident he is terminating our transportation contract and his country will no longer convey our personnel to the space station."

The president then stood up and began to pace across the room. "Why not, I guess I should have expected that as well. You know when they scrapped the shuttle program before we had a replacement vehicle they had no idea what a mistake they made. Don, notify the Kremlin that we agree to their terms and will have Lenoidivic at Heathrow on Tuesday. Also notify them that the International Space Station is property of the United States, built and paid for by Americans and that their occupancy is strictly at our invitation. If we are no longer able to send personnel to the station, we may prohibit other nations including Russia from using the facility as well. Then call a cabinet meeting for this evening and include Admiral McCain."

After a few minutes of small talk and a cup of coffee we left the residence for the short trip back to the White House.

Later that evening a quick meeting of the cabinet was held and during the meeting a lot of shocked expressions were shared around the room. Just before the meeting the press had picked up on the Russian reports of Americans sabotaging the space station at the direct order of President Samuels and it didn't take the liberal pundits long to begin a barrage of condemnation for the president. The attorney general agreed to take the lead on the exchange and she was instructed to contact the Brits to make sure we had viable back up plans ready to go in case there were any problems. Then TJ dropped the bombshell.

"Admiral McCain, have we got a missile that can reach the space station and eliminate it?"

There was absolute silence in the room as the question got everyone's immediate attention.

"Sir, I do not believe our conventional missiles could accomplish that task but the hyper-speed weapon might be able to reach it or at the least deliver a nuclear device into orbit that we may be able to direct close to the station and detonate it in an area that would knock it out of orbit."

The president looked around the room at the surprised faces of his advisors. He then informed them, "I cannot tolerate one of our main enemies having the space station at their disposal. I am not worried about science experiments but I am worried about weaponization of the station. We have developed laser weapons that we can use from planes and ships so I think we would be naïve to believe that they have not been working on some type of advanced weaponry in this same area. If they placed a laser weapon aboard the space station it is possible that the weapon would be used against us should a war develop, which is becoming more and more likely. Admiral, the space station is the property of the United States and is simply leased to other countries for their scientific purposes. When the Russians terminated our contract to transport our personnel we terminated our contract with them for use of the space station. I will have a formal eviction notice delivered to them with Vladimir, once we safely have the astronauts back. I will give them seven days to vacate and inform them that we will take possession back at our convenience after that time. Try to have something ready to go in ten days."

"Yes, sir."

The attorney general then spoke up with an objection. "Sir, with all due respect you realize that if they do not abandon the station, which I really don't picture them doing, you will be murdering their personnel and may start a war."

The president turned to her and replied, "Deborah, I will give them ample time to abandon the station and the death of their personnel will be on them. By the way, I don't know where you have been but we are at war. Only lacking a formal declaration which I will be working on soon."

MAY 23, 2017

HEATHROW AIRPORT LONDON

At the request of the president, I accompanied Vladimir to London along with the Attorney General Deborah O'Connor, six U.S. Marshals, and a host of secret service and other security personnel. We had departed Andrews Air Force Base a little after 10:00 PM on Monday night and were expected to land at Heathrow at about 9:30 AM local time on Tuesday. We were flying on the president's back up to Air Force One, a Boeing 747 decked out with luxurious and functional rooms and the ability to stay in constant contact with the White House. I don't believe Vladimir had enjoyed the flight however, as he remained in handcuffs and leg shackles and was restrained to his seat. The flight was uncomfortable for all of us though as he had a way of staring through you and managed to maintain a sly smile on his face during the night. The man never closed his eyes for a moment like he actually thought someone was going to kill him before he arrived. There was very little said during the flight and the atmosphere on board the plane was tense.

As we approached Heathrow we could see it was overcast and raining. The landing was uneventful and when we reached the end of the runway the plane came to a stop awaiting instructions. We had contacted British Intelligence who had worked out all of the details of the exchange with the Russians. The plane taxied to an area in between terminals three and four and then came to a stop facing north in an open area. From the windows I could see a Russian Ilyushin 96 parked facing south about two hundred yards in front of us. The security people were busy scanning the terminals and surrounding buildings for any signs of a sniper but everything appeared to be clear. An airport shuttle started toward our plane from the Russian plane and mobile steps were rolled up to the door leading into the front cabin. As the door was opened the secret service personnel advised everyone to stand back and would not let anyone outside.

One person exited the shuttle and climbed up the steps to the entrance. He was dressed in a suit and raincoat as he stepped on board and was immediately stopped by secret service. He handed his credentials to the agent who then questioned him for what seemed an eternity and then allowed him on board.

The man approached me.

"I am Thomas Henderson of MI-5. I will be the one responsible for conducting this exchange and getting everyone safely out of London as quickly as possible."

Without waiting for a reply from me he continued; "I have been on board the Russian aircraft and the two astronauts are on board and apparently in good physical condition. The instructions from the Russians are, that I am to bring Mr. Lenoidivic back with me and they will then release the astronauts to me to bring back to you. Is that acceptable?"

"Absolutely not! We do not trust them any more than they trust us. We will hand Vladimir over to them as they hand our astronauts back to us. Simultaneously or nothing."

"With all due respect, sir, they seemed rather insistent about this manner of exchange and indicated that we would do it their way or we could simply take back the bodies of the astronauts after they are executed."

"You see that is exactly what I am afraid they intend anyway. Please return to them and advise them that you have seen Mr. Lenoidivic and that he is in handcuffs and leg shackles and there is a man standing with a cocked gun to the back of his head presently so they should make up their minds quickly to make the simultaneous exchange."

"I do not see that, sir, and will not lie."

I turned and instructed a marshal to bring Lenoidivic forward so that the agent could see exactly what I had just described. Within a few minutes Vladimir appeared with the same smile on his face but with a .40 caliber pistol inches from the back of his head.

"Very well, sir, I will report what I have seen and explain your wishes."

As the agent began to move forward toward the door I shouted at him. "By the way, have you inspected the area to make sure there are no snipers waiting for us to deplane?"

"Oh, there are snipers, sir, but they are all British agents and you have nothing to fear."

I watched as the agent exited the aircraft and returned to the Russian plane. As he walked up the steps to enter that plane security personnel exited our plane and took up defensive positions. If a fire fight was going to occur, we would not be caught flat footed. Despite what the agent had said I was sure that Russian agents were posted somewhere with the capability of destroying our aircraft and my butt was so tight I was sure I would need a laxative to open it up again.

Ten minutes had passed and nothing had happened. A communications specialist came into the cabin area and announced that he had intercepted communications from the plane to Moscow asking for instructions. I was wondering if they were reconsidering Vladimir's worth.

Another ten minutes and I was downright scared at this point. Then one of the secret service agents said that the British agent was exiting the Russian plane and a second shuttle had suddenly pulled up to the plane. The shuttle carrying the agent drove quickly back to our plane and he literally ran up the steps and into the cabin.

"I think you were right not to trust these blokes. When I passed on the information two of their people began to pummel your restrained astronauts and I am afraid they beat them rather severely until I was able to convince them to stop. They were very unhappy about your demand and I made note that they broke out several sniper rifles. I convinced them that if we couldn't do this peacefully then the exchange was over and I would instruct you both to leave. They made contact with Moscow and apparently were told that Vladimir must be returned unharmed so they have agreed to your demands. They wanted the exchange completed at their aircraft and I told them we would make the exchange midway between the two aircraft. I have instructed the shuttle drivers however to make the point of exchange closer to your craft as I have a bad feeling of what might happen immediately following the exchange, if you understand what I mean."

Henderson began to walk away and then stopped and asked if he might inform me of something privately. I agreed and we walked out of hearing range of the rest of the group.

"I sense real danger when this exchange is made so I have taken the liberty to scramble some of Her Majesty's Harriers to oversee this operation and have closed the airspace over the airport for the time being. That information is only known to you but will become apparent to others as the exchange takes place. You will have immediate clearance to leave as soon as your personnel gets back on board so do notify your pilot to be ready. I also believe that there will be a flight of F-16s waiting for you to clear British airspace to escort you back to the States. Do have a safe flight."

Deborah O'Connor and I exited the aircraft and walked to the shuttle as the pilot began to start up the engines of our plane. When we had gotten into the shuttle, Vladimir exited, still restrained, with a U.S. Marshal on either side assisting him down the steps. Once everyone was in the shuttle it began to move forward when I heard the roar of the Harrier jets moving into position. Four of them were hovering about two hundred feet overhead and were positioned facing the Russian aircraft.

Across the way we could see the astronauts being brought down the steps escorted by several Russian soldiers. Their shuttle began moving toward ours and we both came to a stop near the midway mark between the planes. Deborah and I exited the vehicle and Vladimir and the marshals stood just behind us.

A Russian general exited their shuttle along with the astronauts and several other armed soldiers. The astronauts were clearly hurt and bleeding from the beating that had been described by Henderson.

As the general moved forward I immediately asked about the physical condition of our personnel. "It was a rough flight. Now let us conclude our business today."

Deborah then handed a piece of paper to the general. "That is a notice of immediate eviction from our space station. We will give you ten days to remove your personnel before we destroy the facility since we no longer have the capability of using it and feel it is dangerous to leave it unattended."

"This is worthless. The space station is an international facility and we will use it and defend it if we must."

I then entered the conversation. "It was built by American money and American technology. You have been allowed to use it to further science but when you terminated the transport contract you also terminated your ability to use our facilities. Now let's make this exchange."

The restraints were removed from all three prisoners and the exchange began. As Vladimir walked by he turned to me and said, "Tell your weak-minded president that he will now feel my wrath and that I will crush your country." He then turned to the general and shouted something in Russian. Almost immediately I heard Deborah shout something back at the two of them in Russian. That caused each to pause and stare at her and then continue onto the shuttle without looking back.

Our shuttle immediately started back to the plane and I noticed that as the defensive agents began moving onto the plane the chocks had already been removed and the engines were revving up. We ran up the steps as best we could with two injured personnel and the crew closed the door as we began to taxi. The Russian shuttle amazingly stalled as it started to pull out and they had not returned to their aircraft as we began our taxi to the runway.

"What was all that back and forth between you and Vladimir as we were leaving?"

"He told the general to eliminate us. I pointed out that they should consider what the planes above were going to do if they followed through with that instruction."

I had to remember to send a personal note of thanks to Henderson when I got back to Washington. As we were leaving the ground I could see the Russian plane beginning to taxi. Within another ten minutes we had two F-16s on our right and two on our left. The astronauts were being attended to by the plane's doctor and medical crew and I went to my room to take a nap. This had been one long day.

When we reached Andrew's, TJ was there to greet us. An ambulance whisked away the two astronauts who were suffering from broken ribs, internal bleeding, and one from a broken jaw. When I finished explaining everything that had happened during the exchange TJ looked very concerned and said, "Well I guess it is time to declare war. I just want to hold off as long as I can so we can get the country built back up. I guess you can see why I wanted everything back to normal in six months but I am afraid that we haven't even got that much time now."

We had managed to keep the exchange quiet but with all the excitement at Heathrow everyone was buzzing and the media circus had begun at the White House.

TJ just said, "Let's let the press relations people earn their money for a change. I have had enough for this day." So we each were unavailable as the night fell and a new world would greet the day tomorrow.

JUNE 1, 2017

WHITE HOUSE CABINET CONFERENCE ROOM

The president had called for a security briefing of the cabinet and as I entered the conference room at 10 AM, everyone was present except the president.

"Good morning, everyone. When I left the oval office the president was on the phone with President Gryzlovski, so he will be here in a few minutes. Is there any housekeeping items that I can help with before he gets in here?"

The room was silent and no one was joking around. When the president walked into the room everyone stood up as he went to his spot at the table and took a seat.

"Please take your seat and let's get down to business. First, I just ended a phone call with President Gryzlovski. I was hoping that we could work out some type of agreement regarding the space station but he is being very adamant about their position. I have once again warned him that we are considering the destruction of the facility and that he needs to remove his personnel from the facility now. He indicated that they were prepared to defend the facility and would show us their capability very soon. That statement frightens me. For the time being let's discuss the homeland situation. Patrick, you have the floor."

Patrick Simmons, the Secretary of Homeland Security rose from his place and began his report.

"As you all know we have been concerned with security on the southern border ever since the EMP attacks. We had a serious development regarding this early this morning. Yesterday evening a ship came into the port at Gulfport Mississippi, presumably to unload equipment to assist in rebuilding the electrical grid in the area. At about 3:00 AM, local time however, a large number of vehicles rolled out of the dock area carrying tanks and military equipment. In addition, an estimated five to ten thousand individuals presumed to be military troops also pulled out of the area in military style trucks and buses. Gulfport Police attempted to stop some of these vehicles on Highway 49 and were immediately attacked with high powered weapons. Because of the situation they had limited ability to pursue and stop these people who left the area and went east on I-10. The unit was next observed in Mobile, Alabama, and was reported traveling north on I-65. We had drone aircraft dispatched to the area but we have been unable to locate the group. There is a large area of forests in the south and central areas of Alabama and we believe that they are using the forests as cover at the present time. From what we have learned from evidence on the ship it would appear that this group is connected to an extremist Islamic group but we have not been able to confirm which group. We do know that some of the equipment they were moving was American made and most likely captured in Iraq. We are looking into what their exact target may be and we have several probabilities but nothing is certain at this point."

The president interrupts at this point. "Patrick, please explain how an enemy combatant group is able to invade our country and move thousands of troops and heavy equipment well over one hundred miles into our country and we not only don't stop them but we don't even know where they are."

The secretary appeared extremely uncomfortable and frustrated but turned to the president to explain something he had done earlier this morning but he realized he needed to do it again for the rest of the decision makers at the table.

"Sir, we need to remember that Gulfport and the rest of southern Mississippi still have no electrical power. Their police resources are handicapped by having very limited communication and very few operational vehicles. Nevertheless they put up a good fight and lost a number of officers in the process. As soon as possible they contacted the military at Keesler Air Force Base but they also have limited abilities at this time. It took several hours to get a drone aircraft or any aircraft for that matter, into the area and they immediately began a search of the presumed route but the group could not be located. Mobile has limited electricity and does have more vehicles available but again these individuals went through Mobile at four in the morning. There is no traffic on I-10 at the time in this area and very little on I-65. They were able to blow through the area very rapidly since the highways had been cleared for relief groups traveling into the area. They could not have traveled very far on 65 before they turned off. We have ordered surveillance on Islamic mosques in Alabama, Mississippi, and Tennessee but so far there have been no developments in those operations. In addition, a few weeks ago we spoke of freighters traveling unusually north on the Mississippi River and transferring cargo onto barges. At the time it did not appear to be of great concern but with this new activity it raises serious concern that other military units and equipment may have already been transferred into the country under the cover of the power situation. The coast guard is currently stopping barges and inspecting them thoroughly and stopping freighters upon approach but it may be too little too late. I also need to make everyone aware that new smallpox cases have been reported in these areas and we fear since much of the vaccine was destroyed as a result of the attack that the smallpox epidemic might begin to make an upswing again."

The president then turned to Admiral McCain.

"Admiral, do we have the capability to fight a limited action in defense of the country in the southeast region?"

"Not at this moment, sir, but we will have in a few days. I will make sure the equipment and troops we need are repositioned just in case something develops."

The president had a very drawn and concerned look on his face as he stood up and began to walk around the room. After several minutes he stopped and looked at Admiral McCain.

"I believe that we may be looking at the first war since 1865 to be fought on American soil. We need to consider this an eminent threat and make plans for an attack in the heartland of our country. Admiral, I would like you to make a list of probable targets and to develop a war plan just in case a revolt breaks out. I would like all of the rest of you to also submit a list of concerns regarding possible targets and any other concerns you might have regarding a threat on U.S. soil. I need this information as soon as possible. Admiral, I also want you to begin bringing additional troops and equipment home from wherever you can pull them."

THE COST OF LIBERTY

The admiral turned to the president and replied,

"Very well, sir, but there is some additional information that you need to know."

TJ walked back to his seat and sat down and then told the Admiral that he had the floor.

"Sir, in the last forty-eight hours Chinese troops have begun pouring into North Korea. We have been told that they are conducting a joint training exercise but the troops seemed to be all headed to the South Korean border. In addition, the best equipped Chinese Naval fleet is moving into the Yellow Sea and a Russian fleet has put out from Vladivostok and is moving into the Sea of Japan. We currently have insufficient troops and equipment in South Korea to adequately defend the country from attack should that be the plan. Also, once they get into position it will be difficult at best to evacuate the troops we currently have on station. We have our Pacific fleet still in the Indian Ocean after leaving the Persian Gulf and Arabian Sea from the last actions in the Middle East. We are arranging for them to resupply at Diego Garcia but it will be ten days at best before they are close enough to the area to be of any benefit and that will likely be too late. I have contacted Australian Military Command and they are willing to assist with the protection of Japan but again it will be five days before they will be in position and they are not prepared to risk an all-out battle with China over South Korea."

The admiral paused for a moment looking down at his notes and then continued.

"I also want to alert you to the fact that heavily armored Russian troops are congregating on the borders of the Baltic nations and Finland. They have not yet requested our assistance but it appears that an attack in this area is also eminent. The U.K. is sending air and naval units into the Baltic Sea at this point in support of these nations but the number of troops that we have seen make it apparent that this attack will not be turned back by aircraft like the last one."

The president turned to the CIA Director Larry Williams and asked for his input.

"Sir, these developments have occurred very rapidly. Since we made the exchange it seems all of our perspective enemies have put all their possible operations on the fast track."

Jacob Owens, Director of the National Intelligence Agency, also spoke up at this point. "Mr. President, there is more you should know. There is information that Islamist extremist troops are moving close to Manila and they appear to be preparing to overthrow the Philippine government. Pakistani troops are moving toward the border of India and Turkey appears to be gearing up for an attack on Greece. The European Union has had a meeting in the last twenty-four hours to discuss if they would assist Greece and they have decided against any effort to assist Greece and are preparing paperwork to expel them from the European Union based on the economic chaos that has occurred in Greece."

The president then said, "So it would appear that World War III is officially about to begin?"

Owens nodded and said, "That's how I read it, sir, and I don't believe that we are ready based on the current status of our country."

As the conversation continued around the table a marine lieutenant knocked and entered the room hastily moving directly to the president's chair. "Excuse me, sir, but I believe you need to see this message immediately." With that he handed the president a piece of paper and then immediately left the room. The president looked down at the paper and read it. As he shook his head he placed the message on the table for everyone to view and simply said, "It's on."

I looked over and read the message.

1 Jun 2017 1622 Zulu

Six U.S. communication satellites orbiting over the Russian Federation were just

destroyed by unknown means. All satellites were detailed to CIA. EOM

As the president stood up he instructed all of those in the room to prepare war plans for their respective agencies and to begin activation of emergency measures. Then he turned to Admiral McCain and said, "The DEFCON is two."

JUNE 2, 2017

WHITE HOUSE SITUATION ROOM

It was 3:30 AM when I got the call to get to the situation room as soon as possible. By the time I got my teeth brushed and put a pair of pants on there was a marine knocking at my front door. As I opened the door he said,

"Sir, my instruction is to take you to the White House without delay so would you please accompany me."

It is hard to say no to a 6'4" authority figure with a .45 strapped to his side. I grabbed my briefcase and shouted back to the bedroom, "Bye honey, I'll call you later."

My escort walked quickly but I had to jog to keep up with him. No sooner had the door slammed when the car sped up the street. I had never travelled through the streets of DC at such a high rate of speed, meanwhile, there was absolutely no conversation of any sort inside the vehicle. As I entered the door into the White House I was instructed to proceed to the situation room. As I was running down the hallway I was joined by the attorney general, the FBI director, and several military officers. As we arrived outside the room we ran into three marine sentries and several secret service agents. Activity in the White House at four in the morning was not unusual but the number of military and others walking around with exposed weapons was very unusual. In fact, it was frightening to me because I had not seen this level of security since the assassination attempt.

As I entered the room the activity level was unlike anything I had ever witnessed in my relatively short tenure as chief of staff. I still had no idea of what was happening but it was apparent that whatever was going on was something of extreme importance.

The president was huddled with a gaggle of generals or whatever you call a group of six or more military brass. I stood there lost for a few minutes, feeling like the new kid walking into class on the first day of school. After several minutes a military officer approached me.

"Sir, I am Major Harrison Combs and I will brief and bring you up to date on the situation. Please come with me."

With that we walked to one of the few areas of the room that didn't have people hustling back and forth. Deborah O'Connor and Director McLaren also joined us at the small table and all of us grabbed some paper and our respective computer tablets to make sure we took the appropriate notes.

"First of all, I would suggest you do not use your computers as that is part of the problem. Our computer security has been compromised and at this point we believe that we may have little control of the computer system at all and we have instructed all military commands to respond to voice verified commands only."

The Major continued, "Additionally, in the last eight hours there have been several significant military moves around the world. Russian troops have attacked and seized large parcels of land in Latvia, Lithuania, and Estonia. There was a brief naval skirmish between the Brits and Russian Naval vessels. The British vessel sustained significant damage and withdrew from the conflict. The Philippine government has fallen to an Islamic group. Turkey is currently attacking in the north of Greece. South Korea is begging for assistance but the president is refusing to send any additional units. Mexican military units are gathering south of the New Mexico and Arizona border and we still cannot find the military units that entered through Mississippi. According to the CIA and NSA information we have reason to believe that military equipment and soldiers have already entered our country in New York, Louisiana, and Texas. The President is considering requesting a declaration of war but at this point we are trying to decide who should be included in the declaration. It would appear that the fuse is burning and we just don't know when powder keg will explode, but make no mistake it will explode."

As the Major was finishing his briefing I noticed the president was standing patiently behind him. I motioned for the Major to look behind and when he did he immediately jumped up and moved aside.

"At ease, Major, I just want to pass on some updated information to all of you. I just finished a conversation with President Cardoza of Mexico. He has informed me that two of his military bases were attacked yesterday afternoon by what he originally believed to be drug cartels. He now believes that these people are Islamist extremist and he informed me that they have stolen uniforms and weapons from these bases in an obvious attempt to stage an attack against the U.S. and cause it to retaliate against Mexico. I agree that based on recent events it would not be difficult to start a conflict by this method. Based on what President Cardoza has learned they intend to storm the Nogales crossing and move along Highways 19 and 82 into Tucson. They reportedly have about three thousand troops with some heavy armament. I have just activated the Arizona, Nevada, and California National Guard. The plan is a hasty one but we have closed the checkpoint at Nogales and we intend to meet them head on while Mexican troops hit their rear. We should know in a couple of hours, but I am not going to get bogged down in a conflict with Mexico because I think this is a decoy. I am more concerned than ever with the eastern U.S. right now."

Things started happening very quickly at this point as fighting broke out all over the globe. Russian troops had moved into Estonia, Latvia, and Lithuania and fighting outside of Vilnius was described as intense. Chinese and North Korean troops had moved into the demilitarized zone and South Korea reported fighting along the border as well as artillery shelling in nearby cities. As I watched the President you could easily see beads of sweat popping out of his forehead and a concern look had replaced any earlier smiles he might had been forcing.

As the Mexican invasion began we were able to listen to the combat control center radio at Nellis AFB in Las Vegas Nevada. That was the location established as the headquarters for this operation. There were also drone aircraft that was sending a video feed to the command center and the White House so we could watch the action unfold.

Leading the column of invaders as they entered Arizona were four tanks followed by a half dozen armored personnel carriers and then pickup after pickup with men holding semi-automatic and automatic weapons. Some of the trucks had machine guns mounted in the bed and we could see occasional burst of gunfire leaving the barrels of the weapons. As they entered the United States there was no resistance and they sped into the city. The commanders were not sure whether they would head down the business route, get on the interstate as quickly as possible or do a combination of both so they were waiting for a confrontation until the geography was right and they could manage to get the upper hand. The time was 8:00 AM in Washington DC so that made the local time 6:00 AM when the intrusion began.

The Arizona Highway Patrol had closed I-19 at Rio Rico Drive which was north of the city proper. Consequently, there was traffic on the roads as the force moved into the city. The column split with half heading along the business route and the remainder heading straight onto the interstate highway. The first few cars that confronted the tanks stopped dead in their tracks and in at least one case a tank literally moved right over top of a car that had stopped. As the two columns moved down their respective routes there was no resistance but gunfire seemed to erupt periodically as if they were just trying to get everyone's attention.

As they approached the area where the business route and interstate merged back into one highway the columns stopped. In between the two roadways but visible from both was St. Andrew's Episcopal Church. The tanks from both roadways blasted several rounds into the church until they could see it was on fire. Then the columns again started moving forward and merged together on I-19. They began to pick up speed and apparently did not notice the complete lack of traffic as the roadway appeared completely abandoned. As they continued moving they entered an area with a large number of warehouses along the frontage road on the northeast side of the highway. From the feed we were watching it did not appear that they even gave this area a second thought as they must have been concentrating on reaching Tucson.

As I watched the screens with the pictures of what was going on, I looked over at the president expecting to see anger and sadness but instead I saw what could only be described as the anticipation of a child on Christmas morning. I wasn't sure what was about to take place but I knew that something big was about to happen because the president was on the edge of his seat.

Suddenly the radio traffic, which had been minimal, erupted with activity.

"Aztec 2, 3, and 4 you are clear to engage."

The voice that returned simply acknowledged the call.

Then the controller came across with another command. "Apache 4 Delta Charlie, 4 Echo Charlie, and 4 Frank Charlie you are cleared for takeoff and cleared to engage upon arrival." This time the voice was a little more difficult to understand because of the engine noise in the background but it sounded like "Apache flight is clear, weapons hot will engage in two."

I looked back at the video screens and still saw the column moving along the highway unheeded. Then from the corner of my eye I could see something moving from the shadows behind the warehouses. Three M-1 Abram tanks apparently from the National Guard moved along Cale Cristina Drive and Kachina Avenue and immediately fired on the enemy tanks killing two of them before they even knew they were there. The other two tanks stopped and their turrets began to rotate to the right but they were also hit before they could fire a shot. We could see what appeared to be rocket propelled grenades being launched by the invading column at the tanks but machine guns and gunfire was erupting from both sides of the highway as the force and driven right into a textbook ambush. Suddenly from out of nowhere the Apache helicopters entered the fight and it was over quickly. The last ten or so trucks in the column turned around and sped back to Mexico as fast as they could drive. Unfortunately for them they drove into a second ambush just across the border as Mexican troops opened up on them on their side of the border.

Within an hour the Battle of Nogales was over. The statistics were impressive for the good guys. U.S. forces had six people injured but no deaths. The invading force had 1825 people killed by U.S. forces, 1009 injured and 50 captured. Mexican forces had killed 435 of the invaders as they attempted to re-enter Mexico.

The President with a slight smile turned to me and simply said, "And so it begins."

JUNE 2, 2017

OVAL OFFICE
4:30 PM

As I entered the office I found the president sitting at his desk reviewing the concerns and requests forwarded to him by the various members of the cabinet. On the wall across from his desk he had three television monitors on with CNN, Fox, and the BBC all turned on with the sound muted. Every few minutes he would look up to see what story was being covered. The press had praised the United States military for stopping the attempted invasion this morning in Arizona. They gave much of the credit to the Mexican government for sharing their intelligence with our country and TJ was fine with that as President Cardoza could use some good press and we were very appreciative for the help Mexico had provided.

The news out of the Philippines was also being promoted but the other conflicts that were active were barely mentioned. I wondered if the press simply had no real information on them or if there was another reason for the silence about the attacks.

The President stood up and stretched a bit. "I think I am going to head up to the residence and try to take a nap since these next few days are going to make sleep a hard thing to justify."

As we walked toward the door Hillary buzzed the president and announced that Jacob Owens wanted to speak to him quickly.

"Send him in."

As Jacob entered greetings were exchanged and all of us sat down on the furniture in front of the fireplace in the office.

"Sir, I wanted to give you a quick brief on the latest information we have regarding the conflicts that are ongoing."

"What have you got, Jacob?"

"Well, first of all Lithuania, Latvia, and Estonia have all fallen to the Russian troops. The troops in Lithuania are still moving however and have crossed over into Poland. The fighting in Finland has intensified and the Russians have made no headway. Pakistan and Turkey are not making much progress either in India and Greece. In South Korea however, Chinese troops have landed at Incheon, they overran our bases at that location and are moving toward the border in support of the battle there and I believe it is likely that South Korean and American troops may be overrun at the border as well. Tactical air strikes are being made and B-2 bombers are on their way from Whiteman but the sheer number of troops on the border and now the landing are going to prove to be overwhelming. I don't know if an evacuation is possible but I would suggest closing our embassy and moving out whatever troops we can before it is too late. I have no information regarding casualties or prisoners at the Inchon Air Base or Naval facility but both are now in Chinese hands."

TJ gave me a glance and before he could say a word I was on the phone with Admiral McCain of the Joint Chiefs requesting his best information on the situation. He was already on his way to the office when I called.

As Jacob began to explain the situation in the Philippines the President looked up and noticed the "Breaking News" screen had just popped on the Fox News channel. The President said, "Don, turn the sound up on Fox."

"We are getting reports of multiple car bomb explosions in New York City. We have not independently been able to confirm but we have been told that the New York Times building has severe damage from one of them and that the NBC studios, just down the street has suffered . . ."

The screen went black as did the screen on the CNN channel. I went to the phone and contacted the situation room to see if they had any information regarding what was going on in New York. I waited for several minutes before a familiar voice came on the phone.

"Major Combs."

"Major, do you have any information regarding any attacks in New York City?"

"Yes, sir, but it is just coming in and hasn't been thoroughly checked. So far the information indicates that panel trucks of various sizes were parked close to the main entrances of a number of media buildings and detonated leaving the buildings severely damaged and openly vulnerable. What appear to be Islamist militants wearing masks and carrying semi-automatic and automatic weapons entered the damaged buildings and we believe they are taking control of the centers. These attacks occurred nearly simultaneously. The sites hit so far are the New York Times building, the NBC, CBS, ABC, Fox News, and CNN studios and headquarters in New York. As well as the Discovery

Channel headquarters in Silver Springs, Maryland, and the CNN headquarters building in Atlanta, Georgia. All followed similar scenarios. A large explosion followed by trucks with militants storming the buildings and all of the sites are off the air. I will get more information to you as soon as I get it."

I know my face was pale as I put the phone down and turned to the president. He was now watching the only monitor with a picture, the BBC. Nothing was being said yet on the air about the situation but I was sure that would be short lived.

"Mr. President." As I recited back to him what I had just been told I still found the information hard to believe. Both the president and the NIA director looked like they were in shock. It took a few minutes for the situation to sink in and then the president moved into high gear.

"Don, call the congressional leadership and advise them that I would like a declaration of war against the Islamic Caliphate, Russia, and China, and any and all nations that assist them in any way. Call Steven Lambert and tell him we are breaking off diplomatic relations with Russia and China immediately and with any country controlled by the Islamic Caliphate."

As he was continuing to list his requests Admiral McCain walked into the office looking pale as well. "Mr. President, I . . ."

The president cut him off and turned his attention to him with his requests or more appropriately his orders.

"Admiral, raise the DEFCON level to one. I don't know what you have on board the B-2s headed to Korea but it won't be enough. I want you to bomb the hell out of the North Korean and Chinese aggressors with everything you can throw at them short of nuclear. We have to narrow these increasingly numerous conflicts to a manageable number and I think that is where we should start. I don't believe the Chinese will be as committed to this as Russia is and if we show them some substantial resistance they may back down. The problem is they may be the only ones that will. What units have we got capable of urban warfare in New York, Silver Springs, and Atlanta?"

"Sir, we have a number of units trained to fight urban warfare but I want you to know if we go in to get these people there will be innocent lives lost as well."

"Shit, Admiral, innocents are already dying because they're American or Jewish or Christian and I know what you are trying to say but we cannot wait to negotiate with these evil people. When the pundits start pointing fingers at the military you simply need to reply that we followed the orders of the president. I will take the heat because I guarantee if I survive this term it will be my last anyway."

As the Admiral turned to leave the room the BBC was making their first comments on the attack. "We have received a communique from the Islamic Caliphate announcing that they have declared war on the United States of America. They have announced that they now control all of the major media outlets in the U.S. and that they will be moving on government agencies very soon and expect the U.S. to surrender within the week. They went on to state that they intend no harm to most of the American population. That Christians will be left alone as long as they pay jizya tax and that civilian police should not report to work as they are being replaced by an Islamic police force that will enforce sharia law. Police officers that report to work and interfere with Islamic activities will be treated as enemy soldiers. The president and military leaders will be tried under sharia and executed. We have no response from the American government at this time but we do have a call into them for their response."

"Don, I need to talk to Angela. I will be in the residence if you need me."

He left the office walking quickly to the residence. I headed to the situation room because I wanted to be up to date when the president returned.

JUNE 2, 2017

PRESIDENTIAL RESIDENCE
6:15 PM

As TJ entered the residence Angela was in the bedroom finishing getting dressed for dinner. TJ walked up behind her and as she turned around he wrapped his arms around her and just held her tightly. After simply holding her for nearly a minute he kissed her neck and then gave her a long passionate kiss on her mouth.

"Wow! Should I get undressed?"

"No. I just needed to hold onto you and to tell you how much I love you and need you."

"Okay, I knew that but why do I feel that you are about to cause my mood to fall like a load of bricks with your next breath?"

TJ stepped back but kept ahold of her hands and looked directly into her eyes. "You know me better than I know myself. I need you to leave the White House, it is not safe here for you any longer. I will have secret service arrange a safe location for you and I do not want to know where it is so you will remain safe."

"What are you talking about? The White House is probably the safest building in the world. I have no intention of leaving it or you any time in the foreseeable future."

"Honey, where have you been today? Haven't you heard about all the attacks going on? It is not safe here and I think the only way I can make sure you are safe is to let the secret service do their jobs and not to interfere in any way. You have to leave because this is going to be a target and to be honest with you, I don't know how much time we have to get you out of here."

"Well, where are you going to be? I think I will be as safe as possible if I am with you. Besides that, I have no desire to be somewhere away from you and I don't care how safe that location may or may not be, because if I am not with you, I can't be happy."

"Angela, I can't concentrate on what is best for the country and worry about you at the same time."

"Are you saying that when I am out of sight you can forget about me and not worry about me?"

TJ let go of her hands and turned his back while walking across the room.

"Now you are being ridiculous. You know that you are never out of my thoughts but the decisions I have to make are going to require me to disregard my safety and worry about the safety of millions of others. If you are here I don't know if I can make decisions that put me and you in harm's way even if it is the best course of action."

Now Angela moves toward TJ. "Think about what you just said. You are talking as if you could sacrifice yourself and everything will be better. Now you are being ridiculous, not me. I know that Arturo is a good man and will someday make a good president, but if you are killed in this or any conflict while you are in office, the emotional letdown will be devastating to the country. So it is your duty to stay alive and to make sure everyone knows that you are in control of the country. If having me by your side helps you make decisions that keep you alive then that will make me a patriot, live or die."

TJ was now silent has he considered what she was saying. "So I am guessing that no matter what I say you do not intend to be smart and leave?"

"We are in this together. Remember I promised to stay with you through better or worse. If we go down, we will do it together."

TJ went back to hug her once again. "I love you. Get a bag packed because I have a feeling we will be leaving here tonight or tomorrow for destinations unknown."

She looked up at him and said, "I love you too. I will always be ready to follow you anywhere."

JUNE 3, 2017

WHITE HOUSE SITUATION ROOM
4:30 AM

Once again I beat the sun to the White House. As I walked into the situation room it was still bustling with activity. The trip into the White House had been unusual this morning. There was more police within a mile of the White House than I had ever observed before. Not only DC Metro Police but U.S. Park Police, Uniformed Secret Service, and military jeeps with mounted machine guns patrolling the area.

As I looked around the room for someone to brief me, I noticed Senator Jones from Texas was sitting at a table in the corner of the room sipping a coffee. I walked over to him and offered my hand to shake.

"I am surprised to see you here at this time of the morning, Senator."

He looked up at me and appeared a little haggard in his appearance. "I came over to deliver the president's resolution. We met last night at eleven in joint session and after some discussion passed a declaration of war. I think there would have been a whole lot more discussion but New York has a lot of these people really shook up and I think everyone wanted to get out of Washington as quickly as possible. So when some of the democrats wanted to put restrictions into the resolution and set an economic limit there was such uproar it became apparent that a lengthy debate would result. That BBC report about New York was played for a number of the leadership and it was quickly decided to simply give the president a clean resolution with no restrictions. I just brought over a copy to give to the president but he hasn't shown up yet."

"I am sure he will be here soon." I sat down with him for a few minutes of small talk and to keep him company until the president arrived.

As the president walked into the room all of the military officers snapped to attention and the president just as quickly told them to resume their duties. He spotted the senator and myself and walked over to the table. Senator Jones quickly presented him with the declaration of war and they talked about the session for several minutes. It ended and the senator advised him that congress had been adjourned for four weeks. It was their hope that everything would be resolved by then or at least a state of safety would have been restored in the nation's capital.

As the small talk continued for a few minutes between the three of us I noticed an army officer walking toward us and looking at his shoulders I noted three stars. "Excuse me, sir."

TJ stopped talking and looked up at the officer.

"Mr. President, I am Lieutenant General William Hickman, and I am second in command of the Central Command. I will be in charge of keeping you well briefed, sir, throughout the remainder of this crisis and I will also be responsible to keep you in a safe location. I will be working closely with your secret service detail. I know that they are normally in charge of those decisions but we are taking the title Commander in Chief very seriously from this point forward."

The president nodded and simply replied,

"As you should. I also want you to know that my wife will be remaining with me and I am ordering you to make sure that she is safe as well."

"Understood, sir, I promise you that she will be safe with the group of soldiers I will have assigned to her."

"Thank you, general. I appreciate that more than you know."

"Sir, I have a briefing to go over with you, there has been a considerable amount of activity overnight. First, we have secured the perimeters of each of the buildings seized by the enemy yesterday. They are still inside and holding a number of hostages but we have prevented them thus far from broadcasting and they will not be able to leave those facilities. We have no intelligence regarding other units about to attack but we still have not located the tanks and heavy arms which we know were brought into the country. We have units searching the forests and other areas in Alabama, Mississippi, and Tennessee."

"Poland has requested assistance through the NATO alliance. Russian troops and aircraft have pushed several hundred miles into Poland and the city of Gdansk has been captured by the Russian forces. All three of the Baltic nations are currently occupied and controlled by Russian forces. In Finland there is intense fighting outside of the city of Joensuu but the Finnish Army is doing an outstanding job of holding off the Russians. They have not asked for assistance but our reports indicate that they will need supplies very soon if they are going to continue the fight."

"In Asia, the Indian Army and Air Forces have pushed the Pakistanis back to the border but fighting is still intense in that region. In Greece, however, the Turks have taken the Grecian city of Komotini and appear to be moving more heavy weapons into the area for what we believe will be a push south."

"Now in Korea the situation is not good. Preliminary casualty figures indicate that we have lost 3200 soldiers and airmen, primarily in the Incheon area. We have lost two tactical aircraft at this time and the Chinese have brought in several squadrons of tactical aircraft to fight our bombing campaign. Our B-2s, B-1s, and some B-52s have carpet bombed the border area. Korean and American forces withdrew several miles before the bombing was initiated and we do not have any estimates yet on the success of the bombing initiative."

"We are rearming our bombers at air bases in Japan so we can keep the pressure on the enemy. We have also moved several tactical air squadrons to Japan to assist with cover for our bombers. The Chinese Air Force is one to be respected however and fighting has been, and I suspect, will continue to be intense. The Russian Naval units have patrolled between Japan and Korea but have not taken any part thus far in the activity. The Australian Navy units will be in position to assist us within forty-eight hours but our fleet is still four days away."

The president was busy writing notes and occasionally gazing around the room. Senator Jones was gripping his coffee so hard I was wondering if the cup would break. As General Hickman stopped to take a breath, TJ put his hand up to get him to pause.

"General, I deeply appreciate your briefing on what is going on and what will go on today but I need to look at the strategy and what will be going on next week. How long have you been second in command at Cent Com?"

"For three years, sir, before that I was the Commander of the 82nd Airborne Division at Fort Bragg."

"That is excellent, general. I am giving you an additional assignment and that is to be my military strategy advisor. Before you say a word I understand you would never contradict the Army Chief or the Commander of the Joint Chiefs but politics always enters into their decisions and what I want from you is your opinion based on your experience and education and that opinion you will share with me, Don my chief of staff, and that is all. I am not a military expert and I need an opinion other than the joint chiefs before I make my decisions. Will you accept my assignment?"

"Sir, I will give you my best opinion about any military matters but I will never disobey the orders of those commanders above my position."

TJ stood up and shook hands with the general and then said, "Okay, now if you were in my shoes right now what would you be most worried about and what actions would you take?"

"Okay, this is my opinion for whatever it is worth, sir, and nothing more."

The President nodded in agreement.

"As I see the nation is facing three critical situations that need immediate attention. First, the threat within the homeland needs to be eliminated. We should dispatch either troops or paramilitary civilian groups to each of the seized areas to eliminate not capture, but eliminate the threats. These individuals are radical and will not negotiate in good faith so we simply take them out. That will be unpopular and there will be a sizeable number of collateral casualties."

"Second, the problem in Korea requires a massive attack. I would consider using a tactical nuclear device in this matter because the sheer numbers of Chinese forces will be overpowering so we have to display ultimate muscle. The Chinese are much more advanced than we are regarding cyber uses so I would be willing to bet that an EMP would not be a grave event for them because they have undoubtedly taken steps to safeguard their critical computer networks. I would drop that bomb on Pyongyang to show the Chinese that we are willing to use it and with any luck to take the North Korean leadership out. This will have the side benefit of showing the Russian leadership that we are not afraid to use nukes as well."

"Third but possibly the most important is Russia. When we removed the units we did in Germany and Italy we cleared a path for their expansion. I don't believe that Russia will stop with Poland but will continue south and west with the ultimate goal of taking Germany, France, Italy, Austria, the Czech Republic, Slovakia, Hungary, Romania and on and on. If we can control these conflicts we can move on the rest of the Islamic militants at our own speed."

"Lieutenant General Hickman that is a very well thought out and concise summary of your opinion regarding our future strategy. Whether I stick to it or not I appreciate your viewpoint and I will certainly consider everything you said. More importantly, I now know what I need to question when the intelligence people and Admiral McCain finally get out of bed and get in here."

Everyone had a good laugh over the last statement but everyone in the room knew the nation was in serious problems and we were all very worried.

The President then turned to me and gave me an order. "Don, I need to address the nation tonight. Find a way to make it happen."

"Yes, sir."

I had no idea how to pull this off because we had blocked the signals from all the major media groups since the attack on the news media yesterday. There was local stations still up and running around the country, public broadcasting was still on line and the internet. I got on the phone and I called in favors from everyone I could think of. Then I called the FCC and asked them to lift the blocking of the major networks. There was a lot of discussion because of the fear of what would appear on these networks and if the blocking was raised it might be difficult to reestablish. In the end it was agreed that the president's message was important and worth the risk.

While I was working this out, TJ was in the situation room meeting with Admiral McCain and police officials from New York, Silver Springs, and Atlanta.

"I will address the nation at 8:00 PM and the broadcasting blocking will be lifted at 7:50 PM. What I want to happen is an all-out assault on these buildings at about 7:45 PM. Gentlemen, these people are extremists and will not negotiate with anyone. They believe that there is no compromise with their positions. So if we take prisoners we will eventually have to deal with these individuals again and I don't want that, so I do not want prisoners. I want these people eliminated permanently. I realize that if they all throw their weapons down and surrender that you cannot simply murder them and I will not give that order, but I will tell you that for the safety of the hostages and the safety of your country the best course of action is not to ask for surrender but to simply eliminate the threat. I will leave the particulars to all of you but I want the SWAT police units and special operators from the military and hostage rescue from the FBI to work together and put an end to this immediate threat to our country. Don't, for a minute, believe this is the end because it will not be, but it can be a decisive battle in this new war. Now let's get this done."

As the president left the room serious discussions and planning began. There was not enough time to plan this assault like any of the leaders would like but they had no choice because this was an emergency situation.

JUNE 3, 2017

THE OVAL OFFICE
7:45 PM

The president walked into an already crowded Oval Office. Cameras and lights were in place and people were running around finishing the last minute preparations. The president entered the room and turned to me and asked for an update on how many people would hear what he was about to say.

"We will be broadcasting on radio and internet, first of all. We also have PBS stations connected. We have established a link through the internet with major local stations across the country. The BBC is picking up the feed as well and will broadcast it. The block on the transmitters will be dropped in five minutes and engineers with the FCC will work on getting all the major media on line as well but we should still have a sizeable audience if that doesn't work. Last I heard all units were in position for the attack to retake the media centers."

"Be sure and let me know if you get reports on the attacks while I am speaking."

With that the president walked to his desk and sat down while makeup people did their duty and he reviewed his notes once more. At this very moment police emergency services and SWAT units were attacking at street level at each of the media centers while FBI Hostage Rescue units and military special operators were rappelling from helicopters onto the roofs of the buildings. While police units fought their way up through the building the military and FBI were fighting down in hopes that the enemy soldiers would be trapped in between.

At precisely 8:00 PM the cameras went live.

"Ladies and gentlemen, the President of the United States, Tyrone J. Samuels."

"Good evening my brothers and sisters in freedom. We have entered a dark time in the history of the United States. Our country has been invaded by an enemy whose goal is not only to overthrow our government but also our way of life and our beliefs. We cannot and will not allow this to happen. In addition, other major powers in the world, specifically the Russian Federation and the People's Republic of China have worked in conjunction with these radical enemies to seize other countries to both expand their power of influence and expand their borders. We also cannot allow this to happen.

"Before I go any further let me make one important statement. At the beginning of World War II our government under the direction of President Franklin Roosevelt took Japanese-American citizens and placed them in camps allegedly for their safety but in reality because they were unsure if they were agents of the Japanese government. This was not only wrong it was evil. These people were loyal U.S. citizens, many of which had relatives serving in the U.S. military. I mention this because there are many citizens of our country who are good neighbors and co-workers and friends but who happen to be of the Muslim faith. I do not want you to treat them any differently tomorrow than you treated them a month ago.

"Having said that I have to inform you that a military unit comprised of Islamic extremist and radicals have invaded our country and must be eliminated in order to end this threat to our homeland. As I am speaking to you now there are attacks underway in New York, Silver Springs, Maryland, and Atlanta in order to take back the media centers that they seized yesterday. We have already turned back an armed invasion in Arizona yesterday and we have operations underway to seek and destroy other radicals within the country. This is a war and people will be killed as a result of these operations, some intended and some unintended.

"In addition, we are actively engaged in battle with China and North Korea in the Korean peninsula. We are about to engage the Russian Federation in battle in Europe as well. I cannot adequately express how much I would rather be tackling problems with the economy or immigration than dealing with a war.

"Just to make it clear to all of you what this battle is all about, I want you to think about what it means if we lose this war. These extremist believe in cutting the hands off of thieves, and beheading gays and lesbians. They will murder members of the Jewish faith and Christians will have to either convert to Islam or pay a tax. They will take your property and enslave your daughters. So regardless of what you think of me as president or which political party you belong to, consider whether your life will improve under sharia or if you believe with all our problems we have a good country and a fair, equitable lifestyle.

"If you believe that our country is fair and you enjoy the liberty and freedom you now have in your daily lives then I urge *you to do three things. First, make sure you have adequate food and supplies to maintain your household in case transportation becomes an issue. Second, obtain firearms and ammunition to defend your property should that become necessary. Third and most important of all, pray to God for strength and help in overcoming these evil radicals.*

"Thank you and May God bless each of you and the United States of America."

As the lights went off and the cameras turned off TJ turned to me and shouted, "What is going on with the attacks?"

"Sir, I have not heard a word from anyone but I will head to the situation room to find out right now."

TJ didn't wait for me to report to him but stood up and headed out the door with me. We nearly ran to the situation room as the attack had been going on for about forty-five minutes at this point and the president believed we would know something before now.

As we entered the room there were dozens of conversations occurring at once and radio traffic from several different locations blaring in the background. The normal organized chaos of this room was now simply chaos.

Major Combs spotted us and immediately ushered us to a table in the corner of the room. "Sir, there are several intense battles going on at these locations. The Times building in New York was captured fairly quickly. They only had about thirty fighters in the building, all of whom were killed rather quickly but there were a number of improvised explosive devices placed throughout the buildings. Seventy-five of the hostages were found dead but it appeared that most, if not all, were killed prior to our attack.

"At the NBC building the rooftop was lined with explosives. As the operators rappelled onto the roof the explosives were detonated and it appears that all of our agents were killed. The police assault on the ground floor has gone only slightly better as they are still involved in heavy fighting. CBS, ABC, CNN, and Fox buildings are faring only slightly better. All of these buildings had large number of fighters and although the landings on the roof were completed successfully the fighting to get inside was and continues to be intense.

"The discovery channel building in Silver Springs only had about twenty fighters who were easily overcome and that building has been secured. In Atlanta the fighting has ended and we have taken that building with minimal casualties. They had about seventy-five fighters in that building but they have been killed. This battle is not going to end as quickly as Arizona did."

While CNN was struggling to get back on the air using their Atlanta studios Fox and CBS were already up and running but with Islamic prayers and propaganda. Videos of the bodies of the FBI agents at the NBC facility were being broadcast as were videos of Fox and CBS personnel who had been beheaded by the terrorist. Threats were being blared into the living rooms of citizens all across the nation and the FCC was struggling to block the signals once again.

TJ indicated he had to get some sleep because tomorrow he would have to make some serious decisions regarding the direction the country was going to take.

JUNE 4, 2017

WHITE HOUSE SITUATION ROOM
11:45 AM

As I waited in the situation room for the president I was watching the tension mount. Both Lt. Gen. Hickman and Major Combs appeared on edge and were making last minute phone calls and monitoring radio traffic. Pacific Command had set up a temporary command post at Kadena Air Base in Okinawa, Japan. Many of the air missions would initiate from this location but unfortunately the Chinese Navy was floating between Korea and the base. Planes were already leaving the base in preparation for what would be a huge air attack with multiple targets.

The president entered the room and there was a loud "tension" that reverberated through the room as everyone came to attention and awaited the president to say at ease. He did so quickly and moved toward the table where I was located with Major Combs. Before he sat down he turned toward the communications area where the military officers in the room were working diligently and spoke to them once again. "I want you all to know that I and everyone in church with me this morning prayed for the success of this operation. If this operation fails it will be my fault alone. If it succeeds it will be to your credit and God's."

There was no applause or comment just a few polite smiles as they went back to what they were doing.

79

Major Combs then started his briefing. "Sir, we have several electronic warfare planes already in position over the target areas. Their jobs are to simply confuse the radar and other electronics of the enemy as much as possible. We have three main target areas for this operation. B-2 bombers from Whiteman Air Force Base in Missouri will strike Pyongyang firing missiles and dropping other bombs on the Presidential Palace and other government locations in that city. B-1B bombers from the 7th Air Force and originally from a base in North Dakota will attack Chinese warships including a carrier off the coast of South Korea. At approximately the same time B-52s will carpet bomb the approximate area where the North Korean and Chinese troops are currently located. This will be immediately followed by A-10 Warthog aircraft which will attack armored vehicles which have landed at Incheon and have been moving to the front line in an effort to flank the troops currently fighting. All this will begin at noon which will be 4:00 AM, local time in Korea, June fifth."

The radio traffic being heard at the command post in Okinawa was being rebroadcast in the Situation Room and the President began listening very intently to what was going on.

"Baker 16 on the deck on attack run."

"Baker 17 on the deck on attack run."

Major Combs looked at the President and said, "Those are the B-1 bombers and they have descended to an altitude just above the water in order to try to evade any radar which might be still active despite the jamming."

"Baker 16 missiles away, breaking right."

"Baker 17 missiles away, breaking left."

Major Combs again started his explanation. "Both bombers have just fired JDAM missiles, which are air to surface type missiles. The ships they are firing at have defenses to destroy these missiles but hopefully the jamming will prevent this from happening. We will know in a moment."

"Eagle 12, seven missiles destroyed one hit on Liaoning near the rear. Be advised they are beginning to launch."

"Baker 16, roger that, we are returning to drop our load."

"Eagle 12, be advised they have activated ship to air missiles."

"Baker 16 and 17 are approaching at flight level 5, can't miss from point blank."

The President looked up and Combs said, "They are going to fly over the ship at 5000 feet and drop their bombs. This is suicide."

"Baker 16 bombs . . ."

"Baker 17, bombs away, 16 is splashed. No need for rescue I am returning."

"Eagle 12, roger. Be advised command that Liaoning is completely on fire and appears to be listing. Also an unidentified class Luyang II destroyer appears to be damaged and is dead in the water."

"David 6 and David 7 are on our attack run, stand by."

"Eagle 8, roger that. No radars appear to have targeted you at this point."

The President again looked at Combs who simply said, "B-2s over Pyongyang."

Then a new voice came across the air. "Kilo 5, Kilo 6, Kilo 7 beginning bomb run."

Again the President looked up and Combs mouthed B-52s.

There was several minutes of silence before we heard the radio traffic resume.

"David 6 and David 7, delivery complete we will be enroute to refueling point."

"Eagle 8, roger that. Maintain current altitude we see no defensive activity at this time."

"Eagle 8, correction we now see multiple SAMs launched in your general direction. It would appear none will be capable of your altitude."

"David 6, roger that."

"Eagle 10, Kilo 6 you have a SAM launch at your seven o'clock, take evasive action."

"Kilo 6, roger."

"Adam 6, 8, 12 and 16 are beginning an attack run on target location Tango 12."

"Eagle 10, Mike 12 you have two J-15s approaching from your 1600."

"Roger that."

The President was silent as the battle continued for nearly an half hour. In the end we lost one B-1 bomber and two F-18 fighter jets. The crews from the F-18 were both rescued. The Chinese lost their aircraft carrier and an unknown number of aircraft. In addition, the bombing along the fighting seemed to be rather devastating and the Chinese and North Korean troops pulled back into North Korea. The armored units at Incheon were destroyed. The government complex in Pyongyang was also devastated as was much of the city itself. The numbers of casualties were unknown but we were sure that before the day was over the civilian deaths would be exaggerated by the North Koreans. It was not determined how much, if any, of the North Korean leadership had been killed. One other site that had been devastated was a missile launch facility near Wonsan that might have been capable of launching a missile on the U.S. The president had a huge smile on his face as the wrap up operations began.

Lt. Gen. Hickman came over and sat down across the president.

"Sir, don't go lighting any cigars yet. We made a dent. An important dent no doubt, but still just a dent. The Chinese didn't put up much of a fight. I believe they were testing our capability. They were capable of putting up a much bigger fight than they did and that worries me greatly. I believe that they just poked us to see if we would respond and what we would throw at them. Another thing that worries me is that Russia had several warships observing what was going on and made no effort to join in. We are at war with them as well so why didn't they jump in the mix? This was practically one sided. I don't believe either side cared much about what happened to North Korea but were more concerned to see our weaponry in action to judge what to expect in combat situations."

Now the president's smile left his face and was replaced with a look of concern. "Are you telling me we should not have hit them this hard?"

"No, not at all. I am simply saying that this was far easier than I expected and that worries me. They could have easily called in more aircraft from China and the Russian vessels are all equipped with missiles but none were fired at us. Even the SAMs they fired were older models that they knew would not knock our planes down. The aircraft carrier we sank is the oldest carrier they have active. I think they staged this incident as a test run to watch us react and to see where we draw our resources from. I believe we can be certain of an attack very soon with a much more devastating impact on our homeland."

JUNE 6, 2017

WHITE HOUSE OVAL OFFICE
9:00 AM

Monday had been a day for intelligence gathering and assessment of the attacks of the weekend. The president called Admiral McCain of the Joint Chiefs; Jacob Owen, the Director of the National Intelligence Agency; Lt. Gen. Hickman, Secretary of State Steven Lambert; CIA Director Lawrence Williams, Secretary of Defense Donald Rodgers; and Homeland Security Secretary Patrick Simmons for a briefing and strategy session in the Oval Office. The furniture had to be rearranged as a special round table had been brought in so everyone could look everyone else in the eye as the session proceeded.

The president wasted no time in getting down to business. "Patrick fill us in on the homeland situation."

"We currently have control of Fox and CNN networks. The Discovery networks are also in our control. The other networks are also on the air but are in control of the Islamic forces. They have been broadcasting the Islamic prayers at the appropriate times but the rest of the day has been videos of the assaults from their point of view and propaganda regarding Islam and sharia. There have been a number of coded messages that are broadcasted several times a day which we are certain are designed to activate other cells within the country but so far no incidents have occurred since Saturday. Our best intelligence is that these cells will stage a massive attack in several areas simultaneously."

The president then looked over to Admiral McCain and told him to proceed.

"I have not got a lot of good news to share. The Korean operation did eliminate a possible site where a nuclear capable missile could have been launched against CONUS. That site was in Wonsan and was a secondary target but was successfully destroyed. The Presidential Palace and government offices in Pyongyang were destroyed as well. According to information we have been able to obtain, all of the leadership including the president were in Beijing at the time of the attack and they are safe. The city itself sustained what I would refer to as catastrophic damage. South Korean forces are now firmly in control of Incheon, however, Chinese forces are only a few miles away north and east of the Bukhan Mountains and are in control of Highway 39 which runs through the northeast section of South Korea. These forces are within striking distance of Seoul. North Korean government and military command operations appear to have moved southeast to Namp'o. We also have information that there is a large scale troop movement in China from Shenyang south to Dandong near the North Korea border. We also have noted that a number of Chinese naval vessels have departed the port of Quindao with a heading that would take them to the Korean peninsula. Preliminary casualty figures in this operation show 10,575 South Korean military loses 4,786 United States losses as well as several aircraft. Losses being reported from China appear to be 1,265 and North Korea is reporting 12,475 military losses and 85,000 plus civilian losses.

"In other military actions the Turkish forces have advanced in Greece to the city of Salonica, which would give them control of just under a third of the country. The Russians have withdrawn from Finland but have intensified their push into Poland. Russian forces now control everything in Poland north of a line from Bialystok to Poznan. Again, roughly a third of the country."

The admiral then indicated he was finished and there was an eerie silence in the room as everyone pondered for a few moments what he had just reported.

The president looked over at the two intelligence chiefs and asked them for any information they wanted to share regarding the situation.

CIA Director Williams spoke first. "Regarding Russia's intent we have some insight from human intelligence we have been able to gain. First, although I think we all knew it to begin with, Vladimir is calling all the shots. He is supplying weapons and supplies as well as some funding to the Islamist's through Iran. I believe he wants to keep us so occupied with problems in the homeland that we won't become a threat to his activity in Europe.

"Our best intelligence analysis of Russia's intent is very disturbing, to say the least. It appears that Russian forces intend to move through Poland and to continue south into the Czech Republic, Slovakia, Hungary, Austria, and Romania. We have not been able to confirm this yet but we have information that the Turks intend to move north after securing Greece and eventually both Russia and Turkey will meet somewhere in the center either Bosnia or Serbia. We are also concerned that the

Russians could move west as well into Germany, France, and Italy, and ultimately control all of Europe."

The president took a deep breath and looked around the room before asking how certain Williams was of the information and analysis.

Williams looked over at Jacob Owens for a couple of seconds and Owens nodded. Williams then replied, "Eighty-five percent certainty."

The president shook his head from side to side and then picked up his notepad and wrote something down before looking back up at Williams. "Okay, what is your best information on Korea?"

Jacob Owens spoke up this time. "I can give you the intel on this one, sir, and it is not good. We do not have any human intelligence on the ground that is active and reliable at this time. This information comes from intercepted communications so there is less reliability than we would like. We also have some satellite intelligence but as you know we have been greatly hampered by the satellites destroyed by Russia.

"It appears that there is a large scale troop movement in both China and Russia into this theatre of operations. The Chinese appear to be preparing for a full scale invasion into Korea in the very near future. The Russians have what we believe are two or three divisions of military troops gathering outside of Vladivostok. I believe we have a situation where more than South Korea is at stake. I think that while China moves on South Korea that Russia will make a move on Japan. I can't back that assumption up with hard evidence but that appears to be the only other major target that they could be preparing for and the Chinese have more than enough to handle South Korea already. I now believe that during the attack we just completed, the Russian vessel was actually in the area to monitor where our forces were being dispatched from and I believe our forces in that area are in an immediate threat of attack at any time."

The president held his hand up to stop Owens before he went any further. There was dead silence in the room as everyone stopped and looked directly at the president to see what was coming next. He turned toward Admiral McCain and stared directly at him for several moments and then said, "Where is the Pacific Fleet at?"

"They will be coming into Sasebo in the next six to eight hours to restock supplies and munitions."

"How many subs do we have in the area?"

The admiral looked down at some paperwork and then replied, "We currently have two in the East China Sea and one in the Sea of Japan."

The president then turned back to Jacob Owens and told him to continue.

Owens had just started talking about specific units of the Russian and Chinese divisions involved in the build-up when the president again interrupted him.

"Excuse me, Jacob, what if Russia is not interested in Japan but is building up a force to move on Alaska? You realize we have a missile launch facility in Alaska as well as some long range radar facilities and several military units based there. If the Russians moved to take Alaska we could not only lose those facilities but a great deal of oil which they could then use to supplement and supply their war apparatus."

Jacob Owens had a puzzled look on his face at first but then answered the president, "We have not considered that possibility but off the top of my head I think that is unlikely since it is still a long way off to Alaska from their current location."

"Jacob, you might want to take a closer look at the map because the Russians are very close to Alaska already and if they controlled the northern islands of Japan they could stage a multi-directional attack and overwhelm our defenses." The president was furiously writing on the pad of paper in front of him and never even looked up as he made his comment to Jacob Owens. While he was still writing he then called on an update from the Secretary of State, Steven Lambert.

"Sir, there is a lot of concern regarding the recent events but no solid pledges of support. The United Nations is still in the process of trying to re-establish their operations in Zurich but since nearly all of their records were destroyed during the EMP they are moving very slowly. I expect nothing but silence from them. Frankly, I have the opinion that they don't want to back the wrong side and at this point they are still trying to determine who that is going to be when the smoke clears. Most of these countries try to take whatever they can get from us but they could care less what happens to us, especially if there is any chance of them receiving blowback from another country or group like the Islamic Caliphate Organization. The Middle East is as tense as I have ever seen it and I look for an attack on Israel to occur at any time but I am not sure from where it will come. It could be any of the Middle East powers and it could be Russia who would love to control Israel so they could use it as political leverage."

TJ looked at Lambert and asked, "Any recommendations regarding our immediate action?"

"No, sir. I believe that there is no diplomatic resolution available at this time as much as it pains me to say that."

The president stood up and walked across the room with his back to the table. He stood in front of a portrait of George Washington and seemed to be admiring it for several minutes before he turned back around and walked back toward the table. Looking at the defense secretary he said, "Don, I would like you and Admiral McCain to take Jacob and Larry into my conference room and start working on possible attack scenarios."

The defense secretary stood and said, "Okay sir, do you have a particular site you would like us to concentrate on?"

"Yes, our enemies like Russia, China, and the Islamic Caliphate. I will join you in a few minutes and give you more specific information."

As they left the president dismissed the others in the room with the instructions to make preparations for war but asked Lt. Gen. Hickman and myself to stay a few moments.

After everyone had left the room he turned to the general and asked, "General, what do you think my next step should be to end this conflict?"

Hickman looked surprised and a little confused and then said, "Whatever the Admiral and the intelligence chiefs want to do would be a good start."

"General, I want to know what you would do in my shoes and it will stay between the three of us in this room right now. Remember I told you I want to use you as a consultant in these matters."

"Yes, sir." He hesitated a few moments and then said, "Sir, in the history of the United States of America our military has always been used to respond to aggression from some other entity. We have never initiated the attack. I believe that the leaders involved in our current situation believe that this is somehow ingrained in our culture and will continue to be the case. So they will continue to prod us where they are strong and wait for our response. If I were in your shoes right now I would be looking for something unexpected. I would order an aggressive attack in multiple areas where the enemies don't expect us to go. If we attack their weak areas, they will have to reconsider their plans and possibly pull back until they can make sure that their homelands are safe. This is not the nineteenth or twentieth centuries anymore and leaders need the support of their people to secure their position. If the people become more afraid of us than they are of their leadership their domestic issues may become more than they can handle with an aggressive war going on as well. I would hit them in ways that confuse them and stir up their own people against them. This will probably mean the deaths of large numbers of non-combatants though and will be unpopular."

The president looked at Hickman right in the eyes and said, "That is exactly what I hoped you would say. We are thinking along the same lines but I just wanted to make sure I wasn't going down the wrong path. Why don't you come with me while I relate my plan to the others. By the way, you can look on my notepad to confirm that is what I have been thinking and deciding to do even while I listened to the others speak."

"Don, I would like you to go meet with the FBI Director and find out the status of our plans to regain the TV stations as well as what proactive steps they are taking to find and arrest the terrorist cells that they believe are going active."

I simply replied yes, sir, and left. It seemed to me that TJ was a lot more worried about South Korea than he was with the United States at this point. That bothered me but I wasn't really sure if the president and I were on the same page. I was desperately worried about what might take place in the States soon and he seemed to be more worried about South Korea and China.

As I drove to the FBI Headquarters at Quantico I was amazed at the lack of traffic. Since the EMP traffic had been light because so many people lost their cars to the fried computer system and electrical systems that resulted. More and more were having their cars repaired as the parts became available and the auto makers were pumping new cars into the economy as quickly as they could.

As I walked into the lobby Michael McLaren met me just past the checkpoint and ushered me into a conference room on the first floor. After we exchanged greetings and I explained the president's concerns he went right into his briefing.

"Don, we are in very serious trouble here. The intelligence we have gathered points to an attack in the immediate future but we have no idea where it will occur. Coast guard personnel have stopped a couple of ships heading into port and their cargo included munitions and supplies for tanks and heavy weapons but we have not been able to locate either. We have maintained surveillance on many of the mosques and Islamic concerns but have turned up nothing. A judge will not let us search these facilities so we will have to wait until they move them but my biggest fear at this point is that this equipment is not there to begin with and is at another location that we are not aware of at this point."

"So what is our next step?"

"Wait and hope someone makes a mistake before these attacks occur. We have drone aircraft up twenty-four hours a day and we have been able to get a few CIs to go inside these organizations but so far we have learned nothing."

"Do you have an idea of where these attacks will occur?"

"No, but we are certain they will attack locations that will cause the most publicity and lead to the most casualties."

JUNE 14, 2017

White House Oval Office

As I was walking toward the Oval Office I was hoping that today would be different from the last seven days. TJ had really shut me out of whatever was going on in his office lately. He kept assigning me to meet with various directors and department secretaries about what seemed to me to be nonsense. The last thing he told me last night was to clear his calendar for the rest of the week and that he wanted me to stay close so today should prove to be interesting.

As I entered the office TJ was on his knees in front of his desk and praying intensely. I have seen TJ pray before and he frequently read the Bible but I never saw him sweating as he prayed. I stopped dead in my tracks and started to turn around. I decided to simply quietly close the door and wait for him to finish. He continued for several minutes and then stood up and wiped his forehead with his handkerchief before turning toward me.

"Don't worry, Don, you will understand as the day goes on. I know you haven't been in on the strategy sessions we have had in the last several days but I will catch you up pretty quickly. I took Lt. General Hickman's advice to become aggressive and attack rather than respond and we are going to do it in a big way."

As he walked behind his desk I pulled a chair up to the other side and had a seat. That was something I wouldn't normally do without being invited by the president but I had a feeling that I was going to need to sit down very soon. "Okay, sir, what do I need to know?"

TJ leaned back in his chair and then looked across the desk at me and said;

"At noon today we will launch several simultaneous attacks on Russia, China, and North Korea. The hyper-speed weapon will be launched and will deliver a tactical nuclear warhead to the Russian Space Center at Baikonur, Kazakhstan. At the same time Tomahawk missiles will be fired from the USS Antietam and the USS Chosin and deliver non-nuclear warheads on the new space center north of Blagoveshchensk in the Amur province of Russia. The timing has to be just right so that the space station has passed over and is far enough away not to detect the launch. I was going to blow it up but with the laser weapon on board they would be able to destroy the missile before it could get close enough to do any real damage. So the next best thing is to eliminate their launch sites."

"Is that their only two launch sites?"

"No, there is one more in the area of Archangelsk, which is north of Moscow but it is designed primarily for supply ships to the space station and doesn't have all the necessary equipment needed for their manned flights. This won't stop them forever but it will slow them down for a while."

"What about retaliation?"

"Oh, we expect them to retaliate and we know they are aware of where the launch site is located. That's why we evacuated all non-essential personnel yesterday and guidance controls will be handled by another base not from the launch site. As soon as the missile is launched the remaining personnel will evacuate and we have also evacuated everyone within ten miles."

"I am impressed, is there anything else about to happen?"

"We are also going to bomb two Russian Naval Bases, one at Vladivostok and the other at Petropavlovsk. We also intend to send missiles into Dalian Naval Base and to the Chinese Air Base at Haikou on Hainan Island. Except for the space centers, each site is an offensive military site where it is likely the attacks will be launched from, even though they have not done so yet. Our embassies in Seoul and Beijing have been evacuated along with all non-essential American personnel and the embassy in Tokyo is going through the checklist to leave as well."

"So what do you hope to accomplish today?"

The president looked down at his desk for a moment and then looked toward me;

"That's an interesting question and I am not sure how to answer it. I guess the main thing is that we can show both Russia and China that they are vulnerable as well and that they should understand that a war will cost them dearly. I hope that at the end of the day they may want to rethink this whole thing and possibly have a change of heart regarding their world domination."

As he was about to continue that thought the phone buzzed and Hillary announced that Michael McLaren was waiting to come in. He told her to send him in and I pulled another chair up to the desk.

The president said; "Hi Mike, what's on your mind this morning?"

The FBI Director shook the President's hand and then sat down in a chair next to mine. "Sir, I am not sure if you have been watching any of the channels controlled by the Islamic terrorists but they have made repeated announcements which started after midnight last night calling for the soldiers of Allah to take their positions and that the day of destiny will be June fifteenth. Then just a few hours ago they started saying that as of June sixteenth this country will be the Islamic Caliphate of America. I have checked all of our field offices to try to get some intelligence but no one has any information regarding what is coming and we don't have the slightest idea of where to prepare."

TJ leaned back in his chair and looked over at the portrait of George Washington for several moments. When he leaned back forward he said;

"Mike, make a list of the most probable targets and do what you can to beef up security in those locations and naturally alert all the local authorities. Oh, also have HRT set up in a strategic location where they can respond quickly."

Mike looked a little surprised; "Mr. President, only two members of our Hostage Rescue Team survived the New York assaults and they are both in the hospital in serious condition."

The president had a shocked look on his face; "Mike, I am sorry I knew there had been casualties but I didn't know you lost the entire team. I am so sorry."

McLaren stood up nodded and again shook TJ's hand as he started out of the room.

The rest of the morning was spent making phone calls to various governors and warning them of the latest information and assuring them that federal help will be sent should they have an attack. Unfortunately, nearly a third of the country still did not have power and communications were poor or non-existent. We had mixed emotions about the lack of power and communications because we felt if we couldn't communicate to people in those areas neither could the terrorist. At least that was our thought.

Just before noon we both walked to the situation room to observe the attack as it unfolded. In the area of the attack the day was actually June fifteenth and it was nearly sunrise. Like so many times before we entered the room and you could feel the tension at once. As soon as the president entered the room he told everyone to be at ease and then proceeded to the workstation that had been set up for him.

Lt. General Hickman came over to greet us and then advised the president that we would not be able to monitor real time communications because they had been unable to have it set up in time. "Mr. President, the command center for the overall attack will be on board the USS Blue Ridge which is the command vessel of the 7th Fleet. They will be communicating with us through Pearl Harbor and the delay will be minimal but we won't hear the radio communications. As much as possible there will be little radio communications between the units to try to minimize chances of the enemy getting ahead of us."

Just after noon Lt. Gen Hickman indicated that the ISS had cleared the area where they could detect or use their laser weapon to hamper the missile launches. Things started happening very quickly then.

"Mr. President, the hyper-speed weapon has launched and should be on target within fifteen minutes. Both the Antietam and the Chosin have begun launching missiles at their targets. The USS Key West and the USS Chicago are about to launch missiles at Haikou. We also have B-2 bombers approaching the coast of China to attack the Dalian Naval Base at that location. The Fifth Carrier Air Wing has begun operations off of the USS George Washington and will be attacking the Naval Base at Vladivostok, while missiles are being launched at the Naval Base at Petropavlovsk by the USS John S McCain and the USS Fitzgerald. I will let you know as soon as I have any results or other information for you."

The president thanked Hickman who then walked back over to the huddle of generals in the far corner of the room. Admiral McCain had prepared a small book of options and alternative should something go wrong and TJ was busy reviewing the information. Twenty minutes or more had passed as we both sat nervously waiting for some information.

Suddenly a giant cheer went up from the generals and Lt. Gen. Hickman approached us with a grin on his face.

"Sir, we have some good news. The pilots of the B-2s all report a successful delivery of their weapons systems. The missiles were on target and they report significant damage to the Dalian Naval Facility. The B-2s encountered no resistance and are returning to their base. Additionally, we have information from seismograph operators that the nuclear device was detonated and was on target. We have no information regarding the damage to the area but there is no doubt that it exploded on target. A number of the missiles fired at Petropavlovsk were destroyed by Russian defenses but at least four reached their targets and again no information has been received regarding the damage estimates. We are still waiting for reports from the Vladivostok and Haikou operations. I also would like to report, sir, that the Third Expeditionary Forces of the Marine Corp have landed just north of Sapporo, Japan, and will defend the Japanese island of Hokkaido. Intelligence has indicated that the Russians would make an assault on Japan starting here and now they will face stiff opposition should they try."

I glanced at TJ with a puzzling look after that last piece of information but he quickly told me that he had contacted the Japanese Premier and they agreed to the move for their own safety. Despite the good news we both were still tense because the last two operations were both important and the words of Mike McLaren were still haunting us . . . what will the "Day of Destiny" bring?

It was thirty minutes later when we were informed that only two of twelve missiles penetrated the Chinese defenses at Haikou. Damage reports were not available yet and in Vladivostok six F-18s and two F-35s were destroyed. No word was available on their crews. There had been damage at Vladivostok and several ships at that location had been damaged or sunk but those attacks were not the success that anyone had hoped to achieve.

We left the Situation Room at about 4:00 PM and started back toward the Oval Office. TJ turned to me as we were walking and said; "Don, is your family somewhere safe?"

"They're still in town but I was thinking of sending them out of the area."

TJ nodded and said; "That's probably a good idea. I would get them out of here tonight and into a location that is not in a major city."

I nodded as we continued down the hall and before I left that night I called home and told my wife to pack for her and the kids. She had a cousin in Mississippi and I thought it was time for a visit to her. I also told her to pack a separate bag for me because something told me I wouldn't be going home tomorrow or for a long time. The more I thought about the FBI information, the more nervous I became.

JUNE 15, 2017

WHITE HOUSE

I arrived at the White House a little after 7:00 AM, which was later than I had arrived in several weeks. I left my bag in the car but the rest of my family had left for Mississippi two hours earlier. My wife was upset and had voiced her objections about leaving but I held firm and in the end she agreed to leave.

As I entered the office I found Mike McLaren and Patrick Simmons talking with the president. They had informed him of the plans they had designed to try to stop the terrorist threat in Washington, New York, and Boston.

"We can't possibly take measures in every metro area but we are feeling pretty good that these areas will be safe. We have drones combing the area and checkpoints set up near every entry point to the cities. The coast guard has increased their patrols close to the ports. We are just not certain what to expect because we are still lacking intelligence."

TJ looked over at McLaren and said, "Isn't it ironic that I can get better intelligence regarding North Korea than I can from inside our own country?"

Both men looked at the president with a blank stare for a few moments and stood silent.

"As soon as you have any information regarding attacks anywhere contact me and we will set up in the situation room. Am I clear?"

Both indicated they understood and then turned and left the office.

When we are alone in the office again TJ turned and asked, "Is your family safe?"

"Yes, sir, I believe they are. They are travelling to Mississippi to stay with some relatives until this is over."

"Angela is refusing to leave but I am really having second thoughts about that because I am really worried about what lies in store for us before the end of the day."

As we continued the small talk for a few moments the mood seemed to lighten a little, but then the door opened abruptly and a secret service agent came inside. "Mr. President you are needed at once in the situation room."

We jogged to the situation room and as soon as we entered the controlled chaos was obvious. No one snapped to attention because they were much too busy to notice the president's entrance. When Lt. Gen. Hickman noticed he immediately turned and approached with a serious look on his face.

"Sir, we are currently under a missile attack. We have detected multiple launches from Russia and China with a total of sixteen missiles in flight toward Alaska. We are currently tracking and preparing to launch defensive missiles. The Laser Airborne Weapons System has also been deployed and is in the area to hopefully take out at least two of the inbound weapons."

We sat down knowing that it would be only minutes before we knew what the outcome would be and I had a feeling that the rest of the day would progress quickly. The first event was the destruction of two of the missiles by the LAWS which was flying north of Japan. Twenty defensive missiles were launched from various locations within the United States and we sat praying for the other fourteen missiles to be destroyed. Within ten minutes we had confirmation of eleven missiles being destroyed by the defensive missiles, which left three more hurtling toward Alaska.

Lt. Gen. Hickman approached us from the communications corner of the room. "Mr. President, we have confirmed three detonations inside Alaska. All three were Russian devices which were low level nuclear warheads. There will be casualties but at this point the extent of the damage is unknown."

As he started to go further a shout came from across the room and the general excused himself for a moment. He returned a few moments later and reported.

"Sir, a missile fired from China has struck the Antietam and the ship has received significant damage and is in danger of sinking. Rescue efforts are underway."

TJ sat patiently waiting for updates when another shout came from across the room. "Sasebo Naval Base is under attack. Missiles in the air from Chinese destroyer and from Shenyang 15s."

The generals calling the shots were shouting back and forth and there was unintelligible radio traffic blaring in the background. About five minutes passed and then Admiral McCain approached us.

"Sir, we now have F-18s flying cover over Sasebo and the Antietam. Chinese planes have departed the area but the Chinese destroyer, the Kouming, is still on patrol some fifteen miles off the coast of Sasebo. The Chosin and the Blue Ridge are both moving toward the Antietam at full speed to render aid and pick up survivors. The ship has exploded and is on fire and will most likely sink soon. We have an unknown number of casualties at Sasebo as well. Two ships at the Germantown, a dock landing ship and the Warrior, a mine sweeper, have both been hit by missiles and are on fire. The main runway at Sasebo was also destroyed and a number of aircraft that were on the ground were destroyed or severely damaged. It will be awhile before we know the full extent of the damage. The Chinese also fired three missiles into Seoul and all three struck their targets. The capital building was destroyed along with a military facility on the outskirts of the city. Again we have no information on casualties. We have a sub, the Oklahoma City, about twenty miles from Sasebo it was preceding toward the Korean Coast. I would like to have permission to turn it around and take out that destroyer."

TJ didn't even look up but said, "Do it now."

TJ was shaken by this course of events. He expected retaliation but not this significant and well-coordinated. He mumbled something to himself and then looked at me. "How could I have so underestimated their response?"

Limited power was back on in Biloxi and elsewhere along the Mississippi coast. One of the first places to open their doors was the Sea-View Mall. Numerous generators had been brought into the shopping center and all the stores were open even though cash registers amounted to a cash box and a pad of paper and a pencil. No charge cards could be accepted so the crowds were small at the cash and carry shopping experience, but there were crowds.

Only a handful of police cars and fire trucks were operational but amazingly enough it seemed all of the delivery services had managed to bring in trucks and deliveries were continuing as normal. Some services had even replaced their handheld computers, while police officers were relying on landline phones for communications.

A white panel truck pulled up to a delivery door on the north side of the mall and the driver jumped out wearing a brown shirt and blue jeans. He opened the back of the truck and removed a two-wheel hand cart on which he loaded two large boxes. Without a word he went to the delivery door and pushed his load inside. A mall security officer stood nearby smoking a cigarette and gazing into the air. The man entered the hallway which led to the backdoors of a number of stores. He stopped in the hall between two businesses and carefully placed one of the boxes on the floor next to the gas meter and main gas line feeding the mall. He then proceeded down the hallway walking through a door that led into the mall itself. Making a left turn he walked about a hundred yards through the mall before he took the other box and placed it on the floor between two of the most popular stores in the complex. He then pushed his empty cart back to his truck and placed it inside the back. The security officer was finishing his cigarette and the driver waved and smiled at him as he entered his truck and drove off.

Similar events were occurring at the same time in malls in Jackson, Little Rock, Nashville, St. Louis, Chicago, Minneapolis, and twenty other cities across the Midwest and East Coast. Each of the boxes had shipping labels for business near where they were left but each contained explosives equal to twenty sticks of dynamite and thousands of ball bearings and other forms of shrapnel. The boxes were delivered at each location at precisely 9:30 AM eastern time. At precisely 10:00 AM eastern time all of the boxes left in the public areas of the malls detonated. Hundreds were killed instantly. Police, Fire, EMS personnel all responded and immediately went to work trying to save those they could help and sending many victims to the hospital. At 10:30 AM they were still working on aiding the victims and trying to make the scenes safe when the second boxes detonated. The explosion obliterated the gas meters and caused the gas lines to erupt in flames. Walls in the confined hallways crumbled and several of the malls collapsed in the areas where the second explosion had taken place. By the end of the day more than double the number of people who died on 9/11 would die as a result of the explosions.

It was 10:05 AM when TJ stood up and indicated he was going to head back to his office. As we walked to the door one of the generals at the communications table turned and said, "Mr. President, you may want to stay, sir, we are getting reports of coordinated attacks here in CONUS."

TJ stopped dead in his tracks and started toward the communications table. The general who had stopped him turned back toward him and said, 'Sir, we have explosive detonations in shopping malls primarily east of the Mississippi River but these are in numerous locations from Minnesota to Florida. Casualties are high, sir."

TJ turned to Mike McLaren. "Where is the FBI Gulf Stream located?"

"National Airport, sir."

"I need to borrow it now."

"I will make the call, where are you going?"

"It is not for me, it is for the vice president and your pilot is to take him where he wants to go."

"Yes, sir, I will contact them now."

Next he turned to his secret service agent. "Dave, I want you to have the vice president's detail take him and his family to the airport and take the Gulf Stream to a location out west somewhere. I don't care where but it can't be a government facility and you tell them that they are to protect him and his wife above all else."

"Yes, sir."

TJ then walked to his table and picked up the phone.

"Arturo, we are under attack inside the country. It is more than media now. I have a detail coming to get you and your family to take you to the National Airport. The FBI Gulf Stream is waiting for you and I don't care where you go but I would suggest somewhere out west. You and I are targets and at least one of us has to survive this attack. I will leave as well soon but we can't be together so I want you out of harm's way first." I couldn't hear the vice-president's reply but after a few moments TJ replied, "God bless you as well."

He then called the secret service and instructed them to dismiss all non-essential personnel from the White House. He told Admiral McCain to move the command post to the Pentagon as soon as possible.

Next he turned to me. "You know that their next attack will be either on the Capital building or the White House. I want you to go to the Pentagon and stay there as long as you can safely. You will be my contact there, but when it becomes apparent that the Pentagon will fall I want you to get out and disappear. Do you have somewhere you can go that isn't public?

"Yes, I have some friends outside the government in Baltimore."

"That is where you need to go then. I will be heading for Andrews soon and take Air Force One wherever the secret service thinks is safe."

The secret service had called for Marine One to pick up the president as soon as possible and TJ and I started to the Oval Office to pick up the items he would need to take with him. Two FBI agents also accompanied us and were assigned to destroy any document that the president did not take with him when he left.

As the president was quickly going through his files and loading a briefcase, a secret service agent slammed open the door and ran inside shouting at us to turn the television on. TJ was startled at first but then grabbed a remote and turned on the television.

The pictures showed the Supreme Court building and at the top of the steps stood a dozen people carrying automatic rifles and five of the justices on their knees. The men with the rifles had scarfs covering their faces so that all you could see was their eyes. When the sound came up we could hear their demands.

"People of the Islamic States of America, we no longer require a group of elitists Christians and Jews telling us what is right and wrong. The only law we need is Sharia. Submit to Allah or die! Praise Allah!"

With that they systematically went down the line of justices cutting off their heads and allowing the heads to roll down the steps.

TJ looked around and said, "We need to leave. Now!"

Outside we could see Marine One approaching the landing area. Suddenly a rocket propelled grenade shot through the air and exploded near the cockpit of the helicopter. The copter dropped out of the sky and exploded on impact.

The secret service came into the office with Angela and then led us down into the basement and out through a tunnel. When we came out of the tunnel we were in the Lafayette Square Park. There were a number of panel vans waiting for us. I shook TJ's hand and said, "God speed, Mr. President."

JUNE 5, 2018

EMBASSY OF OMAN

Saud had two people writing notes as well as a third videotaping my statement. As I finished my statement he quickly asked, "Is this all you remember of those days?"

"Yes, sir, it is everything I recall. I left to head to the Pentagon but never got there because your soldiers already had the roads blocked. I changed vehicles several times and wound up in Baltimore where I remained until your people captured me."

I sat quietly as he spoke to his aides in Arabic. I wasn't sure what to expect next. I wondered if he was going to be a man of his word or if my life would end very soon. I still wasn't sure what was going on with the rest of the country but I kept remembering that police car moving slowly down the street that I saw from my room. It had been a long time since I had seen any civilian law enforcement but only Islamists moving through the streets in pickup trucks, jeeps, and other vehicles. I could feel the sweat beading up on my forehead and my stomach was becoming nauseous as I continued to sit quietly.

Saud approached me after several minutes and said,

"I appreciate your cooperation and we will be checking much of what you said with others who are in our custody. Should it match up then we will take you to another location until we need you again. As I said, you will not be harmed but we will need you to make some public addresses and we will give you some speaking points that we expect you to promote. You are safe as long as you cooperate, otherwise, you are of no value and I cannot speak to you of your safety should that occur."

He motioned for two men to take me back to my room. As they escorted me out I noticed we did not head for the stairs up to the room where I had been staying but instead headed downstairs into a basement area. There was a long hallway with rooms on either side. We walked about halfway down the hall when one of the men stopped and unlocked a door, motioning me to enter. The room had no windows. A bunk was against the wall to my left and a toilet and sink to my right. There was a desk directly in front of me with a tray of food waiting for me. As soon as I entered the room the door behind me closed and was locked. There was a dim light but no light switch for me to control. I walked over to the desk and looked at the tray. I am not even sure what was on that plate but it did not smell or look appetizing in any way. They may have called me a guest before but I was definitely a prisoner now.

My thoughts were really racing now and nothing positive was coming to mind. I could not hear anyone else so I guess I am alone or these rooms have incredible soundproofing. I did spot a small camera in the corner of the room and was sure I was being watched and listened too. This just made my paranoid feelings that much stronger. I couldn't help but wonder if TJ was alive.

I stared at the floor as I sat on the bunk and I was overcome by a sudden rush of tears. I thought about my wife, Pam, did she make it back to Mississippi? I had not thought of her for months as my sole concern seemed to be my survival. I had indeed been selfish and I was now regretting my attitude. I cooperated with these barbarians to save my life and cared little for those who had been so important to me in the past. I had been taken in by the propaganda of fear that they continually pounded into all of us.

The media had been solely controlled by the terrorists and they had used it to great advantage. When I had arrived at the safe house in Baltimore all of the television stations showed the same coverage over and over again. The members of the Supreme Court being executed and then random people being lined up on the streets and shot simply for not being Muslim. I had no doubt that these were all good people who showed courage and faith in God. What have I shown? Fear, selfishness, and self-centeredness were the only attributes I had displayed. I had to make amends but I didn't know what to do in order to make this right. I just would have to wait for the next opportunity and hope that I can muster some courage. In the meantime, maybe I should follow the example set by TJ in the White House and pray to God for strength.

I made up my mind that I would no longer believe what I was seeing and hearing on television and on the radio. Just because they claim that the United States has fallen doesn't make it so. Instead I will place this whole situation in God's hands and pray that I have truly been a fool and rescue is on its way.

Then I started thinking about the leaflets dropped from the plane, the noise of the jet and explosion, and the civilian police patrol. I realized that I have been a fool but at least I was a living fool.

JUNE 16, 2017

DAVIS-MONTHAN AIR FORCE BASE
TUCSON, ARIZONA

The president was looking out the window from his office on board Air Force One as they approached their destination in Arizona. Andrews Air Force Base was under attack when he arrived and he owed his life to the bravery of the airmen who fought the terrorist along the perimeter of the base. Even on board the plane he could hear explosions as they taxied to the end of the runway and it appeared they would be taking off directly over the fighting. The president could see flashes, back and forth from the combatants and was fearful that they would be blown out of the sky as they left the runway.

The normal run up of the engines was out of the question because this beast made one hell of a target so the plane began to accelerate even before it made the turn. One of the agents ran back to office and shouted to hold on. Just as the plane made a drastic left turn onto the runway there was a tremendous roar from two F-18 fighter jets as they swooped over Air Force One nearly striking the tail and released two air to ground missiles a piece. A bright flash erupted right at the end of the runway as the plane left the ground and climbed so quickly everyone who wasn't buckled into their seats was holding on for dear life. The terrorist had stopped to regroup just long enough for the plane to climb out of range. The F-18s took up a position just ahead of the aircraft and two more trailed the aircraft.

As the plane leveled off the president walked up to the flight deck to talk to the pilots. As he entered the cockpit area they were busy punching a new course into the computer that apparently actually flies the plane most of the time.

"So where are you taking me?"

Colonel Randolph was the pilot and he turned around in his seat to address the president. "Originally, sir, we were heading for Offutt but apparently they are in the middle of a battle with these guys. It appears that there must have been a rather large cell in Omaha and a very well-armed one at that. They have tanks and heavy arms including rockets so I think it would be in our best interest to change our destination. We are now headed for Davis-Monthan in Arizona and we should arrive just after midnight."

"That seems like a lot longer than a trip across the country usually takes, isn't it, Colonel?"

"Yes, sir, but we really don't know what kind of tracking equipment they have so we are taking a rather irregular route. We will refuel at one point over Canada. You know anybody with a computer can tap into programs to track air traffic and even though this plane is not supposed to be able to be tracked we are not going to take any chances."

During the flight, updates were continuously flooding into the communications center. All of the mass media were under control of the terrorists. The terrorist had executed the entire Supreme Court, and then they had paraded people into the street and shot them leaving the bodies lying in the street. They claimed that these were congressmen and senators and members of the president's cabinet but they lied. There were some staff people in the groups of victims but not a single member of congress or the cabinet was among them.

The terrorist had taken control of a long list of cities across the country. New York was the largest but the list also included Cleveland, Pittsburg, Detroit, Minneapolis-St. Paul, St. Louis, Omaha, Memphis, Nashville, New Orleans, Jacksonville, Tampa, Orlando, and Oklahoma City. These appeared to be the area of their greatest strength and it appeared that all the cells that activated in the western United States were quickly put down. Reports were coming in that in Texas, Arizona, New Mexico, and Utah armed public citizens were fighting the terrorists side by side with the police. The president immediately put out a notification to all fifty governors that the National Guard was being federalized across the country. Then Admiral McCain who was on board with the president was notified to use those units as needed.

After the plane landed the president called for an emergency meeting of the staff that was with him. They met in a conference room to discuss strategy. The first thing the President wanted to know, however, was if the vice president and Don are safe.

Mike McLaren answered, "The vice president is at a safe location being guarded by secret service as well as U.S. Marshals. I believe Don is safe as well at a location in Baltimore however we have lost contact with the marshals he was with since there is currently an attack going on in Baltimore."

'Most of the battles have ended for now except in Oklahoma City, Omaha, Baltimore, and Atlanta. There are active firefights in each of those locations. It appears that downtown Omaha has been lost but an engagement is still ongoing just to the south in Bellevue, Nebraska. In Oklahoma City we have achieved a little edge in that battle and appear to be pushing the terrorists out of the city. Baltimore, on the other hand, is solidly in control of the terrorists at this time but the fighting continues and in Atlanta we have lost control of the CNN building but Georgia police have held the terrorists back and they now are only in control of a small section of downtown."

The president turned to Admiral McCain and asked, "Admiral, how do we get our country back?"

McCain had a confused look on his face and shrugged his shoulders. "I will have to confer with the rest of the joint chiefs and develop a plan. We really were not prepared for this situation. It appears that many of these cells consisted of immigrants that had entered the country as refugees after the Iraq and Afghanistan actions."

This was not the response the president had hoped to hear. "Admiral, look around this room. The only thing I can say with certainty right now is that the highest ranking military officers that I am sure are alive and I can trust are in this room. That means you, Lt. Gen. Hickman, and the base commander wherever he is right now. If you like I can call him down here but I need a direction and I need it now."

"I am sorry, sir, but it would be premature for me to give you a strategy without fully examining where our troops are and their strength and equipment."

The president looked frustrated with that response and sat back in his chair while staring coldly at McCain. "Lt. Gen. Hickman."

Hickman rose from his seat and said, "Yes, sir."

The President continued, "Please give me your assessment and your opinion of what steps I should be taking at this time to regain control of the country."

Hickman obviously looked uneasy and turned to the President saying, "Ah, I don't believe I am qualified to make those recommendations, sir."

A big smile came over McCain's face as he shook his head from side to side.

The President was now infuriated and turned to Hickman again. "Sir, I didn't ask you to dispatch troops anywhere but only to give me your opinion. You understand that, don't you?"

"Yes, sir."

"Okay, then give it to me now!"

Hickman gazed over at McCain who was biting his lower lip and shaking his head no as if in a warning regarding what he was about to say. He then looked over at the president who was looking at him with intensity.

"Well, sir, based on what I know and my background I feel that to do nothing is to surrender. So I would follow a number of steps to systematically regain control. First, I understand that Marines from Quantico have secured the CIA and FBI buildings. Assuming that is still correct I would immediately download all satellite imagery over CONUS for the last forty-eight hours. That way we should be able to determine where many of these cells were located when they were activated. I would then dispatch F-35s or F-22s with precision munitions to obliterate those locations. You need to understand that in any of these actions some innocent lives will be lost but many more will be saved. Next, I would activate the airborne troops at Fort Benning and send them to Atlanta to assist in that battle. Many of those troops may still be in training but when they are training for airborne they are already good soldiers or they would not be there. Third, I would put up every drone I have available to start gathering intelligence across the country so we know where we need to send resources. I believe we have been notified that the terrorists have a tank in Omaha, two in DC, and one in Atlanta right now so I would send in either A-10s or F-35s to eliminate them from the battle. Then we can reassess where we stand."

The president listened and liked what he heard. "That sounds like a good plan to start our assault. Make it happen."

Hickman stood there for a moment and then said, "Sir, I will need Admiral McCain's authorization."

The President looked up at him and then over at Admiral McCain.

"No, General, you will not. Admiral McCain you are fired. You are to report for assignment to the new Chairman of the Joint Chiefs. Lt. General Hickman you are now General Hickman and you are assigned as the Chairman of the Joint Chiefs of Staff."

The room was dead quiet. No one could believe what had just happened but the others in the room noted that the president was certainly serious in stopping this attack no matter what he needed to do to accomplish that goal. Hickman and McCain left the room at once and everyone else sat quietly and expectantly of what the next move would be by the president.

"I think we all need a nap before this goes much further. None of us will be able to perform and think at our best if we are sleepy. Grab a bunk and we will meet again at 8:00 AM.

JUNE 17, 2017

COMBAT CONTROL CENTER
DAVIS-MONTHAN AIR FORCE BASE

It was 9:00 AM when the president entered the Combat Control Center for his morning briefing. "I apologize for being so late everyone. I needed the sleep."

TJ moved across the room to his position at the conference table and sat down to start reviewing a stack of memos and newspaper dispatches. None of the news was particularly good so before he could finish his first cup of coffee of the day he was already depressed.

"General Hickman, where do we stand?"

General Hickman's face did not display the stress that he was feeling throughout his body during these past eight hours. General Hickman had been in the Air Force for twenty-two years and had limited experience in combat situations. He had spent most of his career in logistics and intelligence and even though he had excelled in all of his assignments he had never faced anything remotely at the level he was now facing. At six foot five he was the tallest man in the room and his dark brown hair showed not a whisper of gray. As he approached the president he took a deep breath and then began his report.

"Good morning, Mr. President. Overnight since we last spoke we have destroyed the two tanks in Washington and the one in Atlanta. We have numerous drones in the air currently over the areas where the terrorists are active. The drones are being controlled from the combat center at Peterson Air Force Base in Colorado. Information from the satellites is currently being downloaded and we should have some analysis soon. The tanks in Omaha were not actively engaged this morning and they were parked in a residential neighborhood. The pilots aborted because they felt the danger to innocents was too great. We will keep those tanks under observation as well as we can and destroy them when we have a better opportunity."

A Major walked over from the communications area and interrupted General Hickman at this point passing on information that had just come into the center. After their conversation concluded the General turned back to the president.

"Excuse me, sir, I am sorry for the interruption. We have just received information regarding some of the other fronts. The Chinese have taken control of Mongolia, Vietnam, Thailand, Laos, and Burma. They have a fleet moving from the South China Sea toward Japan. The Russians now control all of Poland and are continuing to move south. They have invaded Germany stating that East Germany was theirs for decades and they were going to take it back inside the borders of the country. Greece has fallen to Turkey as has Albania. The Turks are continuing to move north."

"Thanks for the update, General. I would like you to develop a war plan to cover the situations involving Russia, China, and the United States terrorist situation. Please get this together as soon as possible and feel free to use Admiral McCain if you need any assistance but don't let his negativity stand between you and success. Believe in yourself and pray to God for guidance. Now I need some fresh air."

With that President Samuels walked out of the room and went up a tunnel which led to the outside just a short distance from the flight line. There was a cool breeze blowing gently along the flight line as he walked slowly. Gazing up to the sky it was clear blue and seemed limitless. TJ thought about those days between the election and the inauguration, those were the days he believed that his career would be limitless and he felt like nothing could hold him back. Maybe that was why things fell apart so quickly. He felt all powerful despite the fact he knew that was not possible. He had not asked God for help but he realized now that without God's help he could not finish this job with any success but would wind up a significant failure.

As thoughts continued rushing through his head he heard the roar of four F-22s taking off for a combat patrol over the Midwest. As he watched the jets disappear into the sky he turned to walk back inside the Combat Center and see if anything has changed in this fluid situation.

As he entered the center it was very active as it was obvious that a great deal of activity was already going on. He motioned to General Hickman to come over when he got a chance. He went over to a table in the corner and sat down observing the activity.

General Hickman approached and said, "We have a great deal of information coming in from the satellite pictures along with some video from drones that are currently in the air."

"So what does the information show?"

General Hickman again took a deep breath before he began explaining and turned to click a remote which activated a sixty-inch television across from where the president was sitting. "These first sets of pictures are from Omaha, sir."

As he began the photos they showed the tanks nestled between two family homes in a subdivision not far from Offutt Air Force Base. Then there was a series of pictures that showed several churches and businesses on fire. Armored Personnel Carriers with black flags flying from their antenna moving through streets and several fire fights were active between police and terrorists. The last three pictures showed long lines of people leading from a building and moving through a parking lot, into the street, and continuing for several blocks.

"I can understand what I am seeing on most of these pictures but what is the significance of these lines of people?"

"Sir, those are people applying to convert to the Muslim faith and to attend classes. The barrage of propaganda being broadcast over the television media has frightened many people into conversion in order to try to save their families. We have to put a stop to the media blaring the terrorist's message. You know the Christmas and Easter Christians and others that haven't been practicing their faith are giving in from fear and indoctrination. If we don't stop this we will be in danger of losing the country."

The president looked down to the ground shaking his head from side to side wondering what he could do to stop the country from sliding backward in this conflict. "General, get a plan together to take those networks off the air as soon as possible and let's do whatever we can to take back Omaha."

"Sir, we also have a series of photos from DC."

As they played you could see the distress on the president's face. He watched as the photos showed government buildings on fire, bodies piled in the street, and active battles outside the Pentagon.

"I think it is time to pull out all the stops, general."

TJ got up and left the center as he left instructions to contact him with any new information. As he walked up the ramp he had two secret service agents in front of him and two following and just behind them the familiar face of Major Combs. He stopped abruptly and turned around.

"Major Combs."

"Yes, sir."

"I need to see what is going on firsthand. I want you to arrange a covert mission for me to see what is going on in Omaha or some other active site."

"Sir, that is a bad idea and I don't think that we can get that approved."

"Approved? I am the damn commander in chief, am I not?"

"Yes, sir."

"I am sorry to raise my voice but I need to do this so make it happen and if anyone gives you a hard time have them see me. Now get on it, I think I will be safe with these agents."

The Major walked back to the command center as the president walked to his quarters with his secret service escort.

As he entered his quarters Angela rushed over to him to greet him and to ask what was going on across the nation. She had viewed the propaganda on television but had hoped that most of it were lies and that the truth was far different from what she was seeing on the screen.

"It's not good. We are losing the country and we have already lost much of the eastern half. We have to find a way to stop these radicals but they have become so entrenched within the communities that taking them out will require the deaths of thousands of innocent citizens as well and I am not sure I am prepared to do that."

TJ walked over to the refrigerator and opened it, hoping to find a cold beer but instead pulled out a can of Coca-Cola and opened it to drink it.

"Would you like me to have some food sent over for you?"

"No, Angie, I will go to the mess hall like everyone else. I just need a cold drink as I consider the next step. I was actually hoping to find something with alcohol in it so I could calm my nerves a bit."

Angela shook her head and replied, "The last thing you need right now is alcohol. You have some important decisions staring at you and you need to be stone cold sober as you deal with them."

"Yea, I know, did I tell you that I have ordered them to prepare a covert mission to take me on so I can see what is going on firsthand?"

Angela turned her head and looked at him directly before raising her voice in a very emphatic reply. "You what? There is no way in hell you are going at the front lines right now with everything that is going on. Don't you realize that you would be playing right into the hands of the terrorist? If they captured you every television station would be broadcasting your execution and they would probably raise billboards showing your head on a silver platter. Not to mention what would take place afterwards with Russia and China just swooping in here to take whatever they please and then leaving us in the hands of terrorists. You just got finished complaining about having to face a decision which could cause thousands of innocent deaths and now you are ready to make one that could cause millions. Stop and think, TJ!"

"You don't understand, Angela, you just don't understand. I will take your concern into consideration before I make a decision but a leader has to lead from the front not from the rear." He put the empty soda can on the counter and then walked out of the room heading back to the command center.

JUNE 19, 2017

COMBAT CONTROL CENTER
DAVIS-MONTHAN AIR FORCE BASE

As the president entered the combat center he immediately turned to Major Combs with his customary greeting and then asked, "Is this going to be a blue Monday?"

As the Major walked toward the president you could detect a slight smile erupting on his face. "Well, sir, we have some developments on operations that are getting underway but we do have some other information that you need to know."

TJ sat down at a table which had been set up for him in the corner of the room. He invited the Major to have a seat before he started the briefing. He could see concern in Major Combs's eyes as he pulled a piece of paper out of a paper folder. "Okay, sir, please remember I am only the messenger. We have the final figures regarding casualties on June fifteenth. Military deaths in the Pacific attack stand at 643. Most of those were personnel on the Antietam. There were a number of deaths at Sasebo and we lost some air crews as well. There were 8,462 deaths which include both military and civilian in Alaska. There are still fires burning on and around the missile base so that number could rise when we are able to more closely examine the area. We only have a good estimate regarding deaths elsewhere in CONUS as a result of the attacks but that number stands at 13,649. Most of those were in the shopping malls but nearly 5,000 died as a result of other attacks that day by the Islamic State. So nearly 23,000 Americans died in the attacks of the fifteenth"

TJ didn't say a word for several minutes but simply looked down at the table in front of him. He had tears in his eyes as he wondered what he could have done differently to avoid this catastrophe. He said a silent prayer and took a deep breath before looking up at the Major and saying, "Okay, now you said something about some good news?"

Major Combs could see TJ appear to turn the page in his attitude and demeanor. "Yes, sir, first of all, so I don't forget, I have arranged for Tech Sergeant Shaw to take you out to the range this afternoon to train you on weapons you may need to use when you go out on your covert mission. I am still opposed to that but you are the boss so we want to make sure you are as prepared as we can make you before that happens."

The president simply looked up and nodded saying softly, "Thank you."

"Okay, sir, the general had us thinking outside the box and he has decided to use some experimental weapons systems on some missions within the States. We have transported a remote control vehicle we call the Crusher to an area just outside of Omaha. The vehicle is being controlled by a drone operator and appears to be a small armored personnel carrier at first look. It is equipped with cameras and other surveillance equipment but in this case it is also equipped with missiles, automatic weapons, and rocket propelled grenades. The controller will guide it into Omaha using the most stealth route we can manage. Its mission is to seek out the tanks and destroy them. It will also take on any other enemy vehicle or weapon it comes across. It entered Omaha proper about 9:30 last night and has been moving through the city since then and so far has encountered no opposition. According to GPS information we should be close to the tanks within the hour. Atlanta is back under our control and Airborne troops are maintaining the security. They captured about seventy-five enemy combatants during the operation. A combined operation will begin tonight using Army Rangers and Canadian Special Forces to move on New York. A compound used by the Islamists in northwest New York was attacked by F-18 fighters last night and destroyed. Pilots advised that munitions must have been stored at the location as the secondary explosions were significant. National Guard units are currently moving into position to mop up at that location and finish the job. Finally, Texas and Louisiana National Guard units are currently engaged in a battle outside of Shreveport with an enemy battalion. The enemy at that location has been using artillery in this battle and the general has just authorized air strikes to try to finish this battle up."

As the Major finished his briefing TJ took a few notes and then thanked the Major and asked him to express his compliments to the general. The Major went over to the communications area and TJ began reviewing action reports that had come in over the last several days. Suddenly there was a great deal of commotion in the communications area and a large screen television attached to the opposite wall showed a picture of a backyard and a chain-link fence. The vehicle that was carrying the camera moved directly to the chain-link fence and then over it as it continued from yard to yard.

As TJ watched the screen the camera angle changed as the vehicle was apparently turning between two houses and moving toward a street. As the vehicle emerged from between the houses it again turned and there it was ... an American M-1 Abrams tank sat defiantly in the center of a cul-de-sac. The vehicle moved into the front of the house and was no more than fifty yards from the tank when it stopped. A flash, a hint of smoke and then the screen filled with a bright orange explosion. The turret of the tank shot straight up from the base of the tank. Within seconds enemy fighters emerged from the homes in the cul-de-sac and began running toward the camera and firing weapons. Automatic weapons erupted from the vehicle with the camera and began mowing down enemy fighters. What appeared to be rockets were launched at each of the residences where soldiers had originated and within a few minutes all was quiet again.

The picture changed to a similar location and once again an American tank was sitting in the street. This time, however, the fighters emerged before the tank was destroyed and the turret began to turn toward the camera. Once again a flash followed by an explosion and the tank was dead on the spot. This time the camera began moving forward as it fired into the fighters attacking it. A rocket propelled grenade exploded and the camera reflected a slight jump as the vehicle was struck but did not stop. Missiles again took out the homes that the fighters had exited and once again it became quiet after a few minutes of action.

As the Major started to walk to the president, TJ shouted, "How the hell did the enemy get American tanks?" It was obvious that TJ was angry over the fact that American forces had to combat and destroy American weapon systems.

The Major approached TJ and offered the only explanation he could muster. "Sir, we believe these are weapons we left for Iraqi forces to bolster their military. We are finding more American weapons in the hands of the enemy than any other. They do have some Russian and Chinese weapons but their weapons of choice are all from the U.S."

TJ knew this of course, but he was frustrated with the fact that so many American citizens were being murdered by weapons that we gave to others to defend themselves. General Hickman made his way over to the president's corner partially to calm him down but primarily to bring him up to date on new intelligence. The president motioned for him to take a seat.

"Sir, we have some new intelligence you need to be updated on. We have been wondering why there has not been more activity in the west. We know that there are enemy cells that are located there but no appreciable attacks or activity. We now know that a Chinese fleet is moving toward the west coast and a Russian fleet is moving toward Alaska. Both fleets are significant and began their moves when we were still licking our wounds from the attacks on the fifteenth."

TJ considered what he was saying and knew that it was time to begin looking at this situation on a more global basis instead of strictly worrying about the half of the country he has been so consumed with up to now. "So, General, have you got a plan of action for this situation?"

"Yes, sir, I believe I do. First, we have an Ohio class submarine, the Louisiana, trailing the Russian fleet. This submarine is equipped with multiple warhead nuclear missiles. My plan, with your approval, will be to fire missiles from the Louisiana and rain down nuclear weapons on the Russian fleet in sufficient number to eliminate the fleet. In addition, the third fleet has both the Theodore Roosevelt and the Ronald Reagan carriers and their accompanying ships between the west coast and the Chinese fleet. We will stage a head on naval battle in which we hope to destroy the Chinese fleet or at a minimum cause such damage that they will not be able to mount a significant attack. At the same time I am going to attack the Memphis area with Special Forces and Arkansas and Missouri National Guard as well as air units to eliminate enemy strongholds and to cut off the Mississippi River as a mode of transportation for them."

TJ was startled by the massive plans for attack. "General, I am surprised by the size of this attack and the relatively short period of time you have put this together."

"Mr. President, we have been training for this type of scenario for years and it is time we put it all together."

"You understand, General, that a massive nuclear attack like you are planning against the Russians will have serious repercussions, even if it succeeds in its goal?"

"Yes, sir, and that is why I am asking your approval. This could be the spark that initiates all out nuclear war, but the Russians have already nuked civilians in our country and we are using these on a military target that is far enough away from any civilian location that we should not have any long term civilian casualty problem. It could also persuade them that we will not hesitate to use nuclear weapons on their civilian population either and might make them take a step back to reassess. I also have been advised that you have already ruled out a nuclear attack earlier because of your faith, but then you did use a tactical nuke on the Russian Space Center. I know that this is not something you take lightly but I believe that if we are going to succeed we need to take a more aggressive step now. I will be praying as well that God will assist us in overcoming this evil but I was always told that God helps those who help themselves."

"Can I have an hour before I give you a decision?"

"Of course, sir, but I am going to put the weapons systems in position so we will be ready if your decision is affirmative."

"Very good."

As TJ left the combat center he turned to one of the officers in the room and asked for directions to the base chapel.

The president spent two hours in the chapel, most of it on his knees, trying to decide what his decision should be regarding this attack. As he prayed he continued to worry how many would die in the retaliation after this attack and if in fact the attack would cause either Russia or China to change their strategy. Finally, TJ decided that he had appointed Hickman to give him guidance on military action and so far, he has been correct in his strategy, it was time to let the military man do his job and to stay out of his way.

Decision made, it was time to give General Hickman the green light and then to meet Tech Sergeant Shaw and begin his military training as well.

JUNE 20, 2017

COMBAT CONTROL CENTER
DAVIS-MONTHAN AIR FORCE BASE

As TJ entered the Control Center the clock was showing 3:00 AM exactly. The Russian Fleet had crossed the International Date Line and was now approximately 300 miles south of the western Aleutians and travelling north, northeast toward Alaska. It was 11:00 PM on June nineteenth at the fleet's location. The Louisiana was travelling at top speed in a southeasterly course to put some space between the sub and the Russians.

As TJ sat down at his corner table General Hickman looked over and walked over to greet him. "Good morning, Mr. President. It is going to be a long and hopefully exciting day, sir."

TJ motioned for the general to take a seat and replied, "Will see soon. Is everyone in position?'

"Yes, sir. We will be ready to initiate the attack in about twenty minutes unless you have had a change of heart, sir."

"You have my authorization to begin the attack when you are ready, General. God bless our sailors and airmen."

The LAWS aircraft was approaching the Chinese Fleet from the west. The Chinese Fleet was currently about 800 miles east of Hawaii and 1600 miles west of California. B-2 bombers were lifting off the runway at Hickman Air Force Base and would be over their targets very quickly. The Third Fleet was currently heading west and was about 900 miles from San Diego. They were currently launching F-35s and F-18s. Meanwhile, in the control center beads of sweat were popping out on the forehead of President Samuels as he considered what was about to occur.

At the Control Center it was 3:45 AM, when General Hickman walked over to the President and said, "Sir, the Louisiana has launched eight nuclear equipped missiles, we should have some results for you soon. The Chinese aircraft carriers have begun to launch aircraft as they have apparently detected our attack prior to our first strikes."

As the seconds ticked away on the clock TJ's eyes were focused on the back of General Hickman who was standing at the communications desk. TJ noted that as calm as the general's demeanor seemed to be he could see now that beads of sweat were running down the back of his neck. TJ realized now that Hickman was a disciplined officer but was just as concerned about the action they were taking as he was currently.

The general left the communications area and approached the president quickly. "I have an update for you, sir. We have successfully struck the Russian Fleet."

TJ looked up and asked for details.

"Sir, the eight missiles we launched were cruise missiles that fly a few yards over the surface of the waves. The Russian Navy was expecting an attack from Alaska and consequently their radars and early warning systems were primarily focused to the north expecting missiles or aircraft approaching from that direction. They were able to stop three of the eight missiles but preliminary reports from the Louisiana indicates that five of the missiles detonated and it appears that the Russians suffered what the Louisiana describes as a catastrophic destruction. The Louisiana has now gone deep and quiet fearing that if there are survivors that the sub may be in danger of retribution."

TJ looked up at the general and replied, "Thank you, General, please keep me updated on the others actions as well. I guess I should be jumping for joy over this news, Bill, but frankly I am not all that thrilled with the deaths of hundreds of servicemen regardless of what side they are fighting for or against. Let's pray that this is resolved before we have a blood bath on both sides."

General Hickman nodded his head and without a word turned around to return to the communications area.

As time passed TJ became more and more stressed. He rose out of his chair and walked to the communications area to hear firsthand the progress being made in the Pacific and Memphis. TJ stood quietly in the back of the room and listened.

This wasn't like the setting in the situation room at the White House. The transmissions that he could understand at all were obviously in some sort of code and he did not understand what was happening. All the voices were calm and professional, TJ did not hear anything that did not reflect confidence. After several minutes a lieutenant who was writing a running journal of the transmissions nodded to a senior master sergeant and motioned for him to aid the president.

"Sir, can I assist you in some way?"

"Yes, Sergeant, tell me what the hell is going on?"

"Sir, the LAWS plane initiated an attack on a squadron of Chinese Shenyang J-15s which had lifted off a previously unidentified aircraft carrier. The LAWS has only been used against missiles previously but this time they attacked fighter aircraft and were able to destroy three aircrafts and the explosion from the aircraft caused two other planes to crash. The rest of the Chinese planes attacked the LAWS and it has been forced down but is intact. Several F-22s came to their rescue and dispatched the Chinese aircraft. There are now four B-2s approaching the area to release a missile attack on the Chinese Fleet. The general will update you as the operations continue, sir."

TJ took the hint and after thanking the sergeant he walked back to his corner and again sat down to worry. Time passed slowly and TJ realized that even though the air conditioning was going full blast his shirt was becoming very wet from the sweat pouring from his pores.

General Hickman approached TJ who was patiently waiting for some word. The president motioned for him to sit down at the table.

"Sir, we have several operations going on currently and so far, they have all seem to be operating successfully. Navy Seals attacked an Islamic Center in the eastern portion of the Memphis area, an area called Cordova. The Seals approached using the Wolf River and then moved through a wooded area and stormed the center. Seals now control the center and report no casualties. They also reported finding a cache of weapons inside. Marine Special Forces are currently attacking two other Islamic Centers within the Memphis area, we do not have reports yet on their status. The naval battle with the Chinese is in high gear.

"The battle in the Pacific is intense. The B-2s from Hawaii launched a number of missiles at the Chinese ships but less than a quarter of them reached their targets. We have lost several planes from surface to air missiles but our planes have also downed at least fifteen of their fighters. Our ships are still a little far apart to begin a missile attack from the ships but that will begin in the very near future. At this point we know that both the carriers in their fleet have been damaged and they have lost three additional ships that we believe were all missile equipped frigates.

"In Memphis, we have been very successful. A total of 154 enemy fighters have been captured and we have seized several hundred pounds of explosives. Additional National Guard units have been deployed to the area to set up a perimeter in an effort to make sure that we can maintain control of the city. So we are quickly regaining control of the southeast section of the country."

TJ allowed himself a quick smile and a deep breath. "I know this isn't over and I would like you to keep me updated with changes as they occur but I believe I will meet my drill sergeant to continue my training. I very much want to go on a mission myself very soon."

As the president left the center and General Hickman returned to the communications area he was pondering what type of mission he could possibly send the President of the United States on that would not put him in danger and still satisfy this crazy desire he has to get into the action. Hickman realized that this was a no win situation because if he sent his boss on a make believe mission he would certainly see through what he was doing and if he sent him on a real mission and he was killed or injured Hickman would reach the retirement age a little sooner than he intended.

It was nearly two in the afternoon when TJ returned to the Combat Control Center and he entered the room in military fatigues looking a little worse for the wear. As he entered the room he quietly proceeded over to his station and watched the military leaders as they directed the action currently underway.

As TJ sat down at the table at his workstation he noticed that there were several briefing papers on his table with a note attached from the general. "Updated info. Let me know if you have questions. Hickman."

The note was actually a list of battle results.

Russian ships destroyed or severely damaged:

Admiral Pyotr Velikiy	Missile Cruiser	Sunk
Marshall Shaposhnikov	Large Destroyer	Sunk
Admiral Panteleev	Large Destroyer	Sunk
Burnyy	Missile Destroyer	Sunk
Bystryy	Missile Destroyer	Sunk
Varyag	Missile Cruiser	Sunk
Smerch	Missile Frigate	Sunk
Moroz	Missile Corvette	Sunk
Admiral Kuznetsov	Carrier	Dead in water
Omsk	Submarine	Unaccounted
Magadan	Submarine	Unaccounted
Kashalot	Submarine	Unaccounted

In addition, at least 8 landing ships and gunboats are also missing and believed to have sunk. Approximately 28 fighter aircraft destroyed. Approximate number of personnel lost stands at 7,500.

After reading this sheet TJ turned the page and found another briefing sheet.

Chinese ships disabled or destroyed:

Unidentified	Carrier	Damaged but still operational
Changchun	Destroyer	Sunk
Zhengzhou	Destroyer	Sunk
Jinan	Destroyer	Minor damage
Dalian	Destroyer	Damaged but operational
Xuzhou	Frigate	Sunk
Zhoushan	Frigate	Damaged but operational
Wenzhou	Frigate	Sunk
Huaibei	Frigate	Damaged but operational
Shangrao	Corvette	Sunk
Datong	Corvette	Damaged but operational

In addition 37 fighter jets have been destroyed and one air command/control plane destroyed. Personnel lost is unknown.

TJ again reviewed the information and began to feel pretty good about the outcome of the operations. He then turned to the final page of the three.

U.S. losses in the Russian and Chinese operations:

CVN Ronald Reagan	Damaged but operational
SSBN Louisiana	Missing in action
F-22 Raptors	12 Destroyed or missing
F-35Ds	2 Destroyed
F-18Js	6 Destroyed
LAWS Aircraft	Damaged
AWACS	1 Destroyed

Total personnel losses at this time 247 confirmed dead, 315 missing.

TJ looked up from the three sheets of paper to see General Hickman looking across the room at him. He motioned for the general to join him and he nodded and then turned to one of the other officers with him and spoke to him for a couple of minutes before walking across the room.

"Yes, sir, do you have questions?"

"Yes, I do, please have a seat."

General Hickman pulled out a chair across from the president and took a deep breath because he was worried how the president would take the news on the briefing sheets.

"General, I told you to contact me and keep me updated."

"Yes, sir, and this information just came in within the past half hour. I knew you would be back soon so I decided not to place this information over a phone, even a secure one."

TJ realized that was a smart move so he let the manner the information was delivered go and went on to his questions. "What is the status of the Louisiana?"

"We have attempted to make contact with her but we have lost all contact. It could very well be by their design. They inflicted a great deal of damage on the Russians and we know that there are at least three Russian submarines in the North Pacific, so they are probably laying very quietly somewhere."

"How confident are you on these other numbers?"

"The enemy numbers are estimates based on the intelligence we have on the ships and planes destroyed. We have been flying drone surveillance planes over the area ever since the attack and that is what we have based our information on regarding the Russians. The Chinese battle is an active and fluid situation and much of what is reported are again estimates based on AWACS and combat control centers. We lost one AWACS plane by a missile attack and the LAWS plane has landed in Hawaii and is seriously damaged but is fixable. The Chinese fleet has stopped moving east and has set up a combat type patrol trying to keep from losing any additional ships. We assume at this point that they are awaiting instructions. There has been no response so far from the Russians but we are monitoring their missile launch facilities very closely."

TJ sat quietly for several minutes as he tried to digest all of the information he had just been given. He then pushed his chair back and started to get up.

"Sir," General Hickman interrupted his movements, "could I speak to you for a moment about this mission you want to participate in?"

TJ was a little surprised that this was coming up but he was looking forward to going out in the field so he immediately stopped and sat back down. As TJ slid back into his chair the general took another deep breath and began his briefing. "Mr. President, I still wish you would reconsider going out into the field, but you are the boss so I want to inform you that I have a mission that you can participate in. I do have some conditions that I want to go over with you and I know I can't force you to agree to these conditions but I am asking that you do comply with them voluntarily."

TJ had mixed feelings at this point. He was not suicidal and knew that what he was asking was dangerous but he also knew that to be accepted as a real leader and to motivate the people in this country he would have to do something above and beyond what was expected. "I will consider any conditions you have and trust me, I have no intention of leading the charge up San Juan Hill."

"The mission, sir, is an attack on an enemy stronghold in Omaha Nebraska. You will be assigned to accompany a Marine Raider platoon. Raiders, sir, are the Marine equivalent of Special Forces like the Navy's Seals or the Army Green Berets, so you will be in excellent hands. It is absolutely essential, however, that you follow the Marine Commander's instructions without question. You will not be making any strategic or other decision during this mission. This is vital for your safety."

"Agreed."

"Good. Now there is something else that I am not sure you will like. We will have an Air Force Air Rescue Team standing by to evacuate you should things go south. It is imperative that if you are told to evacuate, no matter what is going on, you will evacuate. I don't know if you have considered the propaganda explosion that would occur if the enemy captured or killed you."

"I understand that and yes, I have considered it but I feel the good that will come from citizens seeing their leader fighting for them is far greater than the bad side."

General Hickman took another deep breath and then began again. "Sir, I would like you to make a couple of videos before the mission. These tapes will be absolute propaganda in that you will talk about the mission's success and we will do a little make up work to make it appear that you have just returned from the mission. We may even give you some minor injuries like a cut on your face or something. This way no matter what happens unless you are captured or killed we will be able to build on your statement to raise morale and hopefully turn the tables on the enemy."

"So you want me to lie to the American people to cover up what really happens during the attack?"

"Yes, and no. If the mission goes as planned, and you want to make a different tape to broadcast then that will be fine. I just don't want to have to explain to anyone that you are missing in action or injured if I can avoid it until we control the situation."

TJ thought about this a minute and then came up with another question. "Do we have control of the airwaves now?"

"No, sir, not television, but the enemy never gained control of the internet so I think we can load these up on social media and do podcasts."

"Okay, actually I like the idea although I hope we don't have to send out bad information to the American people. I do understand why you want to do this and it does make sense."

With that the general stood up and as he started to walk back to his station he turned to the president and said, "We will be putting you through a little more training but this mission will take place very soon."

JUNE 23, 2017

COMBAT CONTROL CENTER
DAVIS-MONTHAN AIR FORCE BASE

TJ had been attending eighteen hours of training a day in a remote area off the base for the last two days. He was tired and sore. He had muscle aches where he didn't realize his body had muscles. As he approached the door he felt like he had been in another world for several days and he was feeling very guilty of not being completely up to date on the situation in the world. The training was very serious and had taken a hundred percent of his focus.

As TJ entered the room everyone seemed focused at their workstations so TJ walked to the corner of the room where his table and workstation was set up. As the president began to review the stack of briefing sheets and bulletins neatly stacked on the table an airman approached with a hot cup of coffee and a freshly baked sweet roll from the base kitchen. As TJ looked up to thank the airman he noticed that Major Combs was approaching.

"Good morning, Major."

"Good morning, Mr. President. I have some recent information that you will be interested in digesting."

TJ raised the cup of coffee to his lips, hot steam curling through the air in front of his eyes. He took a sip and quickly lowered the cup while shaking his head. "Boy, I didn't know how hot that was but it will certainly wake you up. So what have you got, Major?" With that the president motioned for Major Combs to sit next to him at the table.

Major Combs very deliberately pulled the chair out and slowly sat down. He had a number of note cards in his hands and he began to shuffle through them as if he was about to deal a hand of poker. "Well, sir, there is quite a bit going on in the world and very little of it is good. I will start with the Pacific, sir. The Chinese have sunk two of our ships in the last forty-eight hours. An Oliver Hazard Perry class frigate, the USS Rentz, was struck by three Chinese missiles including one that ignited the ammunition storage area and caused a catastrophic event. All 210 personnel were lost, sir." Combs paused here because he could see that the president was deeply disturbed by the news and he could see his eyes filling with tears.

After about forty-five seconds Major Combs resumed. "A Ticonderoga Cruiser, the USS Princeton, immediately responded to attempt a rescue operation. When they were still several miles away the same Chinese ship, initiated another missile attack aimed at the Princeton. The Princeton was struck twice and lost maneuverability for a short period. During that period the Chinese attacked with helicopters which were quickly blown out of the sky by surface to air missiles. The Chinese ship that had initiated these attacks was then targeted and destroyed by Tomahawk Cruise missiles fired from the Princeton. Unfortunately, sir, the Princeton has sustained significant damage below the water line and sank before we could get emergency equipment to the scene. We lost seventy-four personnel, sir, but the remaining 280 personnel were rescued and are being reassigned within the active fleet."

TJ took another sip of coffee and a bite out of the sweet roll. The expression on his face at this point was one of absolute focus. His eyes were still watery but he was looking intently at the major's eyes.

"There is also an activity in the North Atlantic, sir. The British Navy is currently engaged in a naval battle with the Russians, approximately 300 miles southwest of Reykjavik, Iceland. Intelligence suggests that the Russians intend to invade Greenland and seize our Air Force and Navy facilities at that location. This would be a convenient jump off point for quick attacks or an invasion of the northeast United States. It would appear that they may be coming to assist the Islamic State units currently operating in the northeast, especially New York. The good news here is that the Russians have pretty much been stopped dead by the British who are waging a masterful fight. If they don't stop them they will, at the very least, significantly slow their advance."

TJ was now writing notes on a pad of paper, fearing that anything he put on his laptop could be hacked, the president had returned to one of the first technological advances he had learned as a child—a pencil and a piece of paper. "How long do you believe the Russians can be stalled?"

"Frankly, sir, nukes have been introduced in this war so it is hard to make a prediction like that since one nuke can trump the greatest strategist in anybody's military.

TJ raised his cup once more and seemed to stare out into space. There had to be a way to bring this conflict to a conclusion before we decimated one another.

The major then continued. "The Russians have now occupied and control all of Germany east of the Rhine River as well as what was once known as the Soviet Block. Poland, the Czech Republic, Slovakia, Austria, Hungary, Slovenia, and Romania all are now under Russian control. The Turks have invaded and control the rest of the Balkan Peninsula. Spain is now under the control of the Islamic State. Portugal, France, Italy, Belgium, the Netherlands, Denmark, Norway, Sweden, and Finland are still free but all have conflicts occurring within the countries. The U.K. has had a number of terrorist attacks but thus far they are still firmly in control of their country."

TJ was having a hard time accepting how quickly the world has seemed to come apart at the seams. He was barely through the first six months of his term and it would appear he may very well be the last President of the United States. He thought about the previous presidents who had spent billions of dollars on solar energy and enforcing thousands of ridiculous regulations. They had grown the government to the point where no one could escape the reach of the bureaucratic tangle that seemed to be attached to every facet of daily life. The real problem had been that elected leaders had found that as long as they stayed in office they could wield power and stuff their pockets with other people's money. This fact had caused them to battle to any length to stay in office and that was the big reason no one would work with a Tea Party backed candidate, even one that managed to get elected as a Republican. It was their attitudes that led to the conditions that allowed this to happen. Of course, he had done nothing to help the situation by failing to find a way to bring the two sides together.

Major Combs interrupted TJ's train of thought as he continued with his briefing. "India is fighting the Islamic State on the west and the Chinese military on the east. The Chinese control Vietnam, Thailand, and Laos. The Islamic State controls the Philippines and Malaysia. So far no one has made any move on Australia and New Zealand. North Africa is in control of the Islamic State and the remaining portion of the continent is being controlled by various rebellious factions that are aligning with the Islamists. South America and Central America have a number of revolts going on involving groups that are mostly aligned with Russia. Israel is in the battle of their lives. So far they seem to be holding their own because the military units of their enemies are spread so thin that they have been able to defend them. At this rate, however, it is only a matter of time."

TJ looked over at the major and said, "I was just wondering if this would be occurring right now if we had worried more about building the military instead of shrinking the military and concentrating on climate change and political correctness. The United States was the force that held the world in check and once we allowed ourselves to become regarded as a paper tiger instead of a force to be reckoned with there was no one left to control the evil in the world."

The major nodded in agreement knowing though that it was a little late to worry about what caused the conflict and right now the president needed to concentrate on how to correct this mess we were involved in fighting.

TJ continued, "So tell me about the continental United States, where do we stand right now?"

Combs took a deep breath and put down his note cards. He knew the status of the U.S. like the back of his hand. "We are continuing to have terrorist attacks along the west coast especially in Washington and in the San Francisco area. With a few exceptions everything appears to be operating normally until we get to Omaha, Nebraska. The Islamists have weak control of an area heading south from there to Oklahoma City. Texas appears secure. We have taken control of Memphis and Rangers are currently attacking New Orleans in the south and Little Rock to the west of Memphis. Chicago is primarily in our control but there are numerous areas in Chicago where the Islamists have taken control. Wisconsin and Minnesota are firmly in control of the Islamic State. Southern Michigan is also in control of the Islamists but Northern Michigan has fought back and is currently under control of U.S. forces and Michigan National Guard. Ohio and Pennsylvania are states that are in conflict. The eastern seaboard from Maine to South Carolina are currently under control of the Islamic State but we have taken Georgia back and Florida. The Gulf Coast except for a few pockets is still ours. Television across the country is still being controlled by the New York networks that are in control of the Islamic State but the internet is still free as most of the controlling points for it are in California."

TJ began shaking his head and said, "So you are telling me that about half this country is free and the remaining half is occupied. What is even worse is that the area under Islamic control has a larger portion of our population."

"That is why we need to take some immediate action to take our country back before it is too late, Mr. President."

"Oh, before I leave there is one more thing, Mr. President." Major Combs said as he began to walk across the room. "We are getting reports that the number of smallpox cases are on the rise again in the southeast quadrant of the country."

JULY 1, 2017

DAVIS MONTHAN AIR FORCE BASE

It was just after seven in the morning and TJ was finishing breakfast with Angela in the kitchen of their quarters on the base. Angela had noticed that TJ was more quiet than usual and had barely spoken a word during breakfast.

"So your back in fatigues again today, I assume you have another hard day of training?"

TJ looked up and Angela instantly knew he wasn't leaving for training from the worried look in his eyes. "No, Angie, I didn't want to say anything until the last minute because I didn't want you to worry any more than necessary. At ten I am leaving on my mission. I can't tell you anything else about it right now but I will most likely be gone for three or four days and Major Combs will keep you advised on how things are going once the operation starts. You have nothing to worry about, I will be in good hands."

"How dare you say I have nothing to worry about? I have a great deal to worry about and you have no right to tell me what I should or should not worry about!" Angela had screamed her reply and her eyes resembled flame throwers. "I think this is a stupid stunt. You know that your place is here leading, not toting a rifle and fighting in the weeds against these professional soldiers. You will probably be more of a hindrance to our professionals and how will you feel if because of some mistake

155

you cause one of our soldiers to die?" By this time Angela was crying and shaking and TJ moved toward her to hold her in his arms.

After more than a minute of holding Angela, TJ whispered in her ear, "Angie, you knew this was coming and we spent a lot of time talking about it. I will be okay. I have gone through some incredible training and I will be with some incredible soldiers so please be brave and when I get back we will spend a long romantic night together."

As TJ left the residence Angela continued to sob and wonder if he would return and if he did, how he would be changed by this experience.

As TJ entered the hangar he heard an immediate and loud— Ten-Hut! As he looked around he was surprised to see two or three hundred marines in fatigues. Not one showing any rank or insignia of any type with the exception of an American flag on the shoulder. "At ease."

Almost as soon as the words left his lips he was approached by a soldier who directed him to a group of fifteen marines who were huddled around in a circle checking their gear.

As he approached a six foot four hulk of a man stepped out of the group and directed him to one side. The man snapped to attention and saluted the president. "That, sir, is the last salute you will receive until we are safely back at this location. I am Gunnery Sergeant Greg Hackborn, I am your team leader. From this point on you will listen to no one but me. You will take no action that I don't direct you to take. You are no longer, for the duration of this mission, the commander in chief but you are a Marine. Is that clear?"

TJ nodded but the sergeant got right up to his nose like a drill instructor and shouted, "Are you clear?"

TJ was surprised but immediately replied, "Yes, sir!"

Gunny Hackborn smiled and then grabbed the president by the shoulder and quietly said, "For the remainder of this mission you will be known as TJ and you will refer to me as Greg. The rest of the team will introduce themselves to you in a moment. While we are operational I want you six steps behind me and to my right at all times. You don't have to worry about anything except what I tell you to worry about. One last thing, sir. I will not let anything happen to you on this mission as long as you don't do something stupid. I have never lost a president yet and don't intend for you to be the first."

TJ smiled and walked over to introduce himself to the group and prepare his equipment as he had been taught during the training over the last several weeks.

For the bulk of the day the men all practiced maneuvers and had one more session on the range. At five each team met separately to begin their final briefings. Greg walked up to the group and began tossing hoods to everyone. "You will put these on when we board the plane and keep them on during the mission. We don't want anyone identifying our guest troop and deciding to take a lucky shot." Next he threw everyone a headset and instructed that all communications once we are on the plane will be over the headset until the end of the mission. "At six we will board what appears to be a cargo plane. There will be three planes and all will land at the Lincoln Nebraska airport. We will land under cover of darkness and with no lights. We will all operate with night vision goggles on during the mission. There will be four teams of fifteen operators each assigned to each group. Each group will have a specific target. Two teams will assault locations at Offutt Air Force Base to take out the command structure that has been set up at that location. One team will assault the Omaha Islamic Center in north Omaha. We believe this is being used as an armory and it consists of a concrete building which is relatively new construction. Our target will be a preparatory school on Western Street. The school is believed to be a training ground for new soldiers and terrorists and as such will have a number of willing fighters and a great deal of ammunition."

The mission was becoming very real now and no longer just an idea. Greg continued, "When we arrive in Lincoln we will exit the aircraft at the north end of the strip. A stealth helicopter will be waiting in a field about fifty yards to the east of the runway. For the last several weeks personnel in the power company in Omaha have been shutting off the power for a couple of hours each night. They have told the Islamic leadership the reason for this is that their main equipment was damaged by terrorists during the initial attacks and they are using backup equipment which needs frequent maintenance necessitating the down time. They have accepted that explanation so the lights go out in this area every night at about ten o'clock and remains off until at least midnight. Our copters will land in an open field near the end of Lake Street and adjacent to Cole Creek. We will travel south along Cole Creek to Western Street and then east to the school. We will be traveling through people's backyards and I don't want to disturb anyone or even a family dog. As we enter the campus area we will move to the northeast and assault the administration building. From that point we play it by ear because we have very little intelligence on what to expect inside. Any questions?"

He looked carefully at each member of the group and then shouted, "Mount up!"

As he reached the tarmac TJ was shocked to be directed to a cargo plane with prop engines. The shocking part was the writing on the fuselage of the plane, part in Farsi and then plainly and boldly in English—Iranian Air. Greg turned to TJ and said, "Don't worry, somebody's idea of a joke but it might also keep someone from taking a potshot at us with a shoulder mounted missile."

The plane lifted off and gained altitude quickly heading northeast as the sun was beginning to set to their west. All the exterior navigation lights on the aircraft were dark as the plane approached the closed Lincoln Airport. The airport had been closed by the Islamic State except for official flights to resupply the units in Nebraska. As the plane approached it was unusually high and then descended very sharply before it touched down sending everyone slightly forward. The plane came to a stop abruptly and the rear cargo door quickly opened and everyone exited. As they reached the bottom of the ramp each operator turned to the left and ran into a field where a very strange looking copter was located. The copter was black with no markings and was formed like a stealth fighter with hundreds of angles to deflect radar. The rotors were turning but there was little engine noise but only a whoosh of air as the blades turned.

As soon as everyone was on board the copter quickly rose but only to a few hundred feet before turning to the northeast and traveling on a course just north of Interstate 80. It seemed odd to see the interstate with so little traffic as they sped toward Omaha. Once over Omaha proper they could see that there were very little lights on anywhere around the area. The commercial areas around Dodge Street still had lights but they presumably had backup generators. The copter made a very abrupt left turn and circled a field once before touching down. Greg shouted, "Goggles and hoods on. Dismount!" As the rear ramp opened up everyone ran from the copter and continued at full speed to a creek just east of where they had landed.

The creek itself had very little water in it. Fortunately for them it had been dry in Omaha for several weeks. The walls of the creek were about eight feet high with tree roots protruding from the walls which would be beneficial if they had to make an emergency exit. Progress was slow at this point as everyone was being extremely careful to be quiet for fear of stirring up dogs or neighbors and calling attention to themselves before they were ready.

As the team reached Western Street they all paused and attached silencers to their side arms, the assault weapons were already suppressed. Eight members of the team went to the south side of the street through a culvert and after Greg contacted his commander via radio they all rose from the creek bed as a unit and began jogging to the school grounds about three blocks away.

As they entered the school grounds TJ saw two people dressed in fatigues and carrying assault weapons strapped on their backs. One was smoking a cigarette and the other was jabbering about something in Arabic. TJ froze but before he could even signal Greg there was a quiet zip noise and then both persons fell straight to the ground. A member of the team across the street checked the bodies and removed the magazines from their weapons and then moved forward.

As they got about fifty yards from the main entrance of the administrative building TJ realized that the front of the building was well-lit. TJ hesitated and suddenly thought this is not the way the plan was supposed to go. Over the headset he heard Greg, "Okay, these guys apparently didn't get the script. It could be a generator or just an emergency backup lighting. Everyone in to defensive position 6." With that each member went to a prone position in what was best described as a semi-circle in front of the main entrance and about thirty yards away. The light was bright enough that they had to remove the night vision goggles. The team had two members, Scott and Jack, who really enjoyed blowing things up. As they watched for anyone exiting the building, Scott and Jack approached the front of the building and set charges. Soon they returned to their previous position and Greg told everyone via headsets to "night vision off."

Scott then came across the headset. "On five look down and away and then place your goggles back on. Five, four, three, two, one!" *Boom!* A bright flash and then absolute darkness. The whole front of the building was simply gone. Glass and brick fragments were scattered everywhere the team looked. Over the headset TJ heard, "Lock and load you are all clear to fire at any target that appears."

It seemed like a lot longer but within about ninety seconds enemy soldiers and what were probably trainees came rushing through the wreckage of the front of the building with weapons firing indiscriminately as they appeared. They were running directly into an ambush. Everyone on the team including TJ fired disciplined short bursts at the emerging enemy soldiers and mowed them down before they could even identify where the shots were coming from. When the initial gunfire ended there were forty or more enemy soldiers dead or dying just outside the entrance of the building. The next thing TJ heard was Greg on the headset, "Move forward, sweep the building but watch for booby traps."

As the rest of the team entered the building Greg and TJ watched the rear just outside the building. TJ was sure that Greg rarely used himself for the rear guard and that Greg was simply protecting TJ from any trap left inside the building. This made TJ feel uncomfortable but he knew that Greg was a dedicated Marine first and foremost and he suddenly felt very secure with Greg looking over his shoulder.

Zip! Zip! Zip!

There was no mistaking that sound. Bullets were flying right past TJ's ear and he fell to the ground like a sack of potatoes. Greg told the team over the headset, "Incoming fire! TJ, are you okay?"

TJ quickly replied, "Yes, Greg. I saw muzzle flashes to the east."

TJ and Greg crawled about ten yards away from the building to get a better view of who was shooting at them. The night vision

THE COST OF LIBERTY

goggles proved to be the advantage they needed as they both saw seven enemy soldiers stand up at the same time and begin to charge the front of the building. They had gone less than twenty feet before Greg and TJ and mowed all seven down. Greg and TJ maintained their position and kept visually sweeping the area looking for any other activity. For about five minutes TJ lied on the grass and felt sick to his stomach. TJ's nerves were stressed and he wondered at this point if he would be able to keep his promise to come home unhurt. His hands shook slightly as his head jerked around at every noise and this night had plenty. Then quietly on the headset he hears Scott, "We have a viewpoint from the roof of the building. Stand by." After about forty-five seconds, "You have twenty-five enemy coming along the west side of the building."

"TJ, reposition quickly. West and south." Greg had calmly commanded. "Scott, keep eyes on them and if you can get a shot at any of them take it. Whoever is still on the first floor head for the entrance but do not exit. Let's try to get them in a cross fire."

Within moments they could see movement as the first wave approached the position they had been at when they mowed down the previous group. As they carefully passed the previous building entrance bullets flew from inside the building and from their position just to the south. The first five fighters fell without ever firing a shot. Scott and Jack dropped several grenades from the roof along the side of the building and right into the midst of the remaining fighters.

By midnight 87 Islamic soldiers were deceased and 315 others were being guarded as they were in a prone position on the grounds in front of a classroom building. The Islamic Center

163

was also captured and a large cache of weapons and ammunition were being loaded into trucks. At Offutt Air Force Base the teams barely had to fire a shot as the leadership council showed no desire to fight once the Marines made their presence known. A convoy of U.S. Army and Kansas National Guard were speeding toward Omaha. As the sun rose on Omaha martial law had been declared and the streets were being heavily patrolled by Omaha City Police and Nebraska State Patrol. The Marines maintained the security of their targets until they were relieved at about noon by Army MPs from Fort Leavenworth, Kansas. Police SWAT units were busy throughout the city raiding suspected terrorist locations.

At about 5:30 PM, a C-130 transport plane landed at Eppley Field and the Marine Raiders along with their newest member went on board for a trip back to Davis Monthan Air Force Base. As the plane lifted off the runway in Omaha TJ noticed flashes of light in the small windows. His first thoughts went to shoulder mounted missiles or anti-aircraft missiles. As he turned to get a better view out the window he heard Greg, who was sitting behind him, say, "Surely you have seen a fireworks show before. Mr. President, did you forget that at midnight the date will be July fourth? It's a little eerie though to be repeating this fight for freedom like the patriots did 241 years ago."

TJ smiled and nodded his head. He then joined a number of the other soldiers on the plane in relaxing and napping during the remainder of the flight.

JULY 4, 2017

DAVIS MONTHAN AIR FORCE BASE

At 5:00 PM, TJ walked to the base communications building hand in hand with Angela. They had enjoyed some private time together after TJ had returned to the base in the early morning hours. As they walked toward the building they were surrounded by military police and secret service. It was hot but there was a gentle breeze that provided some cooling.

As they entered the building General Hickman was waiting in the lobby.

"Good afternoon, Mrs. Samuels, Mr. President."

TJ extended his hand and nodded. "Is it finally time to do the podcast?"

"Yes, sir. As things turned out I am glad we didn't find time for the one I suggested. I know you have a problem with the propaganda I wanted you to talk about but now you can speak from your heart with plenty of good news. I do want to caution you though, do not give out any of the information that has been classified regarding troop strength and location other than the general information we have talked about already."

TJ handed a couple of sheets of information to the general and nodded. "Would you explain once more exactly how this will reach the citizens?"

As they were speaking the group was moving down the hallway toward a small studio. "I will pass your speech on to the teleprompter man so he can prepare it for you. We still do not have control of the major television networks but we can still use the computer networks and social media. You will be broadcasting live on Facebook, Twitter, Instagram, YouTube, Google, MSN, and a number of other computer networks. It will also be taped and sent to several other computer news networks. We hope that it will be rebroadcast thousands of times using individuals that pick up the original. We can cover most of the country with the exception of the deep south and several states in the northeast. So from Boston to Richmond to Philadelphia and from Baton Rouge to Mobile we will be unlikely to get the message out because the EMP damage has still not been significantly repaired in those areas but the rest of the country will at least have the opportunity to hear from you."

TJ squeezed Angela's hand as he entered the studio and Angela left him to wait in another room. TJ looked into the room and noticed a prop desk where he would sit. Behind the desk stood the U.S. flag and the Presidential flag. The president was dressed in a fatigue uniform and instead of walking behind the desk and sitting down he decided to have a seat on the corner of the desk. He turned to General Hickman and asked, "Do you think this less formal look is better?"

General Hickman replied, "I am more worried about how comfortable you are rather than how it looks. If you like sitting there then do it. I have read over what you are going to say and I think it is great, but you really have to sell this so that the people we do reach will get behind us and help. The teleprompter people are putting the information in the computer and it should be ready in a couple of minutes and we will go live unless you want to rehearse it once."

"General, I have rehearsed it most of this afternoon. I am as ready as I am going to be."

A female senior airman came up to apply some makeup to the president's face and several sound checks were made to make sure all the sound levels were correct. The teleprompter flashed on and TJ took a couple of deep breaths to ease his nerves. When the airman applying the makeup was finished she handed the president an earpiece so that he could hear instructions from the control booth. The president placed it in his ear and took a couple more deep breaths.

TJ suddenly heard a voice in his ear. "Mr. President, this will be sort of live. By that I mean that there is a ten second delay. This is not like television so you won't hear a lead in so just start your talk when you are ready. Any questions?"

The President shook his head no and repositioned himself on the desk. Finally, when he was comfortable he took a deep breath and clasped his hands together in front of him nodding to the control room.

"Brothers and sisters in freedom. We are faced once again with a time when we are struggling for our freedom. We are engaged in a Third World War but unlike the previous world wars we are fighting much of this war on our own soil. I am not able to greet you tonight on television because we cannot even control the major broadcast networks. As you watch this tonight on social media or any other computer platform, I ask you to share this message and pass it on to your fellow citizens.

"First, I want to update you on the world situation. The three aggressors in this conflict are Russia, China, and the Islamic State. While pretending to engage in diplomacy and setting up negotiations with various groups around the world, these three entities were preparing for massive invasions and all-out war with the intent of a one world government that will be dominated by the three entities.

"Our previous leaders failed to acknowledge that the radical sect of the Islamic community had become an enemy of all mankind. They failed to show strength when dealing with Russia and China and allowed our country to be looked at with disdain and disgust. They allowed enemy agents to freely walk into our country unmolested and unquestioned. They stripped our military of their weapons when they were on bases within the country and spent more time worried about the ability of same sex couples to be married and obtain wedding cakes than dealing with the developing problems in the world.

"As China invaded South Korea, Vietnam, and Thailand the Russians were invading much of Eastern Europe. The Turks have also invaded Greece and the Balkan Peninsula. The Scandinavian countries have stopped Russia's westward expansion and the U.S. and European troops have held the Russians at the Rhine River.

"We are the real prize that all three aggressors seek. The Iranians began our problems when they teamed with Hamas, Russia, and the drug lords in Mexico to begin the smallpox epidemic. They followed that with nuclear explosions over the northeast and the Gulf coast. The Coast Guard and Navy were able to stop a similar attack on the west coast. Islamic State and Iranian troops entered our country under the cover of the results of the EMP and now have control of much of the eastern part of the United States. The Russians exploded a nuclear weapon in Alaska and sent an invasion force to attempt an invasion of Alaska. The Chinese has sent their Pacific Fleet with an invasion force to California. Their intent has been to have the three dominating forces to occupy the United States as they mop up in South America and Africa.

"Well that was their plan, now let me tell you a little bit about mine. First of all, we are not holding anything back. I ordered submarines in the north Pacific to attack the Russian fleet with missiles equipped with tactical nuclear warheads. I am happy to report to you that the Russian fleet was stopped and largely destroyed about 300 miles short of their goal in Alaska. There will still be a great deal of support needed for our brothers and sisters in Alaska to recover from the vicious attack that had been unleashed on them.

"Our Pacific fleet attacked the Chinese between Hawaii and California and did significant damage to their attack fleet. A number of their ships and aircrafts have been destroyed and as a result, their fleet has stalled and is currently in a stagnate position in the Pacific. We will continue our attack until they turn back or they are destroyed.

"In the continental United States our military has defeated radical Islamic forces in Memphis, Tennessee; Omaha, Nebraska; Oklahoma City, Oklahoma; Atlanta, Georgia and a number of other key locations. Currently the United States is occupied in the Northeast and much of the Midwest, but this is about to change.

"We have Special Forces, National Guard, and other military units moving into regions all across the occupied areas. During the last few days I accompanied Special Forces into Omaha, Nebraska, where we captured leadership targets, weapons, munitions, and captured their primary training base in the United States. If you are hearing this in the occupied areas or if you know someone in these areas, you can be sure of one thing—your nation has not forgotten you and we will come for you too!

"What we need most from you is prayer. This country was founded by people seeking religious freedom and that has always been one of our most sacred rights. We have extended that right to those practicing the Muslim faith as well and will continue to do so in the future but we will not tolerate hatred and terrorism coming from those that practice a radical form of this religion. This always has been and will continue to be a Christian Judeo nation. So I ask all of you to get on your knees and pray that our country may overcome this test.

"It was 241 years ago that the Declaration of Independence was first read publicly. I want to remind you of the last sentence in that document. And for the support of this Declaration, with a firm reliance on divine Providence, we mutually pledge to each other our Lives, our Fortunes, and our sacred Honor. Today I repeat that pledge to each of you.

"May God bless and may God save the United States of America."

TJ again took a deep breath as the lights shut off and General Hickman came bursting through the door with a smile from ear to ear. "That was great, Mr. President. You laid out the situation and encouraged everyone who heard or will hear the message."

As TJ slid off the desk, he noticed Angela come rushing in behind the general. He wrapped his arms around her and squeezed her tightly.

"Mr. President, I have some news that might interest you."

TJ at first ignored the general but after a few seconds he looked over and said, "Okay, what have you got."

The general moved beside the president and spoke softly directly in the president's ear. "Sir, we are receiving additional reports on outbreaks of smallpox. We now have reports in northern parts of Alabama and Mississippi, as well as sections of Kentucky, Tennessee, and Pennsylvania. The interesting thing is that the areas where these reports are located in, are all areas where Islamic groups are strong. The analysts believe that these Islamic fighters didn't get the smallpox vaccine. Smallpox is not a problem in the regions where they were trained."

The president broke in at this point. "Nor was it a problem in any other region before they started passing it around. So you are telling me that they started a smallpox epidemic and then send terrorists and fighters to the same area without vaccinating them?"

"Yes, sir, that is at least the way it appears. We are going to keep track of these trends and examine how they may be useful in our future planning."

"Are we still sending vaccine to the areas where these trends are occurring?"

"We have been, sir, but we will stop until we get complete control of these areas."

As the president and general left the communications building they began walking quickly to the command center. Angela followed them out of the building but was soon left behind as their pace was much faster than she could keep up with. As she looked up she noted that clouds seemed to be building in the southwest. It had been quite a while since they had rain and a good old fashioned thunderstorm and those really occurred rarely in this area. Maybe a little rain would be good right now because the storm in the east was picking up.

JUNE 8, 2018

EMBASSY OF OMAN

I had lost track of time. No windows in the cell and no watch. Worse yet, the lights had been turned off a few hours after being locked in the cell and not been turned back on. Constantly in the dark and not seeing any personnel or hearing any voices had caused my mind to start making me a little paranoid. I was beginning to think the place was abandoned. There had to be a way out of here but I had no idea as to how I would do it.

By this time, I had a less than pleasant odor from not having a bath or shower in a very long time. It seemed like a week since I had eaten although I was sure it had only been a matter of days. The toilet and sink still worked so I was able to get something to drink and although I had no soap I tried to wash what I could in the sink using my hands. I just had to find a way out of here.

I began thinking about what I said to Saud and wondering if my agreeing to speak might constitute treason. Of course I still didn't know what the status of the country was or if there was still a country at all. All I wanted was a few answers.

I couldn't understand why things changed so quickly. One day the Islamists seem to have everything going their way and the next they appear to be gone. Maybe they were better at propaganda than I gave them credit for and maybe they have been on the run for a while.

Worse yet was the fact that I was no longer sure what the date is.

AUGUST 10, 2017

DAVIS MONTHAN AIR FORCE BASE

Angela sat up in bed as she watched her husband walk across the bedroom. "Honey, it is only 4:30, where are you going so early?"

"I am going out for a little run. You know I haven't got much exercise lately and I need to run and think a little before I face the rest of the day."

Angela rolled back over in bed and said, "Okay, if you want to think in private that's fine but don't give me that I am out of shape stuff because you have been on three combat missions in five weeks and I don't think being in shape is an issue."

TJ smiled and made his way out the door. TJ was proud of accompanying the Marine Raiders Special Forces Group on covert missions to fight Islamic Terrorist forces in Des Moines, Iowa, and Milwaukee, Wisconsin, beside the original raid in Omaha. General Hickman had advised him, however, that his combat trips should stop because he was more important in the command post. He knew the decision to go or not would ultimately be his since he was the Commander in Chief. Today was to be the final preparation for raids on Minneapolis, Minnesota, and Dearborn, Michigan. These were major strongholds for the terrorists and these missions would certainly be the most dangerous yet. He knew that the enemy knew he was going on these missions ever since the podcast went out. The general had showed him a flyer offering a half million dollar reward for his head. He continued his run trying to make up his mind because he felt that he might be letting down Greg and the rest of the team.

At 6:00 AM, TJ entered the combat control center. "Ten-Hut!" Someone screamed from the corner of the room. TJ immediately said, "At ease."

TJ walked to his workstation and began going through the briefing information that had been left for him on the table. The first report he read was from the CIA and regarded background information about the targets that were to be hit later today. Amazingly he read that the terrorists had been brought into the United States by our own government. In each city hundreds of Somali terrorist and loyal Al-Qaeda members were brought into the country and resettled in Minnesota and Michigan as part of a program to help refugees. In some cases, there had been known evidence of their association, which had apparently simply been ignored by those in the state department charged with vetting candidates for the program. As he read the information he became angry and wondered if this was simply incompetence or did we have members of the state department committing treason intentionally?

As TJ was studying the information he looked up and saw Gunnery Sergeant Hackborn walking toward him. "Good morning, Greg."

Hackborn stopped and snapped to attention while stating. "Good morning, Mr. President."

TJ smiled and motioned for him to sit down. "At ease and have a seat, Greg."

As he sat down he said, "Thank you, sir. We are finishing up getting everything ready and wondered if you would be joining us today?"

TJ hesitated for a moment and then began to shake his head. "I am sorry but General Hickman has advised me he needs me more here at the command post and he pointed out politely that I might be putting a target on your back as well."

"Sir, we don't fear anyone placing a target on our back. We always have a target on our back. We do understand the value though, of having you in the command post. You did a good job on the last three missions, sir, and you are welcome to accompany us on any mission you wish to help us with in the future. We will miss you, sir, but we will bring you back another successful outcome, sir."

"I am sure you will, Greg." With that Hackborn got back on his feet, shook the President's hand and left to finish with his preparation.

General Hickman then approached to discuss the day's schedule with the President.

"So you have decided to pass on the mission today, sir?"

"Yes, General, I have. So I assume you have a lot of important decisions for me to make today while I sit here wondering what my squad is doing to free our nation from invaders."

"Sir, we will have plenty for you to do today. I know that you were a valued member at Gunny Hackborn's team but I assure you that they will accomplish their mission without you being with them today. In the meantime, we have a number of logistical decisions to make and we need to go over the operations around the world as well."

TJ knew that the general was right even though inside he wanted more than anything to be preparing to leave with the Marines. As he continued to flip through the briefing papers the general turned around to speak to an aide before continuing his discussion with the president.

"The situation overseas has lost ground in the past few days. The U.K. has had several terrorist attacks in London, Birmingham, and Southampton. All of these attacks were carried out by suicide bombers and the number of personnel lost was quite high. The Brits do seem to have the current situation under control but I fear they are getting closer and closer to the breaking point."

The general continued, "I would like to discuss some new strategies with you, sir."

TJ motioned for him to sit down before he continued.

The general pulled out the chair and sat down. He moved closer to TJ and began speaking softly as if he wanted no one else in the room to hear his plans. "I want to approach the Canadians for some assistance in moving troops. With your approval, sir, I will direct the Atlantic fleet with the Coast Guard to establish a naval blockade from Halifax, Newfoundland, to the Bahama Islands. At the same time, we will move infantry and armored units into Canada at Sault Ste. Marie and then using the Canadian Highway System through Ottawa and then south into the northwest regions of New York. We will use Canadian satellites to monitor the operation since the Russians took out our satellites but not the Canadians."

TJ had been writing notes but put his pen down on the table in front of him and leaned back in his chair. As TJ stared at a clock on the wall across the room and said nothing the general continued. "We also will begin blockades of rail routes and highway systems east of the Mississippi and north of the Tennessee – Kentucky state lines. We hope that over time we can cripple the Islamic organization and begin to starve them out. We also intend to fly drones over the area to shoot down any aircraft except for flights authorized through our FAA controllers. If we can isolate these areas, we may have a better chance of citizens staging an uprising and assisting our military operations."

AUGUST 15, 2017

DAVIS-MONTHAN AIR FORCE BASE

The sun had barely risen above the horizon when the front door of the base hospital slammed open startling the nurse at the front desk. She began to scream at the airman rushing into the hallway when she realized who she was about to address.

"Mr. President, can I help you?"

TJ spoke loudly and in an excited manner, "Where is Gunnery Sergeant Hackborn at?"

"I believe he is one of the individuals that just arrived, sir. He will be in the emergency ward, if you could wait just a moment I will call someone to take you there."

TJ ran down the hallway refusing to wait and following the signs posted in the halls. Meanwhile the nurse quickly picked up the phone to alert the personnel in the emergency unit that they were about to have an important visitor.

As TJ entered the unit he saw activity around one bed and instinctively headed to the foot of that bed. There was a doctor and nurse on either side of the bed where Gunny Hackborn lay. Everyone was very busy taking blood, starting an IV and removing dressings to inspect wounds and there were many to inspect. TJ just stood silently watching the flurry of activity.

Greg was silent as well staring at the ceiling of the room but TJ thought he might have glanced at him for just a moment.

As one of the doctors turned to leave he said nothing to the president as if he didn't even notice him. The other doctor looked down at the wounded man and said, "Sgt. Hackborn, we are going to prepare you for surgery in a few minutes. My associate will be attempting to remove the bullets that are close to your spine and that are most likely causing your problems with the feeling in your legs. We won't know the extent of the damage until we get in there to examine exactly what the bullets tore up. When he is finished I will then remove the remainder of the bullets from the other areas. It would appear you are a very lucky man to have survived this incident. Now I am going to give you something for pain that will make you sleepy."

Hackborn very abruptly said, "No. Not yet anyway. I have a debriefing to give to my boss, doc, and I need to be alert to do so."

The doctor began to argue but noticed the president standing there and just backed up while saying, "Make it quick."

TJ moved to the side of the bed and said, "How you doing, Greg?"

"Well, sir, I have had better days but I will be all right, I'm in good hands."

TJ smiled and agreed that he was in good hands and then said, "We will make sure that you get the best possible care so why don't you let the docs give you something to relax?"

"No you need to hear some of this information and I want it coming from me."

TJ pulled a chair over and reached in his pocket withdrawing a notepad and then told Hackborn to go ahead. The President could see the pain in Hackborn's eyes as he turned his head and closed his eyes for a moment to gather his thoughts.

"Sir, it was like being in a Taliban village in Afghanistan. Dearborn is completely Islamic as far as I could tell. The street signs and traffic signs have all been removed. The stores and advertising signs are all in Arabic. I wasn't even sure I was still in the United States. Everyone is armed and there were no friendly faces anywhere we went. We went in under cover of darkness and we were staying in the shadows using alleyways and backyards to move toward our target. Four teams in four different locations were all attacked at the same time. It appeared very much like a coordinated ambush. We were in an alley with little cover when we were lit up with bright flood lights. We were blinded for a few seconds because we were wearing night vision but everything came at us from above, where we were not looking. The coordination of the attack was really surprising. They had automatic weapons and rocket propelled grenades. Nearly everyone on the team was hit at least once in the initial attack. We found a door that we forced open and entered a mom and pop grocery store for cover. We exchanged gunfire for nearly an hour and then I guess they got tired of playing with us and fired a rocket into the building. They misjudged the velocity though and the rocket went through the plate glass window and into and through the wall exploding in the building next door and causing a partial collapse. In the confusion that followed as they charged the adjacent building expecting to find us, we slipped out a side door and withdrew from the area. We received additional sniper fire from several locations as we headed to the exit location and fortunately the evac helo was waiting for us as we arrived. They were accompanied by Cobra's that provided cover. We lost three, sir. I got dropped off here because the neurosurgeon that specializes on spinal injuries happened to be here, the rest of the unit went to other hospitals. We had four teams go in, sir, and after the attacks began I don't know what happened to the other teams. I apologize, sir."

TJ was moved by his last statement. "You have absolutely nothing to apologize for, Gunny. I want you to concentrate on getting better because this war isn't going to be over soon and I need you for missions in the future."

"Yes, sir."

With that TJ stood up, snapped to attention, and saluted Hackborn. "You can return that salute when you walk in my office next time."

TJ walked silently out of the hospital and to the command center. As he entered the command center he saw General Hickman at the communications section busily writing down information for the morning briefing. As soon as the general noticed the president he completed his conversation and walked over to the president's workstation.

"Good morning, sir." TJ simply looked up at the general and stared without a word.

"I guess from your expression you already know much of what I am about to brief you on."

TJ nodded and said, "I just came from visiting Hackborn in the hospital."

"How is he doing, sir?"

"He is in good spirits but the doctors are about to do spinal surgery on him and it doesn't look very promising. I understand he took seven hits including two that are against his lumbar spine. What amazes me is that he was wearing body armor which stopped about ten rounds so he actually got hit seventeen times."

"He is a tough guy and a good Marine, sir, he will pull through. Do you want the rest of the box score, sir?"

"Yes, although I am pretty sure I won't like what you are about to tell me."

"No, sir, you won't. We sent five Special Forces teams into St. Paul, Minnesota, and four into Dearborn, Michigan. The St. Paul teams also ran into heavy resistance but they were able to secure and destroy an armory as well as detain three leadership targets. Those three have been transferred to the Colorado Super Max for interrogation. Out of the 75 special operators dispatched to St. Paul we had 25 killed and 15 injured. In Dearborn we sent in four teams, none of which reached their targets and we had 35 killed and 20 injured of the 60 dispatched."

"You mean only five people got out of Dearborn unscathed?"

"Yes, sir."

"How is your blockade plans coming along?"

"We have an armored division moving through Canada currently and they will be joined by a Canadian group. They will enter the United States again in western New York and begin their assault. Navy and Coast Guard ship are moving into position to begin the blockade of the coast. We intend to have fighter jets destroy rail lines and highways inside the blockade zones in precision attacks. We also have drones already flying in Michigan and Indiana as well as Ohio, Pennsylvania, and New York."

The president was nodding as he was examining a map of the areas. "General, I want to task you with another assignment to be completed as soon as possible."

"Yes, sir, what would you like?"

"I want you to task aircraft to attack the targets in St. Paul and Dearborn which were not reached by Special Forces and obliterate them. You are authorized to use whatever will make the biggest holes short of nuclear weapons."

"Sir, you will be bombing our own country."

"Based on what Greg told me I don't believe these areas are simply occupied. They are a foreign country at this point. I will not sacrifice any more personnel on the ground precision attacks. I want these areas eliminated as a threat."

General Hickman stood up and simply said, "Yes, sir."

The general could see the urgency in the president's eyes and immediately made the necessary calls to get this attack underway. He then informed the president that the attacks would take place at 2:00 PM central time. TJ thanked him and indicated he would be back to check on the status.

As TJ left the command center he felt the need to head to the base chapel to pray that what he just ordered would not turn out to be a mistake.

At 2:00 PM, a group of four F-22s launched multiple missiles at three targets in St. Paul, Minnesota. The missiles hit their targets and numerous buildings crumbled to the ground. In Dearborn six F-35s flew through the sky above the city and released precision bombs and missiles which destroyed large chunks of what used to be working class neighborhoods and have now been reduced to rubble.

As the president walked into the command center he was informed that the missions had been accomplished and without resistance. After discussing the results of the airstrikes with several of the general's aides he began to leave the center. General Hickman called over to the president and stopped him.

"I thought you would like to know that Hackborn is out of surgery and doing well. The doctor says they were able to remove all of the bullets and fragments and that he should make a full recovery."

The president acknowledged the information with a nod and walked out of the center with a smile on his face. Even with the relief of the news about Greg, TJ was worried about the other events of the day. Today opened an all new chapter in this war with the air strikes on American soil and he couldn't shake the feeling that it was very possible that he killed American citizens today with the enemy.

WEDNESDAY, NOVEMBER 1, 2017

DAVIS MONTHAN AIR FORCE BASE

It was 4:30 AM and TJ was finishing his morning run. As he was cooling down and approaching his residence he struck up a conversation with one of his protective detail agents.

"Phil, do you think we will win this damn war?"

"Not my job, sir, to think about that, I am only here to make sure nothing happens to you in the process."

TJ smiled, stopped, and turned face to face with the agent. "Phil, forget about your duty for just a moment, after all there are no enemy agents here, just be a human being and give me your opinion. Sometimes it's good to consider what those out of the loop think about what is going on and I don't have the ability to check the latest polls from the New York Times."

"Well, sir, off the record, I see a lot of people dying and little progress being made. I am not sure what there will be left of the rest of the world by the time we secure our country. I know we have made progress, the west coast is secure, most of the south and Midwest but I am from Virginia, sir, and I want to go home and I am tired of waiting."

TJ looked directly into the agent's eyes and thought for a moment and then said, "Give me six more months and I will try to get you home, I promise." With that TJ turned and went inside to shower.

It's 5:30 AM when TJ entered the command center and immediately called for a complete briefing on the country and the world status. General Hickman approached the president's workstation and sat down to begin the rundown.

"Okay, sir, let's begin with Europe and work our way around the globe. All of Europe with the exception of England, France, Italy, Spain, Switzerland and the western portion of Germany are occupied and being controlled by the Russian Federation. Amazingly the Russians are now attacking the Turks and Islamic State in the Balkans and they are conducting limited air strikes in Greece, Turkey, and Syria. It would seem the original agreements between our three enemies has begun to dissolve. The Chinese fleet has withdrawn and has now taken a position south of Japan. There are occasional strikes from the fleet but they have been easily defended. The Chinese occupy Southeast Asia and the Korean Peninsula. Australia and New Zealand are still free. The Islamic State occupies the Philippines, Southwest Asia, the Middle East, and North Africa. India is still in the fight, however. In South America, Venezuela, Columbia, Peru and the northern third of Brazil are controlled by Russia. Mexico and Central America are still in play. Canada, Greenland, and the Scandinavian countries are still free. As far as the United States is concerned we now control all of the country except the area from New York City to Pennsylvania, Maryland, Virginia, North and South Carolina. It would appear, however, that we are at a standstill in our progress in those areas. The Islamic State has a very strong force in that area including aircraft. They have also gained control of CIA and NIA headquarters and have greatly damaged our intelligence capability. Their leadership has embedded themselves in residential neighborhoods so even if we find them we are incapable of destroying them without killing many of our own citizens. That, sir, is the concise status of the world today."

As the general concluded his briefing of the status of the world he closed a folder he had been using and passed it across the table to the president. General Hickman stared across the table at TJ and was unable to read the blank expression on his face. He expected to see some anger or some excitement but all he saw was a blank poker face like he had not seen on the president's face before.

After several minutes of absolute quiet the president looked up and simply said, "Excuse me for a few moments while I pray for an answer."

The general stood up and walked back across the room to the communications area to check on updates. He checked the weather and found that a freak early snowstorm was crippling the northeast corridor of the country. He thought maybe they can come up with a plan that will use the snow to their advantage.

After about ten minutes time the general noticed that the president was motioning for him to return.

"General, I want to spend the next Fourth of July in Washington DC. I know you have been working hard to keep from harming citizens while attempting to beat back the Islamists. I appreciate that but we can't make a significant difference in correcting the rest of the world and stopping Vladimir unless we control our country. Our whole country. I believe the time is right. The blockade has been very successful they have been weakened considerably. I want an all-out assault with whatever we have available. I would like to see two assault groups, one moving from the south and one from the north. We will squeeze them out of our country."

Now it was General Hickman who stood with a blank look on his face. Slowly ideas began to creep into his mind and after a short time he nodded his head and said, "Yes, sir, but I will need a month or two to assemble the troops and equipment that we will need. Can we plan the assault to begin say February first?"

"That will be fine but I want you to maintain the blockade and continue with precision air strikes to keep them off balance. I am serious about being in DC by July fourth, you understand that?"

"I understand, sir. We will do our best. There is one other thing I think you should know, sir."

TJ looked up and said, "Go on."

"We have an intelligence analyst that believes that Russia is moving toward Syria with the intent of attacking Israel. We think Vladimir intends to remove the Jews from their homeland and turn it over to the Islamic State in return for guaranteed non-aggression from the Islamists. Personally, sir, I believe Vladimir wants to control the whole world and since he believes he has us in an unwinnable scenario he is trying to guarantee peace from his two co-conspirators."

"Interesting. Whoever that analyst is start paying him or her overtime and keep them busy because I agree with their train of thought. I just hope we can resolve this before it is too late because they certainly have the upper hand right now."

NOVEMBER 15, 2017

MOSCOW RUSSIA
THE KREMLIN

It was a bitterly cold day even by Russian standards for November. Vladimir, however, had a very warm feeling running through his body as he gazed out the window of his office watching the snow fall outside. The fresh snow was falling rapidly now and covering the grounds and everything on it. Fresh snow was the one thing that always brought comfort and joy to Vladimir for a reason he couldn't explain but it had always been so since his youth. Vladimir had hot Cossack blood running through his veins which seemed to fuel his desire to conquer and his need to control everything and everyone.

There was a sharp knock at the door and then Ivan, Vladimir's personal assistant, entered the room. "Sir, they are assembled and the meeting is beginning."

"Very good, Ivan, thank you. I will be along in a few minutes but I want them to have a few minutes to get acquainted and size each other up and then I will show them who is in control."

"Very good, sir." Ivan then turned and walked out of the office firmly closing the door behind him.

Vladimir waited another fifteen minutes spending much of the time gazing at the snow. The snow seemed to give him the energy he needed as he knew that he was about to make his allies very uneasy and probably end up having them hate him as well.

Meanwhile, in a lavish conference room at the far end of the hallway from Vladimir's office, President Gryzlovski was welcoming the representatives from China, Iran, and the Islamic State. In the center of the room was a long dark wooden table with several armless chairs on either side. The chairs resembled the type you find in a family kitchen with no formal or ceremonial appearance. At the head of the table was a very ornate leather chair with a high back that resembled a throne.

As President Gryzlovski began the introductions he walked to the left side of the table at the far end. "Gentlemen, let us begin, please. Vice President Xi Jintao and Ambassador Wen Yaobang will be representing the government of the People's Republic of China, please have a seat to my right. Ayatollah Hassan Khomani and General Ali Rouhani representing the Islamic Republic of Iran, please have a seat across from me, and finally, General Mohammad Baqr al-Khoe of the Islamic State if you will have a seat to the left of General Rouhani." Each of the parties took their seat and began to assemble the materials they had brought with them. Their assistants pulled chairs from near the walls and sat behind their bosses. President Gryzlovski sat alone with no assistants but he noticed that everyone at the table looked more than once at the ornate chair left empty at the head of the table.

"I am honored that you have chosen to attend this conference and I am sorry for the short notice but as you will see this is a very important meeting. When we all joined in this glorious project we agreed to certain stipulations when the military phase of the project was complete. We have been disappointed in some of the military operations thus far so we have decided that some changes in the overall plans will become necessary."

Gryzlovski noticed that he now had the complete attention of everyone in the room and as the interpreters were catching up with his statements the eyes of everyone in attendance seemed to become more focused on him. He prided himself in his ability to read people and what he saw in the eyes of those now present at this point was anger.

"Originally, we agreed that all of the conquered states would be divided between Islamic control, Chinese control and Russian Control. However, it is now apparent that Russia is carrying the bulk of the responsibility in the military effort. As a result of our added responsibility, we intend to reap more of the reward. At the conclusion of this conference you will each receive a number of documents for your government to agree to and sign. These documents will consist of an agreement by your governments to cede all foreign policy decisions to the Russian government. You will be free to run your domestic concerns without interference in most cases but you will also agree to grant the Russian government any mineral rights that might be needed without question and for these rights you will be compensated as determined by the Russian government. Finally, we acknowledge the importance of controlling the nation of Israel. Because of this great importance we have decided that Russian troops shall occupy this area. We will allow the Islamic people to move freely within the country and we will not disrupt your religious practices but we will establish an area where the Jewish people may live and guarantee their safety as well."

With that the Islamic representatives rose from their chairs and began shouting at Gryzlovski in Arabic and Farsi. Gryzlovski fully expected their rage and he simply sat back and smiled as they continued to rant.

As if he had been cued Vladimir opened the door of the conference room and quietly, almost regally, entered the room and walked straight to the throne chair at the head of the table. Upon his entrance Gryzlovski and the Chinese representatives rose to their feet out of respect but the Islamist continued shouting and seemed to pay no attention to Vladimir.

As he reached his chair Vladimir held his left hand up and said in a loud stern voice, "Enough! Sit!" He said it twice, once in Arabic and once in Farsi. This got the immediate attention of the men shouting. He then held his right hand out with the palm up motioning for the other representatives to have a seat as well. As they sat down the Islamists continued to voice their complaints but in much softer tones.

"I understand your concern, I, too, am concerned. I am concerned that my allies in China failed to achieve the naval victory that they assured me they would obtain. I am concerned that my Islamist allies have failed on so many issues that I question your ability to assist in world domination. You failed to properly execute your grand EMP scheme, you failed to achieve domination over any of the United States west of the Mississippi River and in fact you seem to be losing ground day by day as their exile government is pushing you back into the sea. I am concerned that the only member of this project who has lived up to their promise thus far has been Russia. So as the overall chairman of the new world government I have found it necessary to enact these changes."

The tension in the room became thick as all of the representatives seemed uneasy in their chairs. There was a great deal of whispering back and forth as the discussions between the members of the Iranian and Islamic State representatives seemed intense. When the whispers stopped General Baqr al-Khoe rose to his feet to address the relaxed Vladimir.

"We have brought the United States to their knees and your only assistance has been to furnish some munitions. We have done the work and suffered the losses. I agree, we have suffered some problems lately but that is due to the blockade and the fact that supplies and munitions have become in short supply. When we are able to break the blockade we will eliminate this government in exile, as you call them. We cannot and will not allow the occupation of Palestine by your government however under any circumstances so you must remove that from the table of discussion."

As the General sat back down in his chair he looked angrily at Vladimir and the remainder of the Islamic delegation also appeared to be looking at Vladimir defiantly. Vladimir, however, continued to appear relaxed and had a smirk on his face that made it appear he was well in control of the situation.

Vladimir looked directly at General Baqr al-Khoe and began to speak, "Allow me to make this clear to you in your native tongue." Switching to Arabic Vladimir continued, "There will be no further negotiations. You will instruct your troops to clear a path for the Russian troops through Turkey and Syria and into Israel. You will not interfere with this movement in any way.

In return for your cooperation, we will break the American blockade and furnish you with munitions and supplies as well as naval assistance along the Atlantic Coast. Your failure to cooperate with my instructions will result in the end of the war for your military sooner than you would like to see."

Everyone else at the table was listening intently to the translation of Vladimir's words. The Chinese representatives were watching closely the reaction of the Islamists. The conference room became incredibly quiet as everyone stared at Vladimir trying to size him up and decide what their next move would be at this point.

As the representatives continued to argue their positions Vladimir stood and placed his hands palms down on the table. "My friends from China, I realize you have been fighting a significant American fleet in the Pacific and I appreciate your efforts but I also see that recently you have been much less zealous in your efforts. I would caution you not to relinquish the gains you have made, but to push on. Even if you don't smash their navy now you will, by attrition, cause them great harm which will lead to our ultimate victory. My Islamic friends, as I previously told you, the negotiations are over. You will comply or you will be defeated by my military. You have been weakened by the Americans where my strength has increased so I would consider carefully your next move. If the documents are not signed and delivered to President Gryzlovski within seventy-two hours I will instruct my forces currently preparing to move into Turkey to proceed and to leave nothing but destruction in their wake. Our navy's Atlantic Group left the waters north of the United Kingdom this morning and are on course for the waters off of New York where they have been instructed to smash the blockade. I also have a number of naval vessels in the Caspian Sea equipped with missiles which we can use on what the Americans left in Iran or against American naval vessels in the Mediterranean. The decision for our future together is in your hands."

As he completed his statement Vladimir turned his back on the Islamists and walked out of the room. All of way out of the room he smiled, having felt like he had just had a major victory. Only he and Gryzlovski and possibly Ivan knew that this had been his plan from the start. He would not share power with anyone and he would make sure that Russia would be the ruling nation of the world. Some may think he was consumed with power but his only goal was to make sure that the homeland would always be safe and secure. No one else ever had the courage to do the things that needed to be done. Now he would control the world and people would give him the respect he deserved, all he needed now was to bring that upstart American President to his knees. If the Islamists couldn't do it, he would make sure that he did and TJ Samuels would find the prisons in Siberia are much less luxurious than the one in Virginia.

NOVEMBER 23, 2017

DAVIS-MONTHAN AIR FORCE BASE

TJ looked at the clock on his night stand and saw the time flashing was 3:08 AM, and he turned to look at a figure standing in the doorway of his room. "Sir, I am sorry but you are needed immediately in the command center."

TJ sat up slowly trying to clear his head and then walked to the bathroom. "Give me a minute to piss and get dressed and I will be right with you. Do you have any idea what is going on?"

"No, sir, but there is a military police escort waiting for you and this request has come from General Hickman who is already in the command center."

TJ quickly brushed his teeth and began getting dressed when he remembered this was Thanksgiving. *I suppose I won't be enjoying turkey after all today if things are starting this early.*

As soon as TJ emerged from the residence he was whisked away in a staff car to the command center. As he entered the center he noticed that everyone was very busy and he saw no smiles on anyone's face.

General Hickman walked over to join the president as he sat down at his workstation. "Sir, I apologize for waking you at this hour but we have a serious problem. We have been monitoring some movement by the Russian Northern fleet and it appeared they were repositioning south of the U.K. and most likely to assume a position off the French or Spanish coast but they suddenly made an abrupt turn to the west. About an hour ago we became aware of several Russian submarines approaching our blockade vessels. They caught us flat footed and two of our frigates working the blockade were sunk by torpedo attack. Since that time the Russians have launched aircraft which apparently were probing because as soon as we launched they turned back. We have now received information from the U.K. that it appears a number of freighters are following the Russian fleet. We now believe that the Russians are coming to break the blockade and resupply the Islamic State troops."

TJ looked down at his desk and the anger on his face was rather easy to notice. "Can I assume, general, that you have a defense plan already swirling around in the logistical mind of yours?"

"Yes, sir, you may."

TJ sat back in his chair and took in a deep breath. He appeared to still be trying to wake up so he could be more alert when the general reviewed his proposed actions. One of the airmen in the center approached from the right side and placed a hot cup of coffee on the desk next to the president's hand. "Excuse me, sir, but I thought this might help you."

TJ took a sip from the cup of coffee and then looked at the general and told him to explain his plan.

"I have spoken to our friends in the U.K. and found that they have submarines trailing the freighters. Upon our request they will sink the freighters. We have identified the Russian's most powerful carrier group heading at full speed for the northeast coast. This will include the carrier Vinogradov, Battle Cruisers, Admiral Lazarev, Admiral Ushakov, and Admiral Nakihimov. They also have a frigate the Admiral Golovko and two corvettes, Steregushchiy and Boikiy. The carrier is equipped with SU-33 Fighter jets and each of the other ships are equipped with torpedoes and missiles. We also know that there are at least three submarines either in the area or on their way. We have intercepted communications with the Yuri Dolborckiy, the Aleksander Nivskiy, and the Knyaz Vladimir. All of these subs are equipped with torpedoes and cruise missiles. The missiles can not only take out other ships but could strike land targets within the country."

TJ just stared across the room and took another sip of the coffee. He couldn't help but remember that today was Thanksgiving Day. This was supposed to be a day of celebration and being thankful for the good things and blessings that they have received as a nation and a people but today it seemed more and more difficult to be thankful. They had so many blessings from God yet their attitude and sensitivity have cost them so much that it is now necessary for them to fight for their very existence.

So general, now that you have given me the bad news I hope you have some good news to follow it up."

"Maybe, sir. It seems this apparent attack by Russia comes at a convenient time for us. We have a carrier group returning for resupply from the Mediterranean and they are only a few miles off the coast of Georgia where they were to dock. I intend to resupply them by fixed wing aircraft and helicopters while they change course and continue north. The carrier in this group is the Harry S Truman and most of the aircraft on board are electronic warfare aircraft. These planes are designed to disrupt radar, sonar, communications and in general just screw with the enemy ships and aircraft. The Truman also has eight E-47Cs which are stealth and unmanned jets which are controlled by personnel on the Truman. They can be and will be equipped with some limited missiles for attack. In addition to these aircraft, we will dispatch a squadron of F-35s to the carrier as it heads north. Also, we were currently in the process of a rotation on the blockade vessels. The Abraham Lincoln just reached station to relieve the George H W Bush which means both carriers and their accompanying vessels are off the coast in the Maryland and New York areas. We also have two destroyers, the Lyndon B Johnson and the Gravely, as well as a guided missile cruiser the Vella Gulf cruising the area."

TJ smiled and nodded his head and then said, "That's a lot of tonnage but tell me why I can be confident that it won't suddenly be lying at the bottom of the Atlantic?"

"I obviously can't guarantee anything, sir, but I do have a plan. I have taken the liberty, sir, of sending two submarines, the Springfield and the Jefferson City, to lay a rather substantial mine field across the path of the Russian fleet as they get closer to the area. The Russians obviously have sophisticated enough equipment that they will be able to detect and remove the mines. This is when our electronic warfare planes will attack. In addition, as they are working on clearing their paths we will attack them with missiles, torpedoes, and aircraft and hopefully the tonnage on the bottom of the Atlantic will all be of Russian origin."

TJ viewed a map of the area with approximate current locations of all the participants and the projected areas where the attacks will take place. "It seems that the bulk of the ships will be a great distance apart when you indicate the attack will take place."

"That's true, sir, but today these naval battles are not fought in close proximity but over great distances sometimes."

"Okay, I will give you that. When will all this take place, general?"

"Sir, you have time to go have your turkey and have an enjoyable afternoon with your wife. Be back here by about six this evening because that is when the fireworks will begin."

TJ sat down at the table with Angela at two o'clock to enjoy some Thanksgiving turkey. The Air Force staff had put together a large feast for everyone at the base and delivered the president's to his quarters. Angela looked across the table and gave TJ a warm loving smile as the airmen began to serve the pair. TJ reached across the table and took Angela's hand and then said a prayer thanking God for the gifts they shared and asking for God's blessing on all of those in service to the United States.

Following the delicious meal TJ and Angela took a walk in the cool fresh air and talked about the good times before the election that made TJ the president.

"I often regret being elected president but then I think what would have happened had I not been elected. These attacks were already planned and beginning before I ever took office and although I have made mistakes, I think we are better off today because of most of my decisions. My predecessor made mistakes that led to the circumstances which made these incidents inescapable. Things like scrapping our space shuttles before replacement vehicles were ready which caused us to rely on the Russians. Neglecting to adequately develop our mineral resources causing us to have to rely on Islamists that lied and cheated us to get their way. Borrowing money from the Chinese to the point of our own bankruptcy. I think if I didn't get elected these issues would have continued and maybe instead of the massive attack that we have tried to withstand they would have slowly taken control of our country politically through illegal immigration and financial control. Would that have been better than what we face today?"

They continued to walk in silence for nearly a mile before Angela turned to T.J. "I know that you have done the best job possible and I think this country is better today because of you and the actions you have taken. You showed the world that this country is not a paper tiger and will not be pushed around at their whim. So no matter what happens tomorrow our country is better off because of you. Maybe you should swing by the chapel before you go back to the command post, you seem to make your best decisions after you pray for a while."

It was 5:30 PM when the president entered the Command Center. General Hickman was busily at work monitoring the events taking place and making last minute decisions regarding the corrections and adjustments that were required. The general's aides were also busy passing messages on to the command staff on board various ships. General Hickman suddenly noticed that the president was looking over his shoulder.

"Hello, sir, I am a bit busy at the moment but I will give you a briefing, sir, at your workstation in just a minute."

TJ took the hint and turned to walk over to his workstation in the far corner of the room. He could see that everyone was very busy so he assumed that the battle was either underway or about to commence.

It was a full twenty minutes before the General walked over to TJ and asked if he could sit down. TJ motioned for him to have a seat and said, "Well, how is the plan going so far?"

"Well, sir, the Russians obviously were not aware of the plan because they attacked us before we were in position. Russian submarines fired a cruise missile that destroyed a Coast Guard Cutter and the Vella Gulf sustained some damage from a torpedo hit, but they were able to make emergency repairs and are still in action. We now have the electronic warfare planes in position and they are jamming the Russian radars. I have also ordered three B-2 bombers from Whiteman AFB to fly a mission over these ships. I believe that as long as the electronic attack is underway that the B-2s will be safe and able to deliver a payload on the Russian fleet. The Russians are currently approaching the area where the mines have been deposited so they will have to change course significantly or slow down enough to get the mines safely removed. As soon as they begin to maneuver we will begin a steady attack with missiles from various ships and F-35 and F-18 Fighters will begin attacks on the various vessels. We intend to have the B-2s deliver a payload on their carrier and possibly one of their destroyers. Our real problem right now is locating their damn submarines. They sunk the two frigates this morning and now have sunk the Coast Guard Cutter and damaged a cruiser. We now have our own submarines in the area and we have submarine hunting aircraft in the area so we will find their subs but I still worry about what damage will be done before we eliminated them."

General Hickman excused himself and returned to the communications area so he could monitor the current situation. It was impossible to monitor the actual radio traffic but they were receiving electronically a blow by blow rundown from the USS Harry S Truman, which was currently acting as the command vessel. The messages were flowing quickly now as the missiles were flying from the Russians and the Americans.

TJ realized that his strengths did not include battle command so he stayed at his workstation and patiently waited for information to reach him. TJ closed his eyes for a moment and tried to imagine what it was like right now in the Atlantic where the battle was looming. He realized that good people were dying for both sides. People who were fathers and sons, mothers and daughters, people who had so much to offer in ways outside of battle. Why couldn't he find a way to resolve these problems without causing the deaths of so many? A very blue feeling was overcoming him as could see in his mind the faces of those who would be left behind from the deaths of those brave people fighting right now. War is so wrong but so often necessary because of the close mindedness of the politically powerful.

It was 7:45 PM when General Hickman approached the president with a number of papers in his hand. "Sir, I can report that the battle is ended for the time being. The blockade is still intact at this time and the Russian forces have withdrawn slightly."

President Samuels nodded but did not show any signs of pleasure or relief. "General, have you got any statistics for me?"

"Yes, sir, I do, would you like to go over the preliminary numbers?"

TJ nodded his head slowly and closed his eyes appearing to already regret what he was about to hear. The general began. "I will start with the Russian losses. The Russian carrier, Vinogradov is dead in the water and has numerous fires on the deck, the Admiral Ushakov and the corvette Boikiy have both been sunk, one of their submarines, possibly the Aleksandr Nivskiy, has also been sunk. All of their remaining ships are in service although several have received moderate to severe damage. They also lost two helicopters and three SU-33 fighters. We have a preliminary estimate on personnel losses for the Russians and it stands at 807. We have also picked up some survivors from the two sunken ships. The Brits sunk all three of the freighters who were following the battle group. Our losses include two F-35s and four F-18s. The Vella Gulf and Gravely each sustained moderate damage but both are underway. All of our submarines are fine. Total personnel loss at this time appears to be 37. Overall I feel our plan worked as well as we could have hoped and the Russian forces appear to have discontinued any efforts to break our blockade."

The president opened his eyes and nodded but did not smile. "I guess that is a win for our side tonight but it is funny because I really don't feel like celebrating. I can only think about all those who lost their loved one tonight."

NOVEMBER 26, 2017

EREGLI KARYAYOLU HIGHWAY
YARMA TURKEY

It was just after noon local time as the Russian armored convoy moved east on the Eregli Karyayolu Highway passing through the southern section of Yarma, Turkey. The convoy commander was Colonel Mika Mendolovich and he was observing quietly from the lead armored personnel carrier. The convoy was made up of more than sixty trucks with troops and ammunition, a dozen tanks riding on flatbed trailers and dozens of armored personnel carriers. Colonel Mendolovich had the task of supervising this movement safely to Aleppo, Syria. From there he would return to Russia and allow other officers to deliver the convoy to Israel where they will set up an occupation force. Colonel Mendolovich was a logistical specialist not a combat officer and once they reach Syria the combat commanders would take charge.

The trip had been very peaceful thus far. The Turkish people have been friendly for the most part although they had received some icy stares from some. Mendolovich had been assured that the convoy was to be given safe passage and if there were any problems to worry about those would be incurred when they attempted to enter the state of Israel. The Jews were expected to put up a fight but would most likely reluctantly allow the Russians into their country when they fully understood that the alternative was to allow the Islamists to move in violently.

207

The Colonel had just settled down to take a nap in the seat next to the driver when he was startled by the roar of a jet fighter buzzing the convoy from west to east. "What was that?" The Colonel shouted as he jumped up.

The driver informed him it appeared to be a Mig-29 with Syrian markings and had flown very low over the entire convoy. The radio began to crackle now with other drivers asking what to do and if this was an attack. The Colonel told the communications specialist to contact the command center for instructions.

The driver calmly looked over and said, "Sir, it is probably just a preventive over flight to make sure there are no surprises waiting up ahead. We are entering the lower levels of the Tarsus Mountains in a bit and they are probably just checking for ambush sites. Are they not the Syrians allies?"

The Colonel gave that a little thought and replied, "Yes, that is probably right. At any rate he is apparently gone now and he didn't fire a shot at anyone so I am sure it is nothing. Just continue on."

The communications specialists suddenly shouted from the rear of the vehicle at the colonel. "Colonel, sir, we have just received information that the plane carrying the combat commanders was just shot down over Aleppo. We are being cautioned to proceed with care and to watch for ambushes!"

As the colonel turned back to look out the front observation area he noticed what appeared to be several helicopters heading toward the convoy from the southwest. As he watched them maneuver he didn't notice the jets suddenly appear from the northwest. The driver first noticed the five planes, three Mig-29s and two SU-22s, dropping down toward the convoy. Suddenly he saw flashes and realized that the planes were firing missiles at the vehicles in the convoy. As the first missiles struck their marks the explosions were loud and bright. Soldiers jumped from their vehicles and ran from the road trying to find a position of cover. The attack had taken place however in an area of open farm fields. The land was flat and there were no crops to hide the fleeing men. The helicopter gunships, Russian made MI-25s began firing and continued until no one was left alive. The Eregli Karyayolu Highway was littered with burning vehicles, huge craters, and bodies.

Many miles overhead a Russian spy satellite recorded the entire event in real time and had sent the pictures to Russian military headquarters in Moscow. The pictures were then dispatched by special carrier to the Kremlin.

NOVEMBER 26, 2017

THE KREMLIN
3:00 PM

President Gryzlovski and Vladimir Lenoidivic were meeting in the President's office and discussing plans for the takeover of Israel. Vladimir was still fuming from the recent setback in the Atlantic and had ordered that the navy to develop a new plan of action to break the American blockade. So far the best option seemed to be an all-out submarine attack but with the number of American ships and equipment in the area at the present time they had decided that would be an unwise move until they relaxed their readiness. Vladimir was hoping that after the Russians stormed into Israel the American Cowboy would divert some additional forces to that area and help to set up a new attack on the northeast.

"Dmitry, how long do you believe it will take to get firm control of Israel?

"I think, sir, it will depend on the cooperation we receive from the Islamists forces. If they do not interfere I believe that we can persuade the Jews to allow us in without much of a fight since we are not the enemy that they are most afraid of and we might be seen as a protective force to them."

"As soon as the convoy reaches Aleppo we will contact the Israeli Prime Minister and begin to make our case to him."

As he was finishing his thought there was a knock on the office door and a military messenger brought in a courier pouch which he promptly handed to the president.

As President Gryzlovski opened the pouch the messenger saluted and immediately left the office. Vladimir sat in a chair directly in front of the president's desk and gazed out the window considering possible snags in his scenario. As President Gryzlovski pulled out the contents of the pouch he got a very serious and disturbed look on his face. He quickly sat down in his chair and the blood seemed to drain from his complexion.

"What is it, Dmitry? Is there a problem?"

"Sir, there are two serious problems with our Israeli project. First, it would appear that the Islamists have shot down the plane that General Ilovich was being transported in to Aleppo. He and his entire staff have been killed. The plane was hit by a missile as it approached Aleppo. At nearly the same time Syrian Air Forces attacked our convoy in Turkey just west of the Tarsus Mountains and destroyed all of the personnel and equipment. There are no reported survivors."

Gryzlovski watched Vladimir closely because he knew he did not react well to bad news and this was the second time in a few days that the news was not just bad but was devastating. Vladimir stood up and walked to the window to look outside without saying a word. The sun was low in the western sky and there were patchy clouds but no snow was falling. Vladimir could feel the blood in his veins beginning to boil but he knew he must control his response.

"Dmitry, this calls for an overwhelming response but one we have complete control of at all times. I believe that rather than chance any additional losses we should mount a large missile attack on Aleppo and Tehran. Do you think that is appropriate?"

"Yes, sir, I do. We have ships in the Caspian Sea that will be capable of delivering such an attack with minimal opportunity for a return attack. I assume you are speaking of a non-nuclear attack on both cities?"

"Yes, I believe that will be best, however, it will be necessary to inflict very serious damage to both locations. I also believe we should put our Islamists friends on notice that we will no longer consider them partners in this venture and will be discontinuing any support we have for their forces in the future. I so much wanted to see the American Cowboy President kneeling in front of me in submission or better yet see his head on a silver platter. I suppose we will have to reconsider how we handle him in the future. You should also contact the Israeli Prime Minister and offer our services in clearing the Islamists Terrorists from his country."

President Gryzlovski nodded and then called for his military staff commanders to join him in his office so he could work out the details and make these attacks happen quickly. He also felt some relief that Vladimir did not seem to hold him responsible. He feared Vladimir as much as others did but had always managed to stay one step ahead in making him pleased and therefore making his career more secure. He could sense that Vladimir was reaching his breaking point, however, and it would not take many more failures to cause him to lash out at everyone. Dmitry never expected to receive a pension but now he feared that his lifetime may come to end much quicker than he had originally planned.

As Vladimir stormed out of the office, Dmitry picked up the phone and contacted his military attaché to pass along the necessary orders for the military operations. He then set up the secure call to the Israeli Prime Minister.

"Good afternoon, Mr. Prime Minister, I trust you are well."

Prime Minister Benjamin Latvin was surprised to be informed that the Russian President was calling him so he answered the phone with a great deal of apprehension. "Good afternoon, Mr. President, yes I am well, thank you. What may I do for you, sir?"

"Mr. Prime Minister, I would like to discuss how we can assist your country with these terrorists that seem to be causing so many problems around the world at the present."

"This is somewhat surprising, Mr. President, since according to our intelligence your country and the terrorists are allied together. Can I assume there has been some sort of falling out or change in your relationship with Iran and the Islamist State?"

"You have misjudged our position, I fear. We have only attempted to maintain some reasonable order and control in the present conflicts in the world. However, today some new arrangements have resulted in our force being attacked by Islamists and a state of war now exists between our two entities."

Prime Minister Latvin had already been briefed on the events of the day in Aleppo and Turkey involving the Russians. His Mossad briefing had included information that the Russians were attempting to change the agreement that had been in effect with the Islamists radicals and the changes apparently had not been well received. "Mr. President, I obviously have some mixed feelings regarding this sudden change of allegiances. While I would not be totally opposed to assistance in maintaining our security, I am cautious regarding how your country might be able to help us."

"Mr. Prime Minister, allow me to explain how we might be able to assist your country. We propose sending a security force into your country to protect your people from the Islamist radicals. Our security forces will guarantee the security of your nation in return for allowing a permanent Russian military base to be built and maintained by our government. You see, it is in our best interest as well to maintain a peaceful existence in the Middle East and we feel we are the best entity to accomplish this important mission. We have no interest or intention of controlling your government or people and will not interfere in any way in the internal workings of your nation. We simply wish to protect your people and to establish a base of operations for our forces in the general area."

"It would appear to me that you are asking for permission to send an occupying force into our nation with my blessing. I am not sure that I can do this. I will have to discuss your proposal with others in our government including the leaders in the Knesset. I will meet with these individuals promptly and will give you an answer to your proposal within a few days."

President Gryzlovski was not totally surprised by this response. "We have information that major attacks are being planned by the Islamic forces so I would caution you, sir, not to take very long in making this decision. We will need some time to put our forces together and to get them properly placed to accomplish this mission. Please keep me updated as to the progress of your discussions."

As the conversation ended there was a chill in the air at both ends of the discussion. In Israel the Prime Minister was ordering a new state of alert among the country's self-defense forces and calling in various ministers and political leaders to discuss the Russian proposal. In the Kremlin President Gryzlovski was notifying the military leadership to develop plans for the hostile invasion of Israel in case Latvin made the wrong decision. He had no doubt that Russian forces would succeed in occupying the small but powerful nation but he also wanted to make sure that the casualty figures would not be a number that would cause Vladimir to become upset. There had been too many Russian lives lost in the last few weeks.

JANUARY 18, 2018

DAVIS MONTHAN AIR FORCE BASE

It was a beautiful Thursday morning as TJ walked from his quarters to the command center. The sky was clear blue and the temperature was in the low fifties, which felt great to the president considering the time of year. Of course, he had never been in Arizona in January so he really didn't know if the weather was strange or not, but that had been one issue he had not had to deal with since arriving here nearly seven months ago. One thing he was certain about, however, was that he was tired of being cooped up on an air force base. A very nice air force base but still a military installation that offered him little freedom to do the things he truly wanted to do. Presidents before him always travelled and visited sites across the country and the world. They talked to citizens and worked out problems but he was limited to military problems and talking to just a few key advisors and of course his wife. TJ yearned to get back to the White House and begin to feel like the president once again.

The holidays had been very subdued with little to celebrate. He had been told of the problems which had developed between Russia and the Islamist State and although he found it a little amusing he knew that it would only lead to greater violence. Russian missiles had left Aleppo in rubble nearly wiping the city off the map. In Tehran the United States had already caused significant damage but Russia finished the job leaving the entire city in ashes and debris.

Israel had permitted Russia to build a military installation in the northern part of the country. This had led to an increase in the number of attacks on the country in and around Jerusalem. The Russian troops also spent a large piece of their day fighting off incursions from Syria and from Jordan as they attempted to build a large base in that location.

The Chinese Naval Forces had withdrawn all the way to the Philippine Sea and although they were still firmly in control of the entire Korean Peninsula, they were no longer an active threat to the United States. Russia also had established firm control of the northern countries in South America. They had established puppet governments in Venezuela, Columbia, Peru and the northern portion of Brazil. So the world was still a mess and he did not even control all of the United States yet. Although the area controlled by the Islamists was becoming smaller in area they still had a long way to go before TJ would be making any speeches in the Rose Garden.

As TJ entered the command center the few officers inside immediately snapped to attention. "At ease." The president stated as he walked toward his workstation. The room was much less chaotic in recent days as major operations had been few since Christmas. TJ sat down at his workstation and began reviewing the briefing papers left for him from last night. The only states still under control of the Islamists were New York, Pennsylvania, Maryland, Virginia, North Carolina, eastern sections of South Carolina and of course the District of Columbia. The television airwaves were still controlled by the enemy. Years ago a system to override any television signals was authorized by the congress and the controls for that system were in New York and Washington so even though they had been able to jam the television signals there was no way to broadcast to the citizens as long as the Islamists had control. As General Hickman entered the room TJ noticed a report from Kentucky noting mass graves being uncovered. The report indicated that examination of the graves revealed that they were of Islamic State soldiers who had apparently died of smallpox. There were similar reports coming in from Ohio, South Carolina, and Georgia.

General Hickman approached the President who motioned for him to have a seat.

"Good morning, sir, any questions regarding the information I left you?"

"No questions, just an observation. It seems quite a few of the enemy are coming down with smallpox."

"Yes, sir. Kind of ironic considering the smallpox virus was brought over reportedly by Hamas. You would have thought they would have made sure their fighters were immunized."

"Who knows what they were thinking but it would appear that the virus is helping us now."

"I know operations in the areas where we found the graves were swift and with less resistance than we expected. We now have National Guard troops and Special Forces moving into North Carolina and continuing through New York. We expect to take control of most of New York City within the next several weeks. They still have strong control of Baltimore and DC. In Baltimore they have a strong contingent of homegrown Islamists who have willingly joined forces with the invaders and this has made it more difficult to determine who the bad guy is much like it was in Michigan. The good news is the blockade is strong and this has greatly reduced their munitions on hand which means they have to be much more specific with their weapons fire."

The two continued the briefing and exchanging ideas for future operations for over an hour. As the president began to get up General Hickman said, "One more thing, sir. I thought you would like to know that Gunny Hackborn is getting ready to leave on his first mission since he was wounded back in Michigan. He is back to one hundred percent and is leading a new team of Marine Raiders."

A big smile crossed TJ's face. "I knew he would be back, you can't keep a good Marine down, can you?"

FEBRUARY 1, 2018

PITTSBURGH PENNSYLVANIA

It was three in the morning local time and the Marine Raiders were targeting two Islamic Centers in Pittsburgh. Both were believed to be the location of several Islamic leaders who commanded two groups of fighters. One was Shia Muslim and the other Sunni. Despite their shared goal of conquering the United States they still could not unify when it came to their religious beliefs. The Marines needed to strike before the Islamist commanders rose for their morning prayers.

The first group of Raiders landed in two stealth helicopters behind the Ebenezer Baptist Church and immediately ran west to the Islamic Center a short distance from the church on Wylie Avenue. The Raiders entered from each entry door with their weapons silenced and nearly immediately encountered resistance. Bodies were strewn across the floor as the Marines made their way through the building. By four AM the helicopters behind Ebenezer Church were again lifting off the ground. Inside the copters were the Marine team plus four Islamic fighters who had their hands zip tied behind their back and hoods covering their faces. The Marines had sustained no injuries and were quiet as the choppers lifted off the ground. It would be more than an hour before anyone would realize that there was a problem as no one would be calling them to their morning prayers.

At the same time two other helicopters were landing southeast of this target in a large residential yard on Francis Road. This group of twenty Marine Raiders was led by Gunnery Sergeant Greg Hackborn. This was his third mission since he returned to duty and the first two had gone without a hitch. Already Greg had spotted a problem as the team approached the landing zone. The plan called for the team to dismount in the rear yard at the residence and then to cross the street through another yard and approach the Islamic Center facing Unity Road from the rear using a grove of trees as cover. As they approached, however, Greg noticed that between the trees and the center was an open field that was very well-lit and could be dangerous to cross. As the team dismounted Greg pulled one of his men aside. "Find the transformer that feeds the power to the center and blow it so we are not attacking through all that light."

Greg and the remainder of the team ran quickly to the grove of trees. The team took cover in the trees and prepared their night vision equipment. There were six guards wandering around the grounds and six members of the team were each assigned one of the guards to eliminate prior to all of them crossing the field. Each member of the team then heard, "Transformer will blow in three, two, one . . ." after which everyone heard a muffled thump followed immediately by darkness.

Within seconds all of the guards collapsed on the ground as the Raiders ran at full speed to the rear entrances of the center. Gunfire rang out as soon as the Raiders made entry. The darkness from the loss of power gave the Marines a distinct advantage at least for a few minutes. A generator came online and the lights suddenly flashed on causing the night vision to become a handicap. Ripping the night vision from their faces the men pressed forward through the building. Progress was slow as the men made their way through the center one room at a time. Nearly an hour later the building had been cleared, there were forty-two Islamists fighters, and five leadership targets in custody. The morning call for prayer would be expected in less than an hour so the team had to depart quickly.

As they disappeared into the tree line they could see several Toyota pickup trucks drive around to the back of the center and start using a searchlight. The men hustled the leadership targets across the street and back to the copters. Two of the prisoners were picked up and tossed over the shoulder of the nearest Marine. The Islamic leaders were doing whatever they could to slow the extraction of the team in hope that they would be rescued.

As the leadership prisoners were taken to the landing zone the others were told to lay flat on the ground with the face down. As the pickup trucks began a second pass eight muffled shots were fired and the trucks slowed to a stop. The spotlights were shining directly on the prisoners. Gunnery Sergeant Hackborn had instructed the Raiders to zip tie each prisoner's hands and then to zip tie the zip ties together. This caused the men to be up against each other as they lay on the ground. A weapons cache had been located inside the center and was taken outside very near the prisoners. The firearms were destroyed and left in a pile. Four of the Raiders carried much of the explosives back to the landing zone but there were several claymore mines located and they were placed on the ground facing the prisoners and just out of their reach. What appeared to be a primer cord was connected to the mines and then run to one end of the line of prisoners where it was connected to the last prisoner.

Hackborn then addressed the prisoners. "You are connected to the mines in front of you and if any of you move or attempt to escape in any way the mines will explode and send you all to meet Allah. When people arrive for morning prayers you can direct them to remove the primer cord if they have the courage to attempt it."

Hackborn then turned to another member of the team, Levi, who was fluent in both Arabic and Farsi and instructed him to repeat his warning in both languages so that he was sure they understood.

In reality the mines were not armed and the primer cord was not hooked up to anything. With any luck these soldiers would believe him and not move until the Raiders were safely in the air. It was a risk but he did not have time to arrange for transportation for the forty-two prisoners, he didn't want to execute them and people would begin arriving within a half hour for morning prayers.

The Raiders loaded onto the helicopters with the five leadership targets that they had captured. The copters quickly lifted off the ground and flew northwest. Hackborn reached down and picked up his night vision goggles and began looking for any threats. He noticed that the prisoners were still in the field and apparently had believed the threat. As the helicopters passed over Interstate 76, Hackborn looked down at a triangular field with trees on two sides. In the center of the field he saw fifteen crosses and each one had what appeared to be a body hanging on them. He turned to the prisoners on board and for a moment considered shooting each of them and throwing them off the copter, but he knew that the information they had might

223

be valuable to defeating this evil. Greg ripped the night vision from his head and sat back. He remembered learning about the horror and evil of World War II but he was wondering if this new evil was not worse.

FEBRUARY 11, 2018

9:30 AM
BASE CHAPEL

Angela turned to TJ and squeezed his hand in hers. TJ had a blank look on his face and was staring at the cross in the front of the church hanging from the ceiling. People were leaving the pews behind TJ but TJ didn't move and continued his gaze. Angela tugged on his arm and began to stand up. "TJ, are you all right?"

TJ nodded his head and then without a word he slowly began to stand up. As he turned and moved toward the aisle he was greeted by the chaplain, Major Charles Jones.

"Good morning, Mr. President."

"Good morning, Major. Nice message this morning. I always find your words comforting but provoking."

"Thank you, Mr. President. You know, most of the time I can tell that you are really engaged in my words as I preach, but this morning there was a difference. I kept noticing that you were staring very intently at the cross. It was almost like you were having a personal conversation in your mind."

"I was, as a matter of fact. I was asking Him why. Why did all of this have to happen? I know we haven't been perfect and we have a lot of problems but I barely got in office when this all started unraveling and it has been one terrible event after another. So many Americans have been killed, so many others from any number of countries have been killed and none of this is necessary. Vladimir is evil and I am sure all of this is directly related to his ambitions. I had him in my custody and if I would have arranged his death then maybe some of this would have been concluded by now."

"Mr. President, if you would have done that, you would have been as guilty as he is in this whole matter. Now the deaths are on him and others but not on you. If you would allow that conversation in your head to be a two-way conversation maybe you would get some answers you can use. It is written in Psalm 81— 'If my people would only listen to me, if Israel would only follow my ways, how quickly I would subdue their enemies and turn my hand against their foes!' You need to open your heart to what the Lord is trying to tell you."

TJ gazed at Major Jones for a few moments with no expression on his face but then broke into a smile. "Thanks, Major. I will keep that in mind. You know somewhere it is also written that you should spend more time listening and less speaking so I think you have a good point."

As TJ and Angela slowly walked out of the chapel, hand in hand, the major followed quietly behind. As the trio emerged from the chapel the sun was shining brightly and the warmth in the air felt good as they moved back to their quarters. Major Jones placed his hat back on his head and turned to walk in the opposite direction.

About 1:00 PM, TJ walked into the command post and found everyone busy with the operations for the day. He motioned to General Hickman to join him and then took a seat at his workstation.

As the general approached he motioned for him to sit down while TJ read the latest briefing papers on his desk.

"How are we coming on plans to take our country back?

General Hickman wasn't prepared for that question and took a moment to formulate a response in his head. "Well, sir, it is a slow process. We currently are training a number of units on urban warfare and we are rounding up the equipment we will need and placing it in the appropriate positions. I think we will be ready for a giant push into these regions by mid-April or the beginning of May. This is not battlefield type stuff that we will have to deal with, this will be house to house searching. We won't be able to clear a path for our soldiers since there is a danger that those people being killed will be our own citizens. It is a much more complex environment than we would face in Iraq or Afghanistan."

TJ sat quietly for a few minutes staring down at a map of the East Coast that was on his desk. "You know, general, I wonder how many of our citizens are being killed each day by this occupying force while we worry how to take this area back without killing any of our citizens. I don't think we can wait until the middle of April or May. I want you to prepare a battle plan for an attack beginning no later than April first. I actually would like to start sooner but I want to make it a clear success and I want to rid our country of these invaders as quickly as possible. So speed up your training and move your equipment because we are going to DC come hell or high water."

The general only stated, "Yes, sir." He moved away from the president wondering if they could possibly be ready in time. The general had reservations about the May timeline but now he knew this rush would more than likely cost more lives, but what could he do. The president made his orders very clear and all he could do was to push to succeed.

MARCH 11, 2018

BALTIMORE MARYLAND

Don Ladner had been living, no hiding actually, in a private residence in the 1500 block of Cherry Street in the south part of Baltimore. He did not leave the house often because of the frequent sharia police patrols through the area. Many people were trying to live their normal lives but there was nothing normal about the current situation. If you drove your car anywhere you took a chance that the sharia patrols would stop you and if they decided, you had done anything wrong you were most likely going to be beaten and your vehicle would be seized for their use. They had a strange fascination with pickup trucks and if you drove one of those onto the streets you would most likely lose it before you arrived back home. Most people left their vehicles in a garage and simply walked to where they needed to go.

Mass transit was not operating and the majority of people in the community were unemployed since most worked in areas that required a commute that was difficult to do on foot. The local grocery and convenience store operators had a tendency to look the other way if you stole food since it was in short supply. If they did report someone stealing and the sharia police found the individual they were often dealt with swiftly and in a gruesome manner, often cutting a hand off the perpetrator without a trial.

There was no network television, only local television operated by the Islamic State and reporting only sanitized information. There were a few who had satellite television who were still able to see BBC newscasts but they were secretive about who they allowed to watch because they did not want to experience the wrath of the sharia by watching what had been forbidden.

Many of the residents had joined Islam in order to seek out a more favorable living status. They had to attend a special school to learn their newly acquired Islamic faith but in return they were allowed to shop at special Muslim only stores and their families had ample food and necessary supplies. They were no better off with regard to the news of what was going on elsewhere in the country but could drive and move around town with little or no restriction. It seemed that many had joined the Sharia Police, some served as interpreters and some worked patrol duty with IS personnel with them. Unfortunately, they were every bit as severe as the IS personnel and it appeared that if they had a grudge against you for any reason, you would be constantly harassed.

Don was sipping on a cup of coffee when there was a knock at the back door. Don's host, Alvin, walked over to the door and after checking to see who it was he opened the door.

"What do you need, Chuck?"

"I just wanted to let you know that I heard a guy on Prudence Avenue has a satellite receiver and he is going to turn on the BBC at one o'clock today. He said that if anyone wants to watch as long as they come quietly he will let them in. His house is the yellow one in the 800 block."

"Thanks but I don't think I will take a chance. That's a little over a mile away and there will be too many opportunities to get picked up."

As Alvin shut the door Don looked up and said, "I'm going, I have to know what is going on."

Alvin shook his head and said. "Look, you're a big boy, but if you get picked up don't lead them back to me. I won't be coming down to try to get you out."

"I know and don't worry I will not lead them here. Remember I escaped DC to get here and was never detected. I think I can pull this off."

Don went to the bathroom, finished getting dressed, and then slipped out the back door of the residence. He began walking, staying as much as possible in the back yards of residences to help stay out of sight of any police patrols. As he approached the intersection of Church Street and Prudence Avenue he noticed that there were four sharia police pickup trucks in the intersection and about thirty people standing in the middle of the street. He got as close as he dared and hid behind some bushes to observe what was going on. Two of the pickups had fifty caliber machine guns mounted in the beds of the truck with IS soldiers manning each one.

As he listened and watched he noticed that there were two priests and three ministers standing in front of the group and speaking with the police commander. It sounded as if the police had interrupted the church services and removed everyone from the services. Those must be the others in the street. Don decided to get a little closer so he could hear the conversation.

The commander was standing in front of one of the priests and shouting at him, "Renounce your faith and praise Allah!" The priest refused and the commander went to one of the ministers. As the commander went up and down the group of clergy he received the same result each time, a flat but confident no. Having no success, the commander was becoming visibly frustrated and angry.

The commander motioned over to the men guarding the crowd and one of them grabbed a young girl and brought her to him. The girl appeared to be thirteen or fourteen years old and was instructed to kneel down facing the clergymen. The commander then shouted again, "Do you renounce your faith and praise Allah?" The girl shook her head from side to side and the commander again shouted at the group of clergy. "Will any of you renounce your faith and praise Allah?"

At first none of the clergy said anything but after a few moments they all began to pray aloud together. "Our Father who art in heaven, hallowed be thy name. Thy Kingdom come . . ." *Boom!* The girl fell forward onto the pavement face first. Smoke rose from the commander's handgun and blood pooled in the street.

The commander motioned to his fellow terrorist and one of the clergymen was being brought to the commander this time. He, too, was forced to kneel while facing the other clergy. The remaining clergy continued to pray and now held hands. Again the commander asked the man on his knees to renounce his faith and again he refused. A second body now lay on the ground and more blood began to pour onto the street.

Don felt the urge to do something to stop this horror but what could he do. He had no weapons and those machine guns would cut him down before he got within twenty feet. As he watched the act was repeated with another student and another clergy man. The commander then spoke into his radio and stood glaring at a priest until a bus rolled up behind the group on Prudence. Everyone was loaded into the bus and the commander posted three sharia police to watch the area with instructions that the bodies were not to be touched for at least three days as an example to these infidels.

Don felt cold and clammy as he reevaluated his decision to continue to the residence with the television and he decided it would be best to return to Alvin's home for the night. For a long while he was afraid to move for fear he might be spotted. Finally, the men guarding the area turned their back to his location and he quickly crawled backward until he reached better concealment along the side of a building.

Once he was out of the guard's line of sight he got off the ground and began running through the backyards again. He carefully made his way back to the residence through the backyards. It had taken him a half hour to reach this location earlier but returning took him an hour and a half since he was being extra cautious. As he reached the back door of Alvin's residence he still could not believe what he had witnessed.

When Alvin opened the door Don rushed inside and explained what had happened. After explaining what happened all Don could think about was that he had to get a message to TJ, if TJ was still alive. All Don could think about was how often this happened in other areas of the country if it could happen in one small area of Baltimore.

MARCH 27, 2018

DAVIS MONTHAN AIR FORCE BASE COMMAND CENTER

It was 6:00 AM, as TJ walked into the command post accompanied by Major Jones. TJ walked to the center of the room and turned to General Hickman. "General, I understand the operations that you have been planning are ready to commence?"

"That is correct, sir. In a half hour we will begin with targeted precision bombing of known IS safe houses and ammunition stores. Following that this afternoon we will begin an invasion of New York City and the boroughs surrounding it with both regular forces and National Guard forces. The Coast Guard has moved in to New York Harbor to block any escape or assistance from the sea. About two hours ago house to house operations began in Boston. We already had control of the Boston area but we have had a number of isolated attacks in that area so we will search out and eliminate any IS units that remain in that area so we can get back to a more routine life in that area. As you know we already have firm control of most of the rest of the region north of New York City including most of the State of New York. Once New York City is secure we will begin a push south through Pennsylvania and Maryland. Tomorrow morning forces that are currently in Tennessee and South Carolina will move into North Carolina and begin to push north into Virginia. If everything goes as planned we will liberate Washington DC by July first, sir."

TJ had a smile on his face as he gazed slowly around the room. "I want to tell all of you that I am proud of the work you have done and I am proud of all of the soldiers, sailors, airmen, and marines that will go forth into this battle to liberate our country from this foreign invasion force. I recall that during World War II the enemy forces thought they were about to defeat an American force at what has become known as the Battle of the Bulge. The great General George Patton instructed his chaplain to write a prayer for his troops in order to make sure there was good weather and the troops would have success in their mission. I have taken the liberty to learn a lesson from General Patton and I have asked Major Jones to likewise develop a prayer to plead to God that this drive will be a success." With that TJ turned to Major Jones and asked him to pray for the troops.

Major Jones stepped to the middle of the room with his cap under his arm. "Please bow your heads and ask for God's blessing. Heavenly and Almighty Father, we come to you today, during a period of great turmoil within the world. A time when evil seems to have conquered so much of the world and evil men appear to be very powerful. We know Father that in fact none of these evil people can stand against You and survive. We are about to send our sons and daughters into a great battle with these evil forces. We do this with great confidence in Your majesty and Your saving grace. Over these next few weeks we will engage in battles to preserve our ability to worship You in the manner You have established for us. Father, we ask that You change the hearts and desires of these enemies but if they have hardened their hearts we ask that You grant us the courage, foresight, and ability to defeat these people and to restore our liberty. We beseech You to watch over and protect our sons and daughters who will be waging these battles. Keep our citizens in these battle zones safe. Finally, Father, we trust that this evil, which we have been unable to defeat without You, will in fact be defeated with Your help and that our liberty and freedom to worship will endure until Your Son, Our Lord and Savior Jesus Christ, returns in glory. We ask this in Jesus name. Amen."

TJ walked over to Major Jones and placed his right hand on his shoulder. "Major, I think that General Patton would have described that as a fine prayer. I have such confidence in that prayer I have already given the order that it be printed and distributed to all of our troops. More important yet I have ordered that this prayer printed on leaflets and dropped over New York City and Washington DC. I want everyone to know that we are on our way and not to give up."

With that there was a smattering of applause from those in the room and then they quickly turned and returned to their workstations.

Major Jones quietly started toward the door, a little uneasy about the situation but feeling good about his prayer.

TJ stopped him momentarily. "Major, just a moment. I know Major Jones that I put you on the spot with this request. I feel very strongly, Major, that it was important that we have this prayer. Maybe if I would have requested a prayer a long time ago this would be behind us today. We will continue to fight this war and generals will continue to draw up battle plans but I have put my faith in God to guide us for the rest of this conflict. For your help in bringing me to this realization and helping me to find this faith I am promoting you to Lt. Colonel, effective on April first. Congratulations."

The Major looked a little stunned. "Sir, I am only doing my job, both to God and my country."

At TJ stuck out his hand to congratulate the Major he said, "I know and if everyone does their job we will succeed."

APRIL 1, 2018

DAVIS-MONTHAN AIR FORCE BASE COMMAND CENTER

At 3:00 AM, TJ entered the command center and started toward his workstation. Everyone in the room immediately snapped to attention and just as quickly were placed at ease and returned to their duties. TJ took a second to look at the improvements made to the room since he was last here yesterday. The longest two walls in the room were now covered from the ceiling to the floor with large flat screen televisions. Below each television on the wall was a piece of masking tape with a unit number written on the tape. In one corner of the room was a stack of recording equipment and on the president's desk was a new television that he could use to watch any of the active screens or to playback any previously recorded operation.

As TJ moved toward his desk he studied the walls of TVs noting the locations that were displayed on each one. The most active screen showed the command center on board the Harry S. Truman, the aircraft carrier currently commanding naval operations about sixty miles southeast of New York City. It was just after five in the morning in New York and personnel on the Truman were actively launching stealth drone aircraft. Two screens to the right he observed a similar scene coming from the George H W Bush where command personnel were monitoring a Marine landing force moving into Charleston Bay. If everything was going according to plan the Marines would be passing the Fort Sumter National Monument and would be landing at Patriot's Point. By the time most people rose to leave for church, those that still dared, the streets of Charleston would be filling with armored personnel carriers and other marine vehicles.

As the call to prayer began at the mosques on King Street and the one on Reynolds Avenue no one noticed the drones flying quietly high above each location and sending pictures back to the Bush. Army National Guard troops were quickly moving along I-26 speeding to both locations as well as others to maintain security both to protect others from a lone wolf attack and to protect worshipers from retaliation now that U S troops were about to control the area once again. South Carolina State Troopers were also moving into the area in a convoy to assume law enforcement duties. As the first Marines were coming ashore predator drones were firing missiles at sharia police patrols throughout the city. The Battle for Charleston would be quick and complete by the end of the day.

As TJ took a seat at his workstation, General Hickman approached to discuss the ongoing operations.

"Good morning, sir. Would you like an update?" The general asked as TJ looked up from his briefing papers.

"Yes, I would, General Hickman. I assume you are having a good morning thus far."

"Yes, sir, it is. We have had no hostile action from the Charleston activity so far. We took the liberty of eliminating all of the armed sharia patrols that we knew about using predator drones. It caused a little mess in the streets but units are clearing those areas up as we speak. We have had absolutely no problem from either of the mosques in town. Neither of them appeared to have any command or control operations on their sites. The sharia patrols had established their command sites at various police stations in the city and those are currently being addressed. The people of Charleston, at least the ones that are awake, have been very cooperative and are assisting our operations in every way they can, even though there is still some risk for them. By the end of the day we will control the entire city, however, then we will start the house to house searches for enemy combatants or sympathizers and that could take several weeks."

"What about operations in the north?"

"Those are just getting underway. We have Marines coming in through Boston Harbor. In addition, you know we have been conducting operations for some time now in western New York State and those units are moving east now. Everything in the region west of I-81 from Syracuse, New York to Scranton, Pennsylvania is under U.S. control. We currently have Special Forces, National Guard, and other Army units moving along I-84 toward Danbury, Connecticut, and the 10th Mountain Division along with a Canadian Army Group are moving along I-90 toward Albany, New York. There is a large area to cover and will take several weeks but once this area is secure we will enter New York City and the surrounding boroughs. This could take a month or more to secure but once it is secure we will be able to broadcast across the country again without trouble and then we should be able to move right down the coast."

TJ was pleased with the professional way this was being handled and was glad that Canada decided to lend a hand. As he listened to the general he was continuing to read over the briefing papers and the intelligence reports.

"General, I see where there appears to be a great deal of Russian naval activity in the North Sea, do you have any additional information?"

"Not at this time but British Intelligence believes that they have detected some troop movement toward ports in the Baltic Sea, including St. Petersburg, Kaliningrad, and Gdansk. We can't confirm this information because of the satellite situation but we are working to determine if it is true and if so what they have in mind. We are also detecting a flurry of activity in the Mediterranean area. The Russians now have an operational base outside of Nahariyya, Israel, and this activity could be a movement to supply and build up the base. From this base Russia could control Israel but could also quickly strike Syria, Jordan, Iraq, and Iran. We still do not have intelligence regarding what they have in mind. I can't believe the Israelis allowed them to move in and construct this base."

"Don't be too harsh because we don't know if they allowed anything yet. It is certainly plausible that they had their backs to the wall concerning the situation. It might be better to have Russians in your country that are currently pissed off at the Islamic movement than to be left alone when Iran or the Islamic State begin to set their sights on Israel."

After a little more chit chat back and forth the General returned to his command console and TJ continued watching the television screens. Most of the screens were now showing activity all over the eastern portion of the United States. TJ felt good about the fact that positive activity was now taking place and he thought maybe this nightmare will be over soon and we will be back in control of the entire country. Of course, even when this ends there will be much more to do because every day Russia seemed to be picking up more power and a broader range of control. TJ was especially worried about the control they were exerting on South and Central America and what that would ultimately mean on the western hemisphere as a whole. What was going to be the next shoe to drop?

APRIL 1, 2018

MOSCOW RUSSIA
THE KREMLIN

At 10:55 AM, President Gryzlovski picked up his office phone and ordered that lunch for two be brought to his office. He was preparing for a special meeting with Vladimir regarding the latest events. It was unusual to have a Sunday morning meeting but Vladimir had called him early this morning to instruct him to meet at the office at 11. Dmitry was certainly concerned because he knew that significant changes in government sometimes occurred at unusual times and this meeting qualified for that.

At 11:02 AM, the door to his office opened without a knock coming first. Vladimir Lenoidivic entered the office quickly and closed the door firmly behind him. He quickly removed his hat and the jacket he wore revealing a short sleeve pull over shirt which left his bulging muscles very obvious. As Dmitry stood to greet him he noted that Vladimir was not smiling and the President was becoming nauseous with worry about what was about to occur.

"Good morning, sir."

Vladimir turned and walked toward the desk without a word. As he reached the desk he pulled a large overstuffed chair to the side of the desk and sat down. "Good morning, Dmitry, did you have an opportunity to attend church this morning?"

This comment did nothing to ease President Gryzlovski's tense feelings. "No, sir, unfortunately after you called this morning I began preparing by reviewing intelligence reports and defense briefings so I would be prepared to answer any questions you might have for me."

"I am sorry to hear that, Dmitry. You know that is a mistake that the party leaders made and which lead to the downfall of the Soviet. You cannot take God away from the people and you must always make them believe you believe strongly whether that is true or not. Now I can see you are tense, please relax. I don't know if you understand why I called this meeting but it is not to replace you if that is what you fear."

President Gryzlovski's shoulders relaxed and he sat back in his office chair noticeably relaxing and breaking out a slight smile. "I was a bit concerned, sir. So why did you call this meeting?"

Now a slight smile appeared on Vladimir's face as well. "I am sorry but I have received some information that I need to pass on to you but I could not do that on the phone because of the sensitivity. I spent yesterday afternoon with a defense scientist Ivan Shotkovich, I am not certain if you have ever heard of him or am aware of his work."

"No, sir, I am not."

"He has been working long hours to find a weapon to put an end to the American threat. I will not be satisfied until America is totally defeated. The Muslim problem we can easily correct when the time is right, but America needs to be brought to her knees because that country has a way of coming back when we least expect it. So Shotkovich is working on a missile that will be coated in a special substance to reflect the laser beam weapon they have used recently. This missile will deliver a nuclear device that will detonate at an altitude of about 200 miles over the middle of the country. This will most certainly eliminate the electrical grid and cause them huge numbers of casualties. We will follow this up within days with a massive invasion force. I want you to confer with naval commanders to find a way to take out whatever naval force they have in the Atlantic so we can gain a quick advantage."

"We have troops moving toward the Baltic ports for transport to the base in Israel. Would you like to change their destination?"

"That is an interesting question. I do not have a firm date on when the weapon will be secure and operational. I believe it would be in our best interest to hold those troops at the ports until we have a better idea of the launch date. There is still much that needs to be done. What is the latest information regarding the Israel base?"

"Preparations are moving forward as expected and on schedule. All electrical equipment will have special shielding to prevent any disturbance due to EMPs. Many of the aircraft have needed to be retrofitted to make sure that they will suffer no injury. My only concern, sir, is that intelligence indicates that much of the Israeli forces also have equipment with special shielding and they will not be disabled as a result of the EMP strike."

"I am not worried about the IDF we will overwhelm them before they even understand what is going on. I have already arranged for the Palestinian forces to stage an attack in Jerusalem that will distract them as we overrun Tel Aviv and begin the push south. Once we control Israel we will move through the region and the Islamist will either conform to our requests or we will overrun them as well."

As Vladimir spoke he stood up and walked to the office window to gaze outside. A light snowfall had just begun and Vladimir always seemed to think best when he was watching the snow. Silence hung in the air for several minutes as Vladimir stared at the snow.

A sharp knock at the door broke the silence.

Dmitry shouted, "Enter!"

The door opened and an army officer walked sharply and swiftly into the office. A quick salute to the president was followed by a taped envelope being delivered. As soon as the president accepted the envelope the officer immediately completed an about face and exited the office as quickly as he had entered.

President Gryzlovski opened the envelope and pulled out a sheet of paper and the attached map. After reviewing the information, he looked over at Vladimir.

"What is it, Dmitry?"

"It would appear that the Americans are making a last ditch effort to push the Islamists out of their country. They have begun operations in New York and South Carolina. In addition, their navy has begun operations all along their eastern coast."

"That is fine. These operations that they are currently engaged in will serve as a distraction while we begin operations in Israel. The more they are concentrating on ridding their own soil of enemies the more time we have to secure our objectives without any type of resistance. Send the troops to Israel immediately while the Americans are so busy."

APRIL 8, 2018

DAVIS MONTHAN AIR FORCE BASE COMMAND CENTER

As TJ entered the command center he quickly noticed that all the screens were active with activity all over the eastern seaboard. Three of the screens displayed the control centers on aircraft carriers that were currently launching aircraft. It was eight in the morning off the Atlantic Coast and while two of the carriers were launching drone jets, the third was launching manned fighters and submarine hunting aircraft.

The president had just arrived at his workstation when General Hickman tapped him on the shoulder and informed him that he had some new intelligence he needed to discuss.

"Okay, general, what have you got for me this morning?"

"We have several Russian submarines moving toward the east coast and are currently within 400 miles of several of our surface ships. Additionally, ten transport ships are now moving south about 100 miles west of the French Coast. We believe that the transports, which are escorted by three cruisers and four frigates, are all headed to the Mediterranean Sea area. I would recommend that we take immediate action against the submarines before they realize that we have located them and that we consider action against the transports."

TJ watched the television screens intently while he considered the information and after a minute of consideration he looked back at an expectant General Hickman. "General, you have my authority to do whatever you think is best regarding the transports but I do not want to jeopardize our current operations for those transports. Of course I think it is best to eliminate the threat of the submarines immediately."

"Thank you, sir." General Hickman replied and turned to walk over to the communications section to give the orders necessary.

The president sat at his workstation and changed the channels on his television screen watching various operations from New York and North Carolina. All of the current operations appeared to be moving successfully. He switched to the view showing the combat control center on board the Bush. He quickly noted that there appeared to be a great deal of activity so he turned the volume up for the feed.

"Bush to Jackson you have permission to eliminate your target."

Several minutes passed of dead silence and then the radio crackled again. "Jackson to Bush missiles away."

Time passed very slowly for the next few minutes as we all awaited to hear if the missile hit its intended target. "Jackson to Bush, target acquired and target destroyed."

The entire control center on board the Bush sent up a loud cheer as did everyone in the room including the president.

As the president was about to switch the channel to another operation he heard a very chilling comment. "Missiles in the air on track for Bush." The commander in the control room then gave the command to launch all aircraft possible. The commander then called for assistance from the LAWS aircraft and tasked all anti missiles systems to begin to track the incoming missile.

The next few moments were some of the tensest in recent history. The LAWS aircraft indicated that they were too far away to be of any assistance. Planes were being launched from the Bush with only the bare minimum of time in between.

Suddenly the radio chatter increased and the president could hear "DDG 1000 to CVN 77, missiles away, stand by." Again minutes seemed to pass quietly before the next transmissions. "DDG 1000 to CVN 77, we have two missiles destroyed by the enemy and we have not, repeat not knocked down your incoming."

Now the commander ordered that all defensive weapons begin to fire. Just as suddenly as all the bad news came some good news. "DDG 1000 to CVN 77, your incoming missile has been destroyed, I repeat your incoming missile has been destroyed." This was followed within seconds by "Nighthawk 10 to Bush, we have fired air to surface at Russian submarine, stand by."

"Scratch one submarine. Target was unidentified but we can confirm it was the origin of the missile and has been destroyed."

Everyone in the control center seemed to relax for a moment when the President shouted across the room. "General Hickman, destroy that transport convoy now!"

The general turned toward the president and simply said, "Yes, sir."

APRIL 10, 2018

DAVIS-MONTHAN AIR FORCE BASE COMMAND CENTER

At 8:30 AM, TJ entered the command center to get a status report. As he walked to his workstation he observed that every television screen had action of some type going on. As he sat down and picked up his briefing papers General Hickman walked up behind him.

"Good morning, Mr. President."

"Good morning, general. Anything exciting going on?"

"Yes, sir. We attacked the Russian transport convoy off the coast of Spain overnight. We sunk two of their transport ships, a frigate, and a cruiser. The remaining transports picked up survivors. We sustained some minor damage to some of our vessels and lost one drone. Most of the attack was by submarine and drone fighters. We launched the fighter aircraft from the Truman and they were controlled by personnel on the Truman. We were able to refuel them in the air and they delivered air to surface missiles which accounted for about eighty percent of the damage to the Russians. Overall it was a very successful attack which took very little away from our Atlantic blockade line."

The president nodded his approval and inquired about what the status was on the east coast.

"Both North and South Carolina are pretty much under control south of Durham. The reason I say pretty much is that we still have some problems with isolated ambushes and what we used to call lone wolf attacks. We have National Guard troops and State Troopers searching for these individuals and their weapons caches. Most of the areas in the southeast are not operating very much as normal, keeping in mind that there is still a great deal of electrical problems and even where power has been restored most people do not have working televisions and electrical appliances. About the only vehicles working are older model cars and trucks that did not have computers aboard. There are repairs going on but they have been slowed as the Islamists stopped those repairs while they were running the show."

"So it would seem that even if we controlled the television broadcasting we would have had a problem reaching the citizens of the area anyway. So let's get people into this area to repair what we can and replace what we can't. We need to make sure that we will be able to reach these people with our message to reassure them and motivate them to assist us in this fight."

"I will make sure we start working on that immediately. We have a number of electrical engineers at a university nearby that we can dispatch into the area. We also will be shipping some new products from California so we will do everything we can to restore the area. We don't want to completely flood the area though because we will need resources for Virginia, Maryland, Pennsylvania, and New York. We also have a number of new vehicles being built in plants in Mississippi, Kentucky, Georgia, and Missouri. Michigan is concentrating on government vehicles. We haven't decided yet on just how these vehicles will be distributed or paid for."

The president was nodding as he listened but was reading the briefing papers at the same time. As the general finished his report he stood next to the president waiting for a question or some type of confirmation that he understood. Silence filled the air for a few minutes as the President finished reading the briefing papers. The President then leaned back in his chair and gazed out looking at no particular place in the room.

"So tell me, General Hickman, when will I be moving back into my house in DC?"

General Hickman walked a couple of steps away and grabbed a chair from a nearby table and then pulled it over and sat down next to the president.

"Sir, the plans for that have been finished but it will still take some time. Urban warfare is some of the most difficult action we could face. So far things have gone well and we have had a great deal of cooperation but once we hit the major metropolitan cities like New York, Philadelphia, and Baltimore things will become much more difficult. We not only have to eliminate the sharia patrols and move troops and law enforcement in place but we also have to do thorough searches along the way. There is a great deal of danger in missing pockets of small cells that might remain behind and ambush and snipe at personnel. The first part of the operation is about to get underway. Personnel from the Tenth Mountain Division will move along I-95 corridor and into Stamford Connecticut, where they will converge on and attack the Stamford City Hall complex at Atlantic and Woodland Avenue. Islamist forces have a headquarters facility at that location and there will likely be a bit of a bloody battle in the streets there. This is largely surrounded by a residential area so there will likely be some collateral victims. After securing Stamford they will continue moving along 95 into New York City. At the same time Canadian Special Forces, Group 124 will proceed by boats south into New York City from Tarrytown Municipal Marina."

The president was listening very closely and nodding his head in approval while writing himself notes about what was being said.

"From there the Canadians will land at Pier 92 on the west side of Manhattan. Meanwhile the Tenth Mountain Division will follow the corridor onto Manhattan Island along the east side following FDR Drive. They will both converge on the Avenue of The America's where they will concentrate first on Rockefeller Center and take back the NBC headquarters and studios. Then they will move down the street and take back Fox before heading for CBS and ABC. Once we are in control of all of the television networks we will attempt to open communications with the world again. New York City and the surrounding boroughs are a huge area and searching out all of the Islamist fighters will take some time. From there we will move through Trenton to Philadelphia and eventually to Baltimore. From there we will launch into DC and take back your house, sir. Once again we will be working with the state and local police departments to place them back in charge of their communities and to leave National Guard and Reserve components to add assistance."

The president had a slight smile on his face at this time and reached over to pat the general on the shoulder. "Well done, general. That sounds like a good plan and you take whatever resources you need to accomplish this mission. This is now your priority, general."

General Hickman stood up and agreed to work as quickly as possible to achieve the liberation of the District of Columbia.

APRIL 12, 2018

BALTIMORE MARYLAND

Don was sitting at the kitchen table enjoying a breakfast of toast and eggs. He was craving some bacon but pork products were forbidden now under the Islamist rule. Even eggs had become more difficult to obtain but food had been a priority and Alvin and Don had gone out of their way to buy or barter for food because they realized that maintaining their nutrition was imperative if they were going to survive.

Don was looking over a bright orange piece of paper. "You say these were dropped from a plane?"

Alvin put his coffee cup down and replied, "Yea, that's what I was told. I got that copy from Jack who told me a C-130 flew just over the top of the buildings and thousands of these came floating to the ground behind the aircraft. His buddy picked one up from the street before the sharia police got there and began confiscating them. Most of those who picked them up were beaten and the papers were taken away from them."

"Well according to these the United States still exists west of the Mississippi and they are preparing to retake the east coast. The problem is how do we know this isn't some kind of trick by the Islamists to find an excuse to kill a bunch of people?"

As the conversation continued Don finally announced that he was going to research just how far the Islamist control extended. With no television and the other media in the area being controlled by the Islamists accurate information was difficult to obtain. "Alvin, I am going to steal a car tonight and see how far I can get travelling southwest. If I find U.S. troops I can give them information regarding strength in this area and maybe return with some encouragement."

It was a little after 7:00 PM when Don walked out the back door and started running through the backyards. It was just becoming dark when he came across an old Ford Fairlane with the key lying on the front seat. Don quickly slid into the car, started it, and started travelling down the street without the lights on. He kept his eyes open for any sharia patrols but he had already made up his mind that he would not stop if they tried to stop him.

Everything was going fine until he got onto Interstate 95 and headed south. By this time it was dark enough he needed to turn on the lights. There was practically no traffic as there were still very few cars that had been repaired and operational. Don had not considered that the fact that any car that was operational most likely was owned by a government official which most likely meant that as soon as it was noticed as missing the sharia police would be looking furiously to find and return it.

Don had the accelerator to the floor and the car was travelling at 90 miles an hour when he noticed a road block up ahead. He pushed hard on the brakes and swerved to the exit ramp at exit 212 in Calverton Maryland. As he turned west off the highway he quickly realized that sharia police were waiting for him and he found his car was surrounded by the Islamists. He made one more turn in an effort to escape but finally stopped in front of the Comfort Inn. He barely opened the door when he was pulled violently from the vehicle and slammed onto the ground. His hands were cuffed behind his back and he was kicked repeatedly in his side. As he was pulled up off the ground someone suddenly appeared with a huge sword and there was some discussion whether to kill him right here or take him back for a hearing.

He was pushed up against the side of a truck when he noticed a rather short dark-skinned man approach the scene. The man was wearing a nice business suit and approached the truck walking professionally and with a purpose. Don thought this guy is someone important but he was not sure if that was going to be a good thing or bad.

As the man got closer the shouting stopped and it was obvious that the thugs that had grabbed him either highly respected or feared this man. As the man stood in front of Don he carefully looked him over as if he was making some sort of assessment.

"What is your name?"

"My name is Don Ladner."

The man looked down at a notebook that he had pulled from his pocket. As he went down a list of names he suddenly stopped.

"You worked for the government of the United States prior recent developments. Is this correct?"

"Yes, sir, I did."

"What was your position?"

"I was the chief of staff at the White House."

The man nodded his head and looked down at his notebook again. His face flashed a slight smile and when he looked back at Don he replied, "Yes, that is where I saw your name. We have a warrant for your arrest, Mr. Ladner. You are to be charged with war crimes." He turned to one of the sharia police standing nearby. "Take Mr. Ladner into custody and transport him back to the nearest holding facility while we make arrangements for transport to DC. Be sure that no harm comes to him, he may be of great value."

As they began to move Don away to another vehicle he turned toward the man and asked,

"Tell me one thing, is the United States government still operating and is the President alive?"

The man stopped and thought about what he was going to say. "Your country's government exists only in your states of Arizona and New Mexico. Your President was killed when the plane he was flying was shot down in Omaha, Nebraska. Any information you have heard to the contrary is merely propaganda being spread to build hopes. By the end of the week your country will be totally crushed and the Islamic State will be in total control."

Don watched as the man gazed intently at him to observe the reaction. Don wasn't sure what to believe at this point but decided that he was not going to show any reaction that might bolster the man's attitude. But what was true?

APRIL 13, 2018

THE KREMLIN

As President Gryzlovski walked into the conference room the generals and admirals at the table barely looked up and none of them stood in respect. For the next several minutes the room was silent. All of the military leaders simply sat quietly looking straight ahead. As the door opened once again Vladimir Lenoidivic entered the room walking quickly toward the head of the conference table. Before Vladimir took a second step in the room every military officer had stood and snapped to attention. President Gryzlovski also stood as Vladimir moved to the head of the conference table. Vladimir allowed all of them to stand at attention while he made his way to the head of the conference table. He then turned and very curtly said, "Take your seats."

Vladimir immediately went into a tirade regarding the most recent incidents. "The Americans have destroyed five of my ships and killed 548 men. This is not acceptable and must be avenged. I am tired of the Americans getting the best of every situation. The next loss we have in the field you should all consider your role in the event. I will hold commanders as accountable. I want you all to consider that when we lose hundreds of troops in a day we do not need many of our commanders to handle what remains. I will not continue to tolerate these losses in every operation. Take care of your troops or you should prepare for your own execution instead."

Vladimir allowed his last statements to sink in some while he slowly scanned the room. After several minutes he continued. "I think it is important that as my top commanders that you understand my vision. When our troops and equipment arrive in Israel we will stage a quick takeover of that country. It is my intention to cause a small EMP over the community of Tel Aviv. This will only inconvenience the Israelis, not cripple them. While they are moving in to Tel Aviv to safeguard it, we will use the attack as a pretense to move troops into Jerusalem and the West Bank areas with the excuse of protecting Israel from the Islamist terrorist. The missile attack on Tel Aviv will appear to originate in Iran and in fact it will originate there but we will fire the missile. We will establish our headquarters atop the Temple Mount, which will cause great distress from both the Islamists and the Jews. We will portray ourselves as protectors not occupiers but we will keep taps on all IDF movements."

As Vladimir looked around the room he noted that he now had everyone's complete attention. "Moving forward we will also send a division into Italy near Rome and we will quickly move an occupying force into Rome and Vatican City. This operation will be supported by air and sea support units and I imagine this will require some destruction as a result of artillery and bombing. At about the same time we will launch a missile with a 50 megaton nuclear warhead at the United States. The warhead will detonate at an altitude of 200 miles above Wichita Kansas, near the center of their country. This will cause an electromagnetic pulse which will destroy America's electrical power grid. Our intelligence shows that the botched EMP attack by Iran and the Islamist Forces was directly responsible for the deaths of 6.5 million Americans. This EMP attack will kill 50 million Americans. This attack will be followed by a massive missile attack from the 154th Missile Division that will destroy their military bases within the continental United States. Within ten days of this attack we will send an invasion force to the east coast of their country and the gulf coast as well. The American empire will be destroyed once and for all. My biggest concern at this point is with their navy and the damage they seem to continue to do to our navy. This trend has to end and end today."

"Within two months of this attack we will shut off the oil and gas pipeline to China. We will destroy the Chinese Navy quickly and starve them into submission. While this is underway we will move into the Muslim nations and we will destroy and kill anything and anyone that gets in our way."

Vladimir looked around the room and saw that he had everyone's complete attention. Most were sitting with their mouths hanging open but everyone was hanging on his every word. He allowed his plan to hang in the air for a few moments for maximum effect.

"Now if any of you feel I am overstepping or have become like a lunatic, well you may leave now and I will see that you are retired from service and given a place to live out your life as long as you don't get in my way. Those who believe that they must object to this plan I ask you to stand as well and I will promise you a quick painless death. Those who want to support me I welcome you and I pledge to you that you will see our motherland, the Russian Republic, will rule the world and will go down in history as the most powerful and successful empire in the history of the world."

Vladimir sat back down in his chair and after another couple moments he looked up at those at the table. "Next week the Duma will meet in special session and suspend the laws concerning the political structure of our nation. Dmitry will be retained as the President of the new Russian State. They will also vote and declare that I will be the new Emperor of the Russian Empire. This vote will be by acclamation. We will now be the new Holy Roman Empire and we will control the world. You are dismissed."

A quiet group of military leaders rose from their chairs and filed out of the room. None were aware that while the meeting was underway over 350 Russian leaders had been arrested.

APRIL 15, 2018

DAVIS-MONTHAN AIR FORCE BASE COMMAND CENTER

At nearly 2:00 AM a sharp knock came at the bedroom door of the president. TJ woke up and quickly sat straight up in bed. "Yes!"

The duty agent pushed open the door and took one step inside the room. As he reached inside and turned the lights on he turned to the president and Mrs. Samuels in bed. "Sir, ma'am, I am sorry to disturb you but you are needed, sir, in the command post immediately."

TJ stood up and put on his pants and grabbed a polo shirt while slipping into his shoes. Then he turned to Angela and kissed her telling her that he loves her and then turned to accompany the agent out of his home. A jeep was waiting just outside and as quickly as TJ was safely inside it started forward driving quickly to the command center.

As TJ entered the room, still wiping sleep from his eyes he looked around the room and saw nothing but serious expressions on the faces of the staff. General Hickman turned and started walking toward him nearly the moment he entered the room. "Sir, please have a seat over here."

TJ looked up and as he walked over to the table he asked, "What the hell is so important to call this unusual meeting?"

"Sir, Vladimir Lenoidivic has declared himself the Emperor of the new Russian Empire. He has ordered that President Gryzlovski will remain as the President of the Russian State which will be one of the states of the new empire. The remaining areas will also be broken into states and will include Western European State, the Southern European State, the Syrian State, the Venezuelan State, the Central American State and others to be named in the future. We have also detected Russian troop movements into Northern Italy as well as Russian Naval forces patrolling off the coast of southern Italy. There has also been numerous transport aircraft landing in the new air base that has been built in northern Israel. All of our intelligence seems to indicate that Vladimir is about to make a move to control the world. We have most of our ground forces in the United States working on the fight against the Islamists. We still have some forces in Germany, South Korea, Japan, Italy, and Great Britain. Our Pacific fleet is patrolling from the Philippines northward to the Aleutian Islands, the Atlantic Fleet is still blockading the East Coast, and we have a battle group in the Mediterranean and a battle group in the Indian Ocean. We are spread very thin sir but it is difficult to pinpoint the exact location we should focus on."

The president looked pale as he listened to the report that General Hickman was rattling off to him. He took several deep breaths and tried hard to focus on what the general was saying. How could he be so wrong about what was really going on. He never really imagined that Vladimir was so strong that he could actually pull this off. Where was the rest of the world?

"General, I know that Vladimir still has dissidents in the country who have some strength, where are they?"

"Sir, our intelligence sources have indicated that several hundred business people and other important leaders who disagree with Vladimir have suddenly disappeared. We have reports that many were arrested and relocated to areas unknown to the public. A number have been assassinated. All this took place within a few hours of this announcement."

"We need a new strategy, Bill. I want you to pull out all the stops and get me back into Washington as soon as possible. I know this means some innocent deaths but if we wait and continue on with the current plans we will be too late. Once Vladimir has control of his new empire we will have great difficulty standing up to him. I don't believe we have a good scenario at this stage no matter which way we go but the current course will deplete our resources to the point that we will be unable to defend ourselves against that mad Russian."

"I fear you are most likely correct about that, sir, but I don't see anyone in this country backing down from a good fight to secure our nation. In 1776, the British looked to be overwhelming to many in this country as well but we managed to fight back and defeat them and we will fight back and defeat Russia and the Islamists now."

The president had a little tear in his eye but he turned and smiled at the general and nodded his head. "You know, general, sometimes it is easy to forget that our country has been the underdog more than once and has always come out on top. Thanks for reminding me of that."

"You're welcome, sir. Now we have control of North and South Carolina, Kentucky, Ohio, West Virginia, and most of Pennsylvania. We are still going door to door in New York but we have units moving into Trenton New Jersey and the outskirts of Philadelphia. I believe we can move more rapidly by using air strikes in some areas however there will be innocent casualties because these leaders are embedded in civilian areas and no matter how much we attempt to use pinpoint strikes we will take out innocents."

"Do whatever you must to wrap up this operation as quickly as possible. I need to go back home and shower. I will be back." TJ then turned and left the command center with his secret service escort.

APRIL 20, 2018

FAIRFAX VIRGINIA

Don Ladner had spent most of the last several days riding in the back seat of a car with a hood over his head and often stuffed into the trunk. When the car stopped he was often taken out and beaten then locked in a room. He had the distinct impression that his capturers had no idea what to do with him.

Ladner was starving as food and water had only been provided sporadically. He heard some noise heading back toward him but he still was prone on the floor with his hands and feet tied and the hood over his head. His pants were soiled as he waited for what he imagined would be a morning beating. He heard the door open and the ropes digging into his wrists and ankles was cut off. The hood was yanked off of his head and his eyes were stunned by the sudden light which flooded into them. He shook his head and his hands trying to restore a sense of feeling. When he was finally able to focus his eyes he observed three men in the room with him. All three had their faces covered and two of the men held AK-47s. The man without a visible weapon then spoke. "Get up! Take off your clothes and you can shower in there." The man instructed while pointing at an adjacent bathroom. "When you have finished there will be fresh clothes on this bed. We will then provide you breakfast before we move you to a more secure location."

Don stood up and said, "Thank you. Does this move mean that American forces are close by?"

The man stopped in his tracks and turned back toward Don. First a big grin crossed his face. "Mr. Ladner, you are being moved for your own protection. Many of your fellow countrymen hate all of those who were responsible for bringing this situation onto them. Your president is hiding in a remote outpost. Most of this country is under the complete control of the Islamic State and will remain that way. You are being moved to a more permanent detention facility for re-education and eventually to a location where you can be debriefed regarding your previous crimes." With that the man turned and walked out of the room leaving him alone.

Don started into the bathroom but first he turned and walked to the window in the corner of the room. Drapes were pulled and blinds closed so Don tried to discreetly raise one blind to look outside. As he looked outside he saw three men holding AK-47s and off to one side he saw a panel van marked Fairfax Virginia Adult Detention Center. He lowered the blind and walked slowly into the bathroom to begin cleaning up. A grin crossed his face for a moment as he realized that the man had just confirmed that TJ was alive not dead as he had been told when he was captured.

After taking a long shower Don got dressed and moved into the kitchen where a hot breakfast was waiting for him on the table. He was unsure of how to respond to this so he sat down and carefully examined the food before he began to eat. When he finished his meal one of his guards approached him and placed him in handcuffs. He was then taken outside and placed in the van. The van departed the area. As the van drove out of the long driveway and turned onto the roadway Don thought he heard a jet in the distance. He had not heard an aircraft of any kind for months now and as he thought about that there was a sudden loud explosion behind him. The guards were obviously startled and the van accelerated rapidly as they sped from the area.

They drove for a little over an hour and Don recognized the area as Fairfax Virginia. They passed the Army Navy Country Club and got off the highway and moved onto Main Street. After a few more minutes they pulled to the front of a building with a front wall of dark glass and gray panels. As he was escorted out of the vehicle onto the concrete walkway he looked up and saw that he was being taken into the Fairfax County Adult Detention Facility. After walking through the lobby he was taken through a secured door and down several halls. When he reached what was previously used as a booking room he was told to undress and to put on the orange jumpsuit that was on the counter.

Don changed under the watchful eyes of several Islamic guards. When he had changed he was taken into a cell block and placed in a cell. Every time he started to speak he was quickly told to shut up. He was thankful that he had not been struck or abused in any way which made him start to question what was actually going on.

Don started thinking about what happened this morning. The sound of the jet and the sudden explosion. The more he thought about it the more he imagined that there was an active war going on. That would explain why he was moved so frequently. Now he was in a government building that most likely would not be a target. With any luck the Islamists were not as much in control as they continued to try to make us believe. After all of this went through Don's mind he thought back to what he had been told early today. Just what did they have in mind when they talked about re-education?

APRIL 23, 2018

COMBAT CONTROL CENTER
USS GEORGE WASHINGTON, CVN 73

"Sir, I am tracking two inbound ballistic missiles that were just launched from Iran."

The watch commander was Commander Steve Evans from Florida. He had been serving on the Washington for nearly eight months. "Give me some details on this missile."

"Sir, there are two missiles both appear to be capable of carrying nuclear weapons but no firm indication what the payload is at this time. The computer indicates with its current trajectory that the possible target could be in Egypt."

Commander Evans walked over to the phone that was a direct line to the captain's stateroom. "Sir, I am sorry to bother but we have . . ."

The radar operator shouted while the commander was in mid-sentence. "Sir, we have Migs launching from the Israeli Russian facility. This appears to be an active emergency launch!"

Commander Evans then returned to his phone call. "Sir, we have two missiles launched from Iran that appear to be targeting Egypt and a massive launch of Migs from the Russian base in Israel."

Captain Samuel Smith took only a moment to respond. "Sound battle stations and launch our fighters immediately."

The commander pressed a red button on the console where he sat. A klaxon began sounding waking the majority of the ship since the time was only 4:30 AM. Still holding the phone in his hand the commander pushed another button that opened his phone to the ship's intercom system. "Battle Stations, Battle Stations, Battle Stations, This is not a drill! Air Boss prepare to launch all available fighters." The commander punched another button on the phone and began to talk again. "Combat Control to the Bridge. Bring the boat into the wind for launch." He then turned to the radio operator and stated, "Notify the fleet to prepare for battle and that we are about to launch."

When Captain Smith entered the command center he immediately instructed that their status be reported to Central European Command who issued their orders and request further instructions.

Captain Smith then punched a button on the phone and he was put through to Aircraft Operations.

"Operations."

"Buck this is Sam where are the Russian aircraft headed?"

"Radar seems to indicate that they are headed north out over the Med."

"I suspect that the missiles may be designed to create an EMP, most likely over Israel so to be on the safe side have our aircraft fly north as well and monitor the Russian aircraft."

"Aye, Aye, sir."

It was slightly more than ten minutes later when the two missiles with their warheads detonated. One missile was about twenty miles west southwest of Tel Aviv. The second missile also detonated when it was about five miles off the coast northwest of Tel Aviv. Special shielding to protect the aircraft and ship had been installed some time back so the ships and aircraft were safe from any problems resulting from the explosion.

At Davis-Monthan Air Force Base it was still April 22, and at about 6:45 PM as the president and the first lady were finishing dinner. Master Sergeant Jones entered the dining area and informed the president he was needed at the command center. The president nodded and rose from the table. After kissing Angela, he walked outside where a jeep was waiting to take him to the command post.

General Hickman greeted the president as soon as he walked into the center. After ushering him to his workstation he began to brief the president on the current situation. "Sir, two missiles were fired from southern Iran and exploded just off the western coast of Israel. The missiles detonated at approximately 26 miles in altitude and the warhead was a nuclear device but apparently a low yield explosive. It caused an EMP that effected all of Israel, Gaza and the West Bank, Jordan, Syria, and a great deal of Egypt. Those are the areas that we know about at this time. The new Russian base was apparently not effected as they most likely had electrical and computer circuitry protected. Prior to the detonation they launched between 20 and 30 fighter aircraft from the base. One last thing, the missiles were not Iranian but most likely Russian."

The president had a very serious look on his face as he listened to Hickman while watching the television screens where he could observe the hurried activity going on in the command center of the Washington. "Did we lose any aircraft or ships as a result of the explosion?"

"No, sir. We are currently monitoring the Russian aircraft and have fighters prepared to engage if necessary."

"Good. Now what is the status in Israel?"

"The Israelis have protected all of their important assets including aircraft and military vehicles. However, this could be a lead in to a Russian takeover of Israel. We know that the Russians have promised protection from the Muslim countries in return for the base. We believe that is why the missiles were fired in Iran to further promote the idea of an Islamic attack."

"Contact the Israeli Defense Forces and offer our assistance should they have any need. Then instruct the Washington to continue to monitor Russian operations and if they begin any type of aggressive move on Israel to take the appropriate action."

Two Russian Mig 21s started moving toward the American fleet. Within minutes they found themselves flanked by F-35s and received a warning to change course. The Migs were already within range of the ships if they decided to fire so the F-35s tried to be diplomatic about the warning but they also armed their air to air missiles in case the warning was ignored.

After only about a thirty second delay both Migs changed direction and flew toward the Syrian coast. The American pilots then backed off and returned to a normal patrol type pattern. At about the same moment four Migs began flying toward Jerusalem.

As they entered Israeli air space they were immediately warned to change their flight plan. They ignored the warning and an Israel missile battery fired on the jets. The first missile missed its target but the next two each hit their mark and two Russian aircraft plummeted to the ground.

Within a few minutes an Israeli mechanized division began an attack on the Russian Air Base. The battle of the Jewish State was underway.

MAY 1, 2018

COMMAND CENTER
DAVIS-MONTHAN AIR FORCE BASE

TJ decided to walk to the command center this morning. It was a bright sunny Tuesday morning and he needed some fresh air to clear his mind. The Battle of Israel had been raging now for more than a week. Much of the Russian Base in Israel had been destroyed but the airfield was still operational. Tel Aviv had been overrun by Russian troops and the battle over Jerusalem was in full swing. Russian forces were also in control of the West Bank area but the Gaza Strip was still an active battle.

China and Japan had an ongoing naval battle in the Sea of Japan. The Chinese Navy had a number of vessels conducting operations and the United States had two ships assisting the Japanese Navy in repelling the aggression. Japan was maintaining superiority in the air thanks to American aircraft that had been loaned to them.

Mop up operations were now occurring in New York as Canadian and American forces were fighting in West Virginia while urban warfare was active in Philadelphia and Trenton New Jersey. Casualties were light for the United States but many of the Islamic forces had been killed or had withdrawn. Since TJ ordered the more aggressive approach he had expected more decisive results and there was no overlooking his disappointment.

TJ and his secret service detail reached the command center and entered with a real sense of purpose. He was becoming more and more frustrated over the length of time this operation was taking to complete. He entered the center and shouted as you were to all of the men and women currently keeping tabs on the activity that was occurring in real time.

As General Hickman began the president's morning briefing TJ held up his hand and cut him off in mid-sentence. "I want to know why it is taking so long to defeat these Islamic Forces on the east coast."

"Sir, we are moving as quickly as possible in a way that reduces casualties as much as possible. To move any faster would require pre softening the areas up through the use of artillery or bombardment from aircraft. We could lose thousands of innocent people if we push this operation too quickly. We already tried that in spots and each time we lost large numbers of civilians and others without accomplishing our goals."

TJ considered that statement for several minutes while staring at the television screens nearby. Finally, he shook his head several times and turned toward General Hickman. "Bill, I think we have to do this. We have to take complete control of our nation so we can put the resources together to stop Vladimir before he is completely unstoppable. I don't want to kill or hurt innocent citizens of this country but I don't see where we have a choice at this point. If we don't stop Vladimir now we won't have a country by the time this is all over. Do your best to minimize our casualties but I want to be back at the White House in a month, get me there!"

MAY 1, 2018

THE KREMLIN

In Russia May Day is a day of great celebration. It is a day of parades and parties in honor of the worker. Normally there are great military parades and political speeches that pay great tribute to the worker and the socialist and communist system. Today was different though because even though the parades occurred and the speeches were made the mood in The Kremlin was somber especially with high ranking members of the military.

The second floor conference room in The Kremlin had two armed posted military guards at each door. The room inside was large and spacious. Bright red carpeting covered the floor providing an obvious comparison to the old Soviet Union era. There were no windows in the room and the walls were covered with a dark wood. In the center of the room was a large round table that could seat as many as thirty people comfortably. Three colonels, eight generals, and six admirals were standing in the room speaking in low hushed tones and awaiting the meeting to begin. As the commanders began to move to their places around the conference table they looked around the room to see who was present. All the major commands were represented except for General Ivan Rostakovich who was the commander of the Russian Middle East Command. Perhaps he had been unable to leave his headquarters at the Nahariyya Military Facility.

As the door opened a major walked into the room and shouted, "Attention! Our beloved Emperor of the New Russian Empire."

Vladimir walked into the room and proceeded to a throne type chair at the far end of the table. Even though the table was circular all the commanders had been assigned chairs that wrapped around one end of the table leaving the other end for Vladimir and his aids. President Gryzlovski was notably not present in the room as Vladimir called the meeting to order.

"As you know we have had some great success over the past several weeks. Our military is now protecting Italy and Vatican City. Troops are stationed at various locations throughout the country and we have taken control of the United States military bases in Italy. We have detained a number of American military and have seized military aircraft and other equipment."

The room erupted with applause and cheers from the commanders in the room as they congratulated each other for the swift and efficient campaign. After several minutes the room became still again and the commanders retook their seats.

Vladimir continues, "Unfortunately, there has also been some setbacks with our plans as well. The Middle East Command has taken control of Jerusalem but is still engaged in fighting to maintain that control. The West Bank area is being controlled but Gaza and much of Israel are still being fought over. In addition, the American fleet has been sending aircraft and causing us a great deal of distress. Now General Rostakovich seemed to be incapable of handling the American and Israeli forces so he is being replaced. The good general has been permanently retired this morning. Are there any questions?"

The room was stone silent. All the commanders looked straight ahead and none of them had any question in their mind about what permanently retired meant.

Vladimir stood up and addressed the commanders one last time. "If anyone wishes to volunteer to correct the situation in the Middle East please let me know. You can be sure that you will be greatly rewarded for successfully turning that campaign around."

Vladimir then walked out of the room while all of the commanders stood quietly. Not one of those officers had any thought about volunteering for the open command. When Vladimir had left the room each of the officers quietly gathered their papers and placed them in their briefcases and then made their way back to their respective offices.

As Vladimir was starting up the stairs toward his office he stopped and turned back. He took several steps back toward the conference room when he saw the officers walking out. He shouted across the room, "Admiral Racic!"

The admiral stopped dead in his tracks. He felt a cold chill run down his spine because he truly wanted nothing to do with any assignment in the Middle East. "Yes, sir."

As the two walked toward each other Vladimir addressed the admiral. "You are to move some ships into the Middle East area and eliminate this threat we face from the Americans. I care not how you handle this but I do not want to hear any more about lost aircraft or naval vessels at the hands of these Americans. Am I clear?"

"Yes, my Emperor. I shall handle this situation immediately."

As Vladimir turned and returned his trip back up to his office he had a slight smile on his face. He liked the emperor thing and he was growing in confidence every day.

MAY 4, 2018

Davis-Monthan Air Force Base

It had been a beautiful Friday afternoon in Arizona and TJ had been making arrangements for his victorious return to Washington. He had secured a special train that would take him across the country through a number of large cities so he could speak to the people and confirm that the United States was secure and ready to do whatever it would take to bring this new so called Russian Empire to its knees.

TJ had arranged to board the train in Phoenix Arizona, and from there he would travel to Las Vegas, San Diego, Los Angeles, San Fransisco, Portland, Seattle, Butte, Denver, Kansas City, Little Rock, Memphis, Jackson, New Orleans, Mobile, Jacksonville, Atlanta, Lexington, Chicago, Detroit, Cleveland, Boston, New York, Philadelphia, Baltimore, Richmond, and end up in Washington DC. He was depending on the General Hickman to have all the operations completed and mopped up by the time the trip was to end. By his calculations he would arrive in DC on June twelfth, so the general had better step up his activities.

As he entered the command center TJ saw General Hickman give him a worried look and after finishing his conversation with another officer General Hickman made his way to the president to brief him.

"What is going on this afternoon, general?"

"It has been sort of an up and down day, sir. Stateside we have made considerable progress in New York and Trenton but we have come against some stiff resistance in the outskirts of Philly. We have some more serious problems though in the Med. Russia is hitting back with a bit of a vengeance. Two cruisers have sustained damage as a result of torpedoes fired by Russian submarines in the area. Two of our F-18s have also been shot down. More Russian vessels are heading into the area and they are significantly stepping up operations against our resources. The Israeli Defense Force has requested our assistance in defending their country. Specifically, they wish for us to fly as many flights as possible to harass the Russians."

TJ looked surprised but he was actually more alarmed than surprised. "General, what is your recommendation regarding this development?"

Hickman looked down at the floor for nearly a minute focusing on what he was going to say next. "The aircraft carrier Abraham Lincoln has entered the Persian Gulf within the last eight hours. Her battle group includes a guided missile destroyer, two guided missile cruisers as well as a number of submarines. I suggest that we begin to make use of her to take the heat off of the George Washington. We will never receive permission to overfly Syria or Iraq but I think we need to do it anyway. We can employ both air to ground, air to air, and ship to ground missile strikes from the Lincoln. We also have Marines on board which can be deployed to assist Israeli forces. I would also like to use our subs to aggressively attack the Russian ships coming down from Italy. I am also developing a plan to bring Marines into

Italy by landing them on the east coast from the Adriatic Sea. It will take a while however to get those forces prepped and ready."

TJ was quiet for a moment and then replied, "Okay, get those plans underway but remember we can't pull forces from the states until we have full control of our country."

"Understood, sir."

MAY 5, 2018

NORTH PHILADELPHIA, PENNSYLVANIA

Gunnery Sergeant Hackborn was leading a patrol of Marines in a house to house search along Germantown Road. The plan was to meet another patrol that was working the area on North 16th Street. This area was more business and warehouse than residences. The two patrols were going to take a break for breakfast in a parking lot at the corner of Germantown Avenue and Kerbaugh Street. It was still dark with just a few rays of light beginning to emerge from the east. The Marines parked their two armored personnel carriers at opposite ends of the parking lot. They sat down in various places on the parking lot in groups of two or three and began eating their breakfast. It was almost 5:30 AM and they had already been searching homes and structures containing businesses and warehouses for nearly four hours. This type of activity was often safer and more efficient in the middle of the night than it was in the daytime. The Marines worked as quietly as possible and as efficiently as possible. They had taken a few prisoners earlier but had failed to find any important documents or weapons.

Suddenly there was a *whoosh* sound and an explosion. The APC parked on Germantown Avenue guarding the northeast flank jumped from the ground as a bright yellow flash enveloped the vehicle. Then came the whizz of bullets filling the air as a machine gun atop a building just northeast of their location had opened up on the men. The Marines immediately grabbed their weapons and moved to defensive positions striving to find whatever cover they could find. As soon as the men had cover and found a target they began to return fire. The aggressor however was on the roof and while the machine gun could fire over the lip the Marines could not target anything but the barrel of the weapon.

Hackborn tried to determine the best way they could cross the street and fight their way up to the roof to eliminate the threat. Just as he was ready to start barking orders he heard the sound of a mortar being fired and in just a few seconds an explosion from the mortar shell went off on Kerbaugh Street just a few feet from the property where the Marines were located. Then a second machine gun began firing from a rooftop southwest of their position on Kerbaugh Street. Now they were pinned down and would be hard pressed to move forward or backward.

Hackborn made his way slowly to the patrol radio operator. As soon as he got close he shouted, "Get us some air support now!"

PFC Ryan Smith was already on the radio trying to get some help. "Eagle base this is Owl 2."

"Eagle Base go Owl 2."

"Eagle base, Owl 2 and Owl 5 are both pinned down at stop Charlie 6. We have incoming heavy weapon fire from the northeast and southwest. Both targets are on building rooftops and are actively engaged. We can't move. Over."

"Roger that Owl 2. We will dispatch air support stand by,"

Smith then turned back toward Hackborn and shouted, "Gunny, air support is on the way!"

Hackborn turned to the rest of his patrol and shouted, "Keep under cover and conserve ammo until help gets here. Make sure you watch for any ground movement toward us!"

The machine gun fire continued for several minutes. Two Marines were now wounded and at least one appeared dead. Greg was trying to account for all of the men who had been with him and he knew that he had two in the APC prior to the explosion and he had observed no one get out of the vehicle.

He could hear radio traffic again, "Owl 2 and 5 this is Falcon 8—put your heads down men I am about to take care of your problem."

Greg still did not hear any noise from the helicopter but realized the hellfire missiles that they had been armed with could be fired from a long range as long as they could see the target. Twenty seconds passed. The weapons fire stopped from both buildings and five seconds later the building on Germantown erupted in flames from the third floor and roof and there was a loud explosion. Five seconds later the same thing happened to a building on Kerbaugh Street. It got very quiet very quickly.

The radio came alive again. "Owl 2 and 5 this is Falcon 8. Your immediate targets have been eliminated but you have additional targets on their way, Sharia Police types. Do you want me to eliminate that problem for you as well?"

Greg nodded quickly and PFC Smith began to speak into the microphone when Hackborn shouted, "We need air evacuation for at least two!"

Smith then replied on the radio, "Affirmative Falcon 8, please eliminate those threats and then get us an air evac for two."

"Roger that Owl 2 but your location is too tight with the overhead wires and close buildings. Move your injured to West Pine and McFerran Street and your air evac will be able to land in there."

Gunnery Sergeant Greg Hackborn stood up and began to survey the scene. He ran to the overturned armored personnel carrier and found both Marines inside injured but alive. He then confirmed one dead Marine and found two more wounded but alive. As the others in the patrol gave first aid to the injured he looked for the leader of Owl 5, Gunnery Sergeant Daren Agara. He located him near the street a few feet from the other armored personnel carrier. He was dead as well from a piece of shrapnel that had sliced into his body just below his left ear.

Hackborn coordinated the loading of the APC with the wounded and dead. Before they were finished they heard several explosions in the distance. The radio operator shouted, "Gunny all threats have been eliminated!"

Hackborn nodded and continued his work. It was 6:15 AM and there was still much to do today before they could head back to the base. Now he knew that the mission would be much more difficult as there was no longer any chance for surprise. The sun was now beating down on his skin and the warmth felt good.

MAY 28, 2018

FAIRFAX VIRGINIA
ADULT DETENTION FACILITY

The boredom was the worst part of being incarcerated. No television to pass the time and Don was never allowed to leave his cell for any reason. Don had been given a few books to read but there was nothing interesting because the books had to pass the Sharia inspectors before he could read them. Don spent a lot of time exercising in his cell but still his imagination had come up with hundreds of conspiracy theories and ideas of how the American military would suddenly swoop in and save the day.

Don kept playing back the events of the last year over and over again in his head. Each time trying to find where they could have changed things that would have resulted in a different and better situation today. He also imagined frequently what he would do when the sharia police came for him to execute him because he knew in the back of his mind that they would never let him live.

One thing Don had been very careful to keep track of mentally was the date and the day of the week. He did not know why it was so important to him but he continued to keep careful track. Today he realized was Memorial Day. The day that all Americans celebrate the lives and efforts of those brave people in the military who gave their lives to protect our country and to keep it free. How could he possibly properly celebrate in a way that would pay tribute to their great sacrifice?

His thoughts were interrupted by a buzzing at the door and his cell door opened. A man entered his cell that he had never seen before.

"Mr. Ladner, you are to be transferred to another facility tomorrow. We need you to be prepared to leave at six tomorrow morning."

"Where are you going to take me?"

"You will be taken to a facility in Washington where you will be interrogated regarding your crimes against the American people and the Islamic people. After that I do not know what will happen to you."

"Okay, I will be prepared to go."

With that the man turned and walked out of the cell closing the door behind him as he left. Don realized that this was most likely the end of his life. He realized that this could very well be his last ride into DC. What crimes were they going to question him about and is there any possible way he will survive this entire ordeal?

Even with the concerns of torture and possibly death streaming through his mind his primary concern was whether or not he will be able to have a view while he is transported. He did not want to travel with a hood over his head or in a panel van. He needed to see what DC looked like after the attack and terror of those last hours in the White House.

MAY 29, 2018

PRESIDENTIAL TRAIN
SEATTLE, WASHINGTON

TJ had finished a long day of talks, speeches, and negotiations. He entered his rail car and sat down at the beautiful wooden desk located in this room where he could relax and get some paperwork completed. A steady rain had begun and was pelting the windows in the rail car. He took a couple of minutes to catch his breath before reaching for his satellite phone to call the command center to get his evening updates. After punching in the number he pushed a toggle switch that activated an encryption system to keep the call safe from anyone listening that should not be.

It took several minutes before he heard anyone on the other end of the phone. After some beeping and static, a voice came across. "Mr. President, this is General Hickman."

"General, can you bring me up to speed on the current status."

"Yes, sir. First the fighting in the Middle East is significant. Russians have troops in Syria, Lebanon, Jordan, Iraq as well as Israel. The air base in northern Israel is still active but the Russians have sustained some serious losses at that location. Tel Aviv is controlled by Russian troops but Jerusalem is still controlled by the Israelis. The Russian Navy has been giving us some problems in the Med and the Persian Gulf but we are holding

291

our own. The Iranians have also got patrol boats active in the Persian Gulf again. Russia now controls all of Italy and Vatican City. They have also invaded Austria, Slovakia and the Czech Republic. In South America the Russians control Venezuela, Peru, Columbia, Chili and Brazil north of the Amazon. Chinese warships have increased their activity around Japan. Southeast Asia seems to be firmly in their control as well."

"Have we lost personnel or assets in any of these areas?"

"Yes, sir, but our losses have not been significant."

The president sighed and then replied, "General, you know that even if only one member of our military is lost then it is significant."

General Hickman hesitated before he replied, "Yes, sir, you are correct and I am sorry to phrase it that way. What I should have said is that we have lost a minimal number of personnel and that we are continuing to take safeguards to protect our forces."

"Okay, now that I am up on the international problems how are we doing nationally?"

"Well, sir, on the home front we have made some real progress. Our troops are doing a fantastic job of urban warfare. We have lost very few and have taken a large number of prisoners as well as seizing several caches of weapons. We have established two prisoner camps for those detained one in southern Pennsylvania and one in North Carolina. Strangely enough a lot of the Islamic soldiers are surrendering as soon as we approach. We now control all of the continental United States with the exception of an area within 100 miles of Washington in every direction. We are currently making preparations for one final push. Not to mislead you there are some isolated areas of fighting in and around Baltimore and Philadelphia, but I believe we can start making plans to deploy troops to areas overseas where they can begin to push the Russians back into Russia."

"That is wonderful news, general. Let me ask you, have you seen or heard of anything that would lead to the location of Don Ladner, my chief of staff?"

"I was notified that during some intelligence interviews one person indicated that a man claiming to be the president's chief of staff was hiding in a residence in Baltimore. When a patrol found the home that was described they did a number of interviews and found that he did in fact live for some time at the residence but had left the area a number of weeks before the troops took the area. No one was sure where he went but only that he took a neighbors' car and disappeared."

"That's great news. Hopefully, he was able to survive that long so he should be able to keep his wits for a while longer."

A smile crossed the president's face and he took another big deep breath.

"Now, general, I have some information for you. I spent part of the day negotiating with some people from Boeing. They have agreed to convert six of their 787s to LAWs. We have some engineers and equipment being flown into Seattle where they will start an immediate process to equip these planes with the lasers needed and to modify the cabins to carry extra fuel. With any luck we should have the first two in the air within a month. I have also arranged for permanent land based lasers to be placed in strategic locations within the country so that we can eliminate any incoming missiles."

"That is wonderful, sir."

After a few more minutes of friendly chatter the phone call ended. TJ placed the satellite phone on the desk and turned off the encryption device. He sat back in the chair and took a long slow deep breath. He turned slightly and looked out the window to his left to enjoy the view as the train pulled out of the station. The sun was just setting as the train sped off to the east. The sky was a bright orange and somehow it brought about some peace to TJ and for the first time in a long time he was able to relax. He stood up and walked back to his private quarters where he decided to finally get some deep sleep.

The train rolled onto Butte as TJ fell asleep.

MAY 29, 2018

FAIRFAX, VIRGINIA

Don had been pacing the floor in his cell all morning. He kept thinking that maybe if he was to be moved things would get better or it could be to an execution site but at least this episode of his life would be over. Don had no idea of what time it was but it must be late afternoon already and the move was supposed to be this morning.

Suddenly the cell door opened and two large black men walked into his cell. Each of the men had to be at least six foot five and they were both built like professional football players. Don walked toward them and as he did one of the men grabbed him by the upper arm and spun him around. As the force of the motion caused him to face away from the men he felt the other man grab his free arm and his arms were pinned behind him and handcuffs applied. As he turned around the man on his left pulled a black hood out of his pocket and Don shouted, "Please, no hood I will not cause you any problems. I just want to see what Washington looks like now."

As the hood was pulled down over his face one of the men said in hush tones. "If you are no problem then I will remove the hood for a few minutes when we get to Washington but it will be dark by then so there will not be much to see."

Don felt both of his upper arms gripped in a very tight manner. Each was being held just below the shoulder and the men nearly raised him off the floor. He was manhandled down the hall and into the elevator and then out of the building. It seemed he was being placed in a van or SUV and after being buckled into the seat he heard the door slam behind him. The vehicle began to move and there was no conversation as the ride began and continued in silence.

The only vehicle noises he heard during the drive was the sound of large trucks and that noise seemed to be infrequent. The hood covering his eyes caused Don to be disoriented and confused regarding his location. It was a long drive with a lot turns and it had been made at various speeds but in absolute silence. The vehicle slowed down and came to a stop. The door opened and a voice said, "You have cooperated so we will allow you to do some sightseeing now that we have reached Washington." With that the man pulled the hood off of Don's head.

Don simply replied, "Thank you."

As the vehicle moved forward again Don gazed out the windows of the van he was riding in. It was dusk and becoming dark quickly. There were only a few lights and he was struggling to see as much of Washington as he could for the remainder of the ride. The first landmark he noted was the Lincoln Memorial. He could see it had been seriously damaged and appeared to have been struck with some type of explosive charges. As they sped forward he noted numerous storefronts that had windows broken out, interiors damaged by fire, and various other damage. In several places cars and small trucks were overturned and often burnt out. The District of Columbia was certainly a war zone.

When he did see a flag flying the flag was the black flag of the Islamic State. Finally, he saw the Capital Building. Huge gaping holes could be clearly seen in the building exterior. There were large holes that may have been made by artillery shells in the parking areas in front of the Capital. The van once again slowed to a stop. The man in the passenger seat turned and slid the hood back over Don's head. Once again there was only darkness.

The trip continued for another ten or fifteen minutes before stopping for the last time. Again he was roughly escorted out of the vehicle and into a building. The helped him up some stairs and down a hallway. When the hood was removed he found himself in a nice room with a bed and bath. The cuffs were removed from his hands by one of the men who had escorted him to the location. As they left the room the door slammed and was locked.

Don looked around at the rather spacious room. The bathroom was clean and the bed had clean sheets. There were two windows in the room and they were both nailed closed. Looking outside he could see he was about twenty-five feet off the ground and there was no roof outside the window but just a sheer drop to the parking lot below. Looking around Don could see that there was a parking lot and courtyard and the entire facility was surrounded by a brick wall and iron gates.

Somehow Don realized he had been in this building before but the exact location escaped him. It was dark and maybe tomorrow morning he will be able to get a better idea when the sun is out and he has a clearer view of the surroundings. But for now Don was tired and that clean bed looked very inviting. Tomorrow is another day.

JUNE 1, 2018

LOS PINOS
MEXICO CITY, MEXICO

President Cardoza was reading from a stack of newspapers sitting on top of his desk. He looked up from his reading for a moment to gaze outside. The sky was overcast and the morning was unusually dreary, but this was Friday and the weekend would give him a chance to relax for a couple days. He was expecting General Montez to arrive in ten minutes to give him a briefing on the current status of the American military as they were working to free their shores of the invasion force which had occupied so much of their land these last months.

A loud knock at the door announced the arrival of the president's secretary, Carlos, who entered the room abruptly. "Sir, you have a phone call."

President Cardoza looked back down at his newspapers and replied, "I am not taking any calls this morning until I have completed my briefings."

Carlos appeared disturbed by that reply and even though he would normally simply say yes sir and leave he knew this required the president's attention. "Forgive me, sir, but I believe you may want to take this call. It is from President Gryzlovski of Russia."

Cardoza looked up and said nothing while he thought about why Gryzlovski would be calling him. After a few moments he simply nodded and Carlos returned to his office where he connected the phone to President Cardozas's office.

Before picking up the receiver the president pushed a button on the phone base which automatically began taping the phone conversation. He took a deep breath dreading what the topic of the conversation would include. "This is President Cardoza to whom am I speaking?"

"This is Dmitry Gryzlovski, President of the Russian State in the Great Russian Empire. I trust you are well President Cardoza."

"I am, may I ask why you have contacted me?"

"I have a very unique opportunity for you. Should you agree to my proposition I can assure you that Mexico will benefit and the Russian Empire will be very generous to you and your country in the future."

"You have peaked my interest, Mr. President, so what is it that you need of my country and myself to do to earn these great rewards?"

"President Cardoza the United States during the last year has invaded your soil, killed many of your countrymen, and has made numerous accusations against your government that have proven to be at best misstatements of facts or perhaps outright lies. They have also been a thorn in our side during this period of time but we have been preoccupied with other matters. Now as we conclude some of our ventures that have consumed so much of our time we are ready to conclude our American problems."

Cardoza sat back in his chair and the color drained from his face as he was fearful of what was coming next. "Our country, as you must be aware, has corrected the problems that we had with the United States. Our relations at this time are much better and unlike your country we have to survive while living next to them. So what is it that you are proposing?"

"President Cardoza the Russian Imperial Army and Air Force will be landing an invasion force at the Chihuahua International Airport in eleven days. All we are asking of you is to close your airport at that location prior to our arrival and to provide free access to our forces between that location and the American border. We expect no interference whatsoever from your military. If you agree to this stipulation, then as I said earlier you and your country will be richly rewarded for your service."

"And if I don't?"

Gryzlovski chuckles prior to answering and then says simply: "We will be at the Chihuahau airport on June twelfth, Mr. President and if we must fight our way in it will simply be another inconvenience for us but not an insurmountable problem. For you, however, I am afraid it would prove to be a very poor decision for the future of both your country and yourself."

"I understand, Mr. President. I am sure you understand that I must confer with my advisors prior to announcing my decision, after all we still are a republic not an empire."

"I do understand please contact me as soon as your decision is made, sir, so I can notify my military leaders as to how to approach this situation. Good day, sir."

The phone line went dead at that point and Cardoza just stared across the room in disbelief. So many thoughts racing through his head as he considered the consequences of what he was going to have to decide. Why wouldn't the rest of this screwed up world simply leave his Mexico alone?

This situation was beyond his level of diplomacy and he knew he had to decide which side he would come down on. All things considered the choice was easier than he originally thought it would be. "Carlos, get President Samuels on the phone and tell him it is urgent."

"Yes, sir, and General Montez is here."

"Send him in."

General Montez was six foot and trim. Tall for most Mexicans and very muscular with dark focused eyes and known for being serious and to the point. His sense of humor was hard to find as he took his new position of Commander of the Mexican Military very seriously. He approached the president's desk and snapped to attention with a salute.

"Please take a seat, general, we have much to discuss."

"Yes, sir, where do you wish me to start the briefing?"

"I am not as concerned with the status of the American forces right now as I am with our own situation currently."

"Sir, we have recovered nearly completely since our earlier skirmishes with the Americans. Our forces are back in their normal locations and are operating at full strength with the exception of the Air Force which has had difficulty replacing a number of our fighter jets. We also have lost several patrol boats on the Gulf of Mexico but we see little threats in that area. In fact, sir we see very little probability of any threatening action against our nation in the foreseeable future. American forces seem to be concentrating on their East Coast area and there are minimal signs of troop activity in the southwest area of their country."

"How would your assessment change general if you were to learn that a Russian invasion force would be landing in Chihuahua State within the next two weeks to prepare and initiate an invasion of the United States?"

"Sir, that information if correct would trouble me greatly. We could not stop such a large force and we would have to drop the bulk of our forces to the Mexico City area to protect the capital. I would not suggest placing any aircraft in harm's way since we could not ultimately win a battle with the Russian military any better than we could against the United States."

Both men sat silently for several minutes staring across the room and each wondered whether they would still be around in two weeks. The phone buzzed and the president pushed a button opening the intercom. "Yes, Carlos."

"Sir, I have President Samuels on the phone for you."

General Montez stood as if to leave but Cardoza motioned for him to sit back down and wait.

"President Samuels this is President Cardoza. How are you, sir?"

"Mr. President, I am fine but I am a bit busy on my national tour to encourage the people of this country to rise up against the invaders. So what is on your mind?"

"Mr. President, I have just finished a phone call with President Gryzlovski of Russia. He indicated to me that he would like to see me close the airport in Chihuahua prior to June twelfth as his country would be in need of the facility for the transfer of troops which will be moving to positions north of that location as they eliminate what he referred to as a thorn in their side."

The phone line was silent and Cardoza patiently waited taking deep breaths waiting for a reply.

"President Cardoza, I appreciate you sharing this information and I understand sharing this with me puts you in great risk. I need to discuss this with my military leaders because I expect that if they are going to hit us from the south they are also planning activity in other locations at the same time. We will get prepared. Mr. President, you have proven yourself to be a true friend and a solid ally. I mean no disrespect sir but I do not believe that your military will be capable of standing up to the Russians, I am not even sure about our military, so please cooperate with the Russians. I would greatly appreciate any additional information you may become aware of but I insist that you do not put yourself in danger to get the information to me."

Cardoza smiled for a moment and then continued. "I will certainly keep you informed Mr. President but I would not be surprised if I have company here at Los Pinos from the Russian government very soon which may keep me from contacting you on the promptest basis."

"Mr. President, I also want you to understand in advance that any military action we take to stop the Russians on you soil is not directed at you or your country. I would think it would be best if you evacuate as many of your citizens from the area as you can because we will need to take action before the Russians are prepared for it. Again I do not wish to engage Mexican troops or citizens if we can help it and if we do I can tell you now it will be with great regret, sir."

"May God be with you, President Samuels."

"And with you and your countrymen, President Cardoza."

As President Cardoza placed the phone back on the cradle he looked up to see General Montez stand at attention and state, "I await your orders, sir."

"See that the airport in Chihuahua is closed and begin a quiet evacuation of the city and surrounding area. Meet with your other commanders and design a plan to protect Mexico City and to stop any possible movement by the Russians to the south from the airport vicinity. Also move troops away from the border and along the most probable path that the Russians might use to move into the United States."

The general stood and simply said, "Yes, sir," as he left the office.

JUNE 1, 2018

UNION STATION
KANSAS CITY, MISSOURI

As the Presidential train moved into the station it was early evening. The rain was coming down steady and TJ was simply gazing out the window wondering what to do next. The real question now was how many operations this country could possibly fight successfully at one time.

An aide came into the room and announced that General Hickman was on the secure line.

"General Hickman, I am just arriving in Kansas City but we have quite a bit to talk about so give me a quick briefing."

"Sir, I have nothing but good news for a change. We now have control of Baltimore and Philadelphia and we are mopping up in some of the suburban areas. We also have control of the southern and western portions of Virginia and we are holding over 3,200 prisoners at various detention centers. Residents are seeing what is going on and are being very helpful now in assisting us in locating the fighters that stay behind to sabotage. Drone overflights have indicated that the forces holding DC are considerably smaller than we originally believed and it would appear we will be able to move into DC within the next several days. Naval forces have detected and destroyed a Russian submarine off the coast of New York. We believe that the sub was meant to find a hole in our blockade."

TJ smiled briefly and then said, "Very good job, general. Your efforts and those of our forces are truly commendable. Regrettably I have just received some new information that may push us to the brink. President Cardoza has informed me that President Gryzlovski notified him that within the next two weeks Russia will be sending an invasion force into Mexico, specifically Chihuahua International Airport, for an operation against the United States. I figure that they will not just hit us from the south but they must have other operations planned for the same time or in close proximity. So can we stop Russia after what we have been through lately?"

"Sir, we have no choice. I will get with the staff and we will develop a new plan but I believe it would be best to shorten you trip. We will work to get you back to the White House before this next operation begins."

As the conversation ended TJ placed the phone back in the cradle and then looked out the windows of his railcar. A small smile crossed his lips as he said a silent prayer. He had confidence in General Hickman but even more importantly he trusted God would not let all of the efforts of his countrymen be for nothing.

General Hickman also was saying a prayer but his was for a miracle because he knew that stopping a Russian force would be impossible with the status of the military currently.

As TJ put the phone down and turned off the encryption device his mind began running through scenarios that would prevent this attack by Russia. Maybe he should bluff his way through this and he could come up with a plausible story that would give Vladimir second thoughts. No Vladimir was already having delusions of grandeur and TJ was sure that after naming himself emperor that his confidence level was off the chart.

The door to his railcar office opened. "Sir, we are ready for you now. We will be heading to the Convention Center for your talk." TJ stood and walked to the door with the agent.

JUNE 3, 2018

CLEVELAND, OHIO

The sun was shining brightly and the temperature was already in the mid 70's as the Presidential Whistle Stop Train pulled into the Cleveland Amtrack Station. TJ was gathering paperwork together to prepare to make a speech at the Rock and Roll Hall of Fame, a very short distance away. There was a knock on the door to his suite followed by the immediate entry of a secret service agent and Major Combs.

"Mr. President, your speech has to be delayed. We have an emergency meeting with General Hickman, Director Owens, and some others at the Cleveland City Hall. We need to leave immediately, sir."

TJ looked a little surprised and stood there for just a few moments and then replied, "Let's go."

Waiting just outside were three black Chevrolet Suburban's and as the trio stepped into the vehicles they sped away toward the east and turned onto Ninth Street. Within five minutes the vehicles pulled up to the Cleveland City Hall on Lakeside. The group quickly moved into the building which had already been surrounded by Cleveland Police and secret service agents.

Once inside they were ushered into a conference room that was crowded with military staff and intelligence analysts.

Everyone in the room stood quietly when the door opened and the president walked inside.

"At ease. What is going on?"

General Hickman stood as everyone else took a seat.

"Mr. President, we have been working closely with the intelligence people to try to find a way to prevent Russia from escalating the situation any more. One of the questions we all seemed to focus on was how the Russians seemed to continually bounce back with large numbers of troops even after repeated catastrophic defeats? They lost an invasion force heading toward Alaska, then they lost an invasion force heading to Israel. We have repeatedly destroyed naval vessels and we have destroyed two of their three space centers. CIA and National Security Agency personnel both agree that total Russian military personnel losses exceed two hundred thousand. That is nearly half of their total estimated strength when this began which was approximately 450,000. They have only slightly more than a third of their naval vessels still in operation and have lost nearly a fourth of their total aircraft. So our assessment is that we are spread thin but the Russians are spread thin as well and if they try an invasion of the United States it will mean that their homeland is very vulnerable and they cannot absorb another significant setback."

TJ was listening intently to the assessment but then interrupted and asked, "That is very interesting information but have you got a plan to take advantage of this situation?"

"Yes, sir, we do. We currently have assets in position for simultaneous attacks on the Russian base in Israel and numerous strikes in various Russian bases and ports. Submarines in the

Baltic Sea will fire numerous missiles at the space center in Archangelsk, missiles will also strike Rovtov-da-nova where the Russians currently have numerous ships in port. There are reported large troop movements toward either Kalingrad or Gdansk and a number of naval vessels moving into these ports as well. We believe that these troops will be part of the invasion of the U. S. so we will dispatch B-2 bombers to destroy these port facilities as well as the vessels. These attacks will not only bring significant distress to the Russian military but will hopefully turn the Russian people against Vladimir. All we need is your approval sir. The details of all of these attacks is contained in this binder sir but I realize you don't have time to go over everything so I wanted to give you the highlights prior to your speech. We will also begin the formal attack of the District of Columbia tomorrow morning."

TJ was trying to take all of this in as quickly as possible. TJ quickly browsed through the binder to see if there were any questions that popped out to him. After several minutes TJ looked up, closed the binder and looked directly at General Hickman. "General, you have my blessing. Go for it."

As he was saying to go for it TJ was standing up to leave. Major Combs slid a series of formal military orders across the table in front of the president along with an ink pen. TJ signed the bottom of each order and slid them across the table to the general. TJ then walked out of the room and back to his waiting vehicles which then took him to the Rock and Roll Hall of Fame for his speech.

As the President left the room General Hickman picked up the phone and simply said, "Go on all targets."

JUNE 4, 2018

MONDAY

As the sun burst over the horizon Special Forces, National Guard and Virginia State Police SWAT officers were moving into Washington DC. The Islamic State troops had used vehicles that were disabled as a result of the EMP to blockade a number of roadways and highways leading into the city. Each time American troops approached the blockades they were met with automatic weapons fire and rocket propelled grenades. It was a tedious trek into the city but at each stop they were able to defeat the ambushing forces. All morning and afternoon these isolated and small battles continued making progress slow. By five in the afternoon gunfire and explosions could be heard in various places around the city but the black IS flag still flew above the Capital and the White House.

In Knob Noster Missouri, a different kind of roar could be heard. A low rumble could be heard all over the small town as a result of the fifteen B-2 bombers preparing to launch from Whiteman Air Force Base. As the bombers left the base the residents watched the flying wings swoop low over the town. It was not unusual to see three or four of the bombers to lift off on missions but today was different because fifteen of the unique planes were on their way to targets. What the residents did not know was that each plane carried 40,000 pounds of bombs and missiles.

In England refueling tanker planes were being pumped full of fuel for a rendezvous with the B-2s in a few hours. The bomber crews would fly for seven hours to reach their targets.

JUNE 4, 2018

11:00 PM
MEMPHIS, TENNESSEE

TJ had given his stump speech to encourage supporters in Nashville, Tennessee, and was now catching some sleep as the train arrived in Memphis. As the train came to a stop it was immediately invaded by military brass including General Hickman. They quickly revamped the communications car of the train and began working on keeping track of current information. About twenty minutes elapsed before General Hickman turned to the secret service agent. "Agent, we will need the President present as we are about to have some major operations kick off."

The agent left the communications car and returned ten minutes later with TJ. The president appeared to still be trying to wake up as he entered the car and appeared slightly disoriented by all the changes that took place so quickly. "General, I really need to get some sleep tonight what is going on?"

"Sir, the attacks we discussed in Cleveland are about to occur and I thought it was best that you were present to get a first-hand update on the action."

TJ walked to a chair in the corner of the train car near the rear door. As he sat down he pulled out a handkerchief and blew his nose and then gave a large long yawn. As he sat down he looked toward the military officers who continued to work and paid little attention to the president. He then turned to General Hickman and said, "Okay, General, what is going on?"

"Well first of all, sir, we now have control of much of the outskirts of Washington but it is still a slow haul. All of the main government buildings and a number of embassies are in control of the Islamic State and they are defending these positions with their best troops. There are several other attacks about to take place however that are relatively certain to cause a response from the Russians. The units are in position and about to launch the attack."

"Okay, give me the rundown."

"In about ten minutes three submarines in the Mediterranean, the South Dakota, Illinois, and Colorado, will fire Tomahawk Cruise missiles at the main Russian base in Israel. At the same time two submarines in the Persian Gulf, the Hawaii and the Jimmy Carter, will fire their Tomahawks at Russian positions and bases in Iran, Syria and Israel. Each missile is carrying a conventional warhead equal to one thousand pounds of TNT. After the missiles detonate the base in Israel will be attacked by A-10 Warthogs that have orders to destroy anything mechanical that is moving. During this attack C5 transport aircraft will be bringing in a Marine invasion force. They will land at Beirut Lebanon and Haifa Israel. The Beirut units have already landed and are currently in convoy to the Russian base. The units going in at Haifa will be landing in few minutes. Both groups will converge on the Russians following the A-10s and we intend to take that force out of action.

Within the next ten or fifteen minutes three submarines in the Baltic Sea, the New Hampshire, New Mexico, and Missouri, will fire their Tomahawk missiles at the Russian Space Center in Archangelsk. We have contacted Finland and received permission to overfly their country with the missiles. We also have a number of attack submarines that are hunting for Russian Naval vessels in the Atlantic.

It is going to cost us a couple of billion dollars but by noon today we should have completed inflicting serious permanent damage to the Russian military and space program.

We also are aware of troop movements toward the ports of Gdansk, Poland, Kaliningrad, Russia, and Rostock, Germany. We currently have B-2 bombers in the air heading to those ports to destroy them and to destroy any Russian convoys that are detected prior to their arrival. We believe that the consequences of these combined attacks will discourage any Russian movement into Mexico. In fact, we believe that this attack will cripple the Russian military severely.

The two men then sat silently for nearly ten minutes when the first reports began to come into the communications center. Major Combs approached the two and noticed how both looked very uneasy. "General Hickman, we are receiving the first reports."

"Very good, so what is the news?"

"The A-10 pilots are reporting that the Russian base in Israel is totally destroyed. They indicated that there were very few targets left for them and that the cruise missiles had been devastating. The Marine convoys are still an hour away so the A-10s will remain in the area to watch for any activity on the base. We also have unconfirmed reports that the space center has also received devastating damage but we know of at least four missiles that were destroyed by Russian air defenses. The B-2s will be on target within twenty minutes."

TJ stood up and motioned for his personal agent that he was ready to leave. "General, Major, it appears that everything is in good shape with your leadership. I have to get some sleep before my next speech later on this morning. Please make sure that my residence in DC is ready for me to arrive in two or three days." A big smile crossed TJ's face as he turned and walked toward the door.

JUNE 5, 2018

10:30 AM
WASHINGTON D.C.

Marine Gunnery Sergeant Greg Hackborn was leading thirty Marine Raiders in an effort to take the White House back. As they approached the north lawn Hackborn could already observe at least five armed soldiers roaming the north lawn area. There was a considerable amount of open lawn to cross before they could enter the building and unless they could eliminate the troops on patrol it would be a suicide mission to approach.

The Marines made their way down H Street NW by using the cars parked along the side and in the street for cover. The cars had not moved for nearly a year as their electrical systems burnt up during the EMP. As they reached Jackson Parkway Hackborn sent a sniper and spotter to get on the roof of St. Johns Church to oversee the assault. The next stop was the front of the White House Visitors Center. Hackborn sent two more snipers and two more spotters to the roof of this building. Hackborn's mind was now racing trying to adjust his plan of attack. He was now about to storm the White House with 24 Raiders against a force that he had no real idea of the numbers, equipment, or skill level of one of the best defended buildings in America. If those inside knew how to use the built-in defenses, Hackborn knew he would be in for a tough fight and he was sure that the Islamic forces did not use anyone but their best for this mission.

Hackborn moved into a position behind a broken down pickup truck, taking out his field glasses he slowly took in the whole scene on the north side of the White House. The iron fence was missing and the lawn was torn up with military vehicles parked at various locations on the north lawn. He counted five guards wondering in different locations, all were armed with automatic rifles and two of them also had rocket propelled grenade launchers. As he looked at the building itself the first thing he noticed was that the north doors were missing. Was that a booby trap or an easy entrance? He also noted that a number of the windows on various levels were gone and it appeared that explosives had caused a number of large gaping holes in the structure. Flying from the roof was the black flag of the Islamic State. He had to decide quickly how to approach the structure.

Hackborn sat on the pavement with his back against the front right wheel of the Ford F-150 he was using for cover. He didn't see anyone on the roof but if they were there they might be able to spot him and at least in his present position he had the engine block to slow or stop the bullet. Reaching down on his belt Hackborn retrieved his radio and raised it close to his face. "White Horse One are you in position?"

"Affirmative White Horse. I see two snipers on the roof and five guards on the ground."

"White Horse two and three are you in position?"

"Affirmative. We can see the five on the ground but have no targets on the roof."

"Clear. Stand by."

Hackborn contemplated how to conduct the assault to keep his Marines alive but to take out the enemy. It was almost noon. They would expect an assault at dusk or overnight but not in the middle of the day. With any luck they will be eating or praying at noon so that would be when the attack begins.

"White Horse One at noon take out the roof targets. White Horse Two and Three at noon take out the ground targets."

Each unit replied affirmative. Hackborn then passed the word along to the rest of the Raiders that at 12:01, the attack was on. Everyone checked their equipment and made sure their magazines were full while they waited for the sign to go. At exactly noon three shots rang out from all three positions. Hackborn gave the signal and all of the Raiders began to run to the northwest corner of the White House. A large gaping hole now existed where a large window once stood. The Marines entered the White House through the hole not chancing any traps waiting at the door. Once inside they split into six teams of four Raiders each and began a room to room search of the structure. Each of their weapons were equipped with suppressors and their orders were to eliminate the enemy, not to take prisoners. It was one in the afternoon when the teams had completed their sweeps of the White House. None of the Americans were injured but there was a total of 56 enemy lying dead throughout the building.

Hackborn reached into his backpack and pulled out an American flag and handed it to one of the Raiders. "Replace that damn black flag on the roof now."

He then reached into his pocket and pulled out a cell phone. He quickly dialed a number and when the phone was answered he simply said, "Sir, the White House is ours. No casualties among U S forces."

In the Oman Embassy Saud was talking on the phone in the library as Abdul returned after locking Ladner in a detention space downstairs. Saud placed the phone back in the cradle and calmly stood up before picking up a chair and throwing it across the room. Abdul stood in the door and did not say a word because he had seen Saud become angry before and he realized that something was very wrong.

As Saud turned he noticed Abdul standing in the door. "Pack up all of the important records and destroy everything else. Place the records in the back of the van and make sure this happens quickly."

"Right away, sir, but can I ask has something changed?"

"The Americans have a force in Washington and they have retaken the presidential palace. We have to move before they completely cut us off. There is a plane about to land at the airport in Baltimore and we must meet it and leave the area before we are captured. It would appear that they are becoming more successful in retaking their country. The damn Russians failed to hold their end of our agreement."

Abdul quickly located his other agents and they began to gather the materials they needed to take with them. The shredding machines were going as quickly as possible. The tapes of the Ladner interviews were all placed in locked diplomatic pouches. As soon as the records were packed and loaded in the van Abdul calmly walked through the structure shooting all of the employees as he and Saud prepared to leave. He forgot about Ladner in the cell downstairs as they pulled out of the embassy grounds and headed toward the airport in Baltimore.

JUNE 5, 2018

9:00AM
MOSCOW, RUSSIA

President Gryzlovski was nervously going through the papers on his desk and placing them in the order that he wanted to present them to Vladimir. Early reports of the morning's activity appeared to be devastating and the president looked for something promising to report. So far there was nothing. He knew that Vladimir was already angry because he believed the United States would collapse but even though it appeared they were on the verge of doing just that, they had come back and were close to being in full control of their country.

It would appear that America was mounting an all-out campaign to defeat the Russians. He now had reports of attacks on their positions in Israel, in port cities where Russian vessels were docked, and most devastatingly in Archangelsk where the space port and missile defense center were located. He also had early reports that as many as 35,000 troops had been killed or wounded in the attacks.

A loud knock came from his office door and almost immediately the door opened and in walked Ivan, Vladimir's aide.

"The Emperor is requesting a briefing on the military status this morning. He is hearing reports of numerous attacks on our positions and is concerned you have not briefed him yet today."

Gryzlovski took a deep breath while looking down on the papers on his desk. "Yes, Ivan, I have been trying to assemble the most up to date information. I will accompany you directly."

Dmitry gathered the papers on his desk and followed Ivan out of the office. He dreaded each step up the stairs to the Emperor's office. Ivan opened the office door and announced the arrival of the President.

Vladimir turned around and walked over to his desk while motioning Dmitry into the office. "Please have a seat. I have heard nothing good about the world situation this morning and I was counting on you to provide me with some updated information, perhaps some good information as well?

Dmitry swallowed hard and then began the rundown of the morning's events. As he explained the problems that had occurred Vladimir's face went from stern and concerned to one of anger and disgust.

Vladimir with the palms of both hands flat on his desk stood and shouted; "Where were our intelligence people? How did the Americans pull this operation off without us receiving any warning? I would have thought our Muslim friends would have kept them so occupied that they would not be able to put this type of operation together. Still I underestimate these western cowboys and now they make me appear a fool!"

Vladimir turned his back on Dmitry and walked across the room. His anger was obvious but who would he direct it at?

Dmitry was worried about who would pay the price because he was without a doubt that people would soon disappear to be forgotten. He did not want to be one of those people.

Dmitry sat silently for several minutes, not sure what to say under the circumstances. Finally, Vladimir turned around and walked back to the desk. His face had returned to its normal color and he had regained his composure.

After taking a deep breath Vladimir calmly stated, "I will correct our intelligence problem. You, Dmitry, need to make sure our invasion force is dispatched on time.

"Sir, I thought it would be best to delay that activity for a while since we have lost so many troops recently."

"You think that advisable, do you?"

"Yes, sir."

"Well, I do not share your thoughts regarding this situation. I need to punish the United States and remove them from my side like the thorn they have become. With Archangelsk not operational I am limited to how I can strike back. So the invasion is to be accomplished without delay. As short of troops as we are, they have even less at their disposal. Do you fully understand what it is that I am saying, Dmitry?"

"Yes, I do, sir. Would you like to hear what has been prepared to dispatch to the Mexican American border, sir?"

"I would like to hear what you are planning and I trust it will meet my approval."

"We have two AN-224s and three Airbus 380s in Kiev preparing to transport the Fourth Army to Chihuahua Mexico. The planes will carry the initial invasion force including the 131st Motor Rifles, the 10th Tank Division, and the 21st Reconnaissance Unit. The transports will be carrying 20 tanks, 50 APCs, 2 portable short range missile launch vehicles, and 35,000 troops all under the command of Colonel General Anatoly Galen. They are currently assembling in Kiev and should be ready to transport in several days. The Mexican President has indicated he will evacuate the area around the airport and will offer no resistance."

"Will just five planes be enough to transport such a large force?"

"The AN-224 is the world's largest transport sir, as you undoubtedly know, and it can carry 600 thousand pounds of cargo each. There are only two operational and we have both awaiting this troop movement. The Air Bus 380 is the next largest civilian air transport. Together they will be able to transport this force quickly. We are making arrangements for midair refueling for all aircraft. Once they land and offload they will quickly return to Kiev to make additional trips as needed. In addition, they will be escorted by fighter aircraft and we will have two missile cruisers in the Gulf of Mexico for additional assistance."

"So the plan is to enter American soil from the Mexican border?"

"That is correct, sir. We will take out several air bases that are located close to the border and then use these bases as forward bases for our own units and aircraft. We will not make the mistakes of the Muslims."

Vladimir stood looking at a map which indicated the troop movements. "It looks like a good plan, Dmitry, but I hope you are sure that the Mexicans did not tip off the Americans because if we send this force into a trap it would be devastating."

"We will be prepared for all scenarios, sir."

"Dmitry, I believe you forgot one important piece of information regarding the attack on Archangelsk. During the missile attack Professor Shotkovich was killed and the special missile he was working on was destroyed. Did the Americans know about this project or did they simply get lucky? I will have to think hard about that."

JUNE 5, 2018

9:30 PM
BALTIMORE-WASHINGTON
INTERNATIONAL AIRPORT

Abdul and Saud were in the front seat of the van as it sped down Aviation Drive. The trip had been interesting as they passed numerous convoys of military vehicles and witnessed large numbers of state and county police units establishing checkpoints. They had been fortunate to miss all of the checkpoints and were almost to the plane. As Abdul made a right turn on Aronson Street he began looking for Henderson Flight Services where the plane was supposed to wait for them.

As they drove around the corner of the building they saw a Gulfstream G-650 being loaded and refueled in front of the hangar. They drove to the rear of the plane and exited calling to the men working at the location in Arabic to remove the boxes of records and computers and load them onto the plane. As they turned and walked toward the plane a man wearing a pilot's uniform greeted them.

"Good evening. I am Hadid and I will be your pilot tonight. We will be flying at about 42,000 feet to London, and we should arrive there at about two tomorrow morning. After we refuel we will be able to resume our flight to Baghdad or where ever you wish to fly."

Saud looked at the man and then asked him, "Are you Muslim?"

Hadid replied, "Yes, does that make a difference?"

"No, I am glad you are." With that Saud and Abdul boarded the plane and got settled in.

As the doors were closed and sealed Hadid walked back to his two passengers. "I wanted you to know that the FAA has issued an order forbidding any private flights for the next two days. I understand the urgency of your travel so I am going to try to leave without permission. Obviously no one at this airport has the capability to stop us and I am hoping that the military is much too busy to worry about a Gulfstream leaving a busy airport. Usually private planes from the location are carrying politicians or CEOs so I don't believe they will be much of a problem."

Saud nodded and replied, "Very good. I believe we will try to sleep on the way to London."

The engines of the plane roared to life and the plane began to move. It was a long trip down the taxi way to the end of the operational runway. The pilot had left the radio playing over the cabin speakers so there would be no surprises for his passengers. The first thing they heard was "Gulfstream 650 you are not cleared to taxi. We have no flight plan. Please turn at the next exit and return to your gate." The message was repeated several times but the plane continued down the taxi way.

As they reached the end of the taxi way Saud observed a Delta airliner land and then the Gulfstream started up and turned onto the runway itself.

Once again the radio traffic began "Gulfstream 650 you are not cleared for takeoff. Stop the plane at your current location, shut down the engines. Police units are on their way to your location. Prepare to have them come on board."

In the tower the controller shouted for the supervisor and explained what was going on. At about the same time they received a phone call from the Airport Police reporting that units at the hangar where this plane originated are reporting that the occupants are Middle Eastern males and they had boxes of material marked Secret and White House. The supervisor immediately called Air Defense Command.

Hadid shouted back, "Buckle up this could get risky!"

The plane began to move and quickly gained speed before suddenly leaving the ground and traveling nearly straight up to gain altitude quickly.

At Langley Air Force Base the first group of pilots to serve alert duty at this location in nearly a year were playing cards. A klaxon horn sounded and was followed by "Scramble, Scramble, Scramble, Charlie 1, Charlie 2, Charlie 3, Charlie 4, possible Islamic State command target just departed BWI, coordinates will be fed to your computers."

Within two minutes all four pilots had entered their aircraft and had their helmets on. As the canopy's closed they quickly moved onto the runway and received clearance. Within five minutes of the card game all four F-18s were airborne and their afterburners engaged.

As the Gulfstream passed over the Delaware coast they had already passed an altitude of 28,000 feet. The pilot turned to a more northerly course and shut off the planes lights and transponder. After placing the plane on autopilot Hadid walked back into the cabin. "Gentlemen, I don't think we are out of the woods quite yet but I don't believe that the U S air defenses are back to normal yet so I have taken steps to make it more difficult to find us and I am confident that we will be clear of any problems soon."

Eight minutes later Hadid was relaxing in his seat and allowing the autopilot to do the work. The plane was flying at 40,000 feet and was nearly 85 miles off the coast of New York. All he could see were stars as the sky was black. Suddenly a voice came over the radio that got his immediate attention. "Gulfstream 650 this is the United States Air Force. We need to have a chat sir and we would appreciate you turning on your lights and transponder. You then need to make a left turn to a new course I will give you when I see you will comply."

Hadid sat up straight and started checking the windows around the cockpit but he could see nothing. He shouted out to the cabin, "Did you both hear that? We have Air Force planes moving toward us but I can't see them and they are not on my radar. What would you like me to do?"

"We will not return so I think you should see how fast you can fly this plane."

Hadid fastened his seatbelt and gripped the wheel as he switched off the autopilot and quietly prayed to Allah. He realized the foolishness in what he was about to do and could only hope the Air Force would not pursue them much further. The warning sounded two additional times before he finally replied. "I am no longer in U.S. air space so I would respectfully ask you boys to back off so I can continue to my destination."

"Gulfstream we are about to cause you to divert your destination. You can turn your lights and transponder on and begin that left turn and we will direct you to a location in the U S or you can maintain your current situation and we will divert your destination to the Atlantic Ocean. Your call, sir."

Hadid placed the plane into a dive for about 2000 feet and then an immediate climb of 5000 feet but did not comply with the fighter pilot's request. Again that voice came across the radio. "Sir, this is the United States Air Force and we will destroy your plane in 30 seconds should you not comply. We will give your crash location to the Coast Guard."

"Charlie 1 to Langley. Do you have our position recorded?"

"Affirmative Charlie 1."

"Langley, you will want to start rescue units toward this location. Do we have permission to eliminate this threat?"

"You are cleared for weapons hot. Target has been confirmed as Islamic State Command and a high risk."

"Charlie 1 to Langley – missiles away."

Thirty five seconds passed and then the radio traffic began again. "Target destroyed Langley, we will continue to circle the area until rescue units arrive. Target was destroyed at flight level 420, sir, there will be no survivors."

There was no doubt that air defenses were operational and effective on the east coast.

JUNE 8, 2018

9:00 AM
MOSCOW, RUSSIA

Vladimir was having a bad morning already. How could things go this far off track? Every success seemed to be followed by a major defeat somewhere else. This has to end if we are to end successfully we have to get on track. That is why he had called a meeting this morning with the president and the chief of intelligence and now they were late.

A loud knock on the door and Vladimir looked up from his desk and shouted, "Enter!"

As the door to the lavish office opened President Dmitry Gryzlovski entered quickly followed closely by General Leo Stanski of the Military Intelligence Department. They both walked quickly to the front of Vladimir's desk where they stood at attention. Vladimir looking down at his desk ignored them for a full thirty seconds. Finally, he looked up at them and said, "Mr. President and General please take a seat."

As they sat down Vladimir's tone became harsh. "As you are both undoubtedly aware we have suffered several setbacks recently that are primarily the result of poor intelligence. Now I must confide that my first thoughts included replacing the intelligence staff with those more capable at accomplishing my goals. Then President Gryzlovski assured me that the staff I currently have at my disposal is excellent and not likely to be overshadowed by a new staff. He informs me that the recent American victories were the result of bad information from the Islamic State and a matter of luck by the Americans. He convinced me that the Americans good fortune will be short lived and that as new information is developed we will once again be victorious. So General Stanski do you also share this great optimism?"

The general's body stiffened as he understood the message very clearly and now worried that his results would most likely effect not only his life but others as well. "Yes, sir, I do share his optimism on this matter and I believe there will be some major changes ahead. Even as we speak I am ready to bring you information that will change the course of our activities, sir."

With this comment Vladimir's eyes opened wide and he leaned back in his chair. He clasped his hands across his chest and looked at Gryzlovski and then directly into the eyes of Stanski. "Well, please, general, do not hesitate to enlighten me."

Stanski opened the portfolio that he had placed on his lap. He looked down at the information in the folder for a moment and then looked back at the Emperor. "I believe I know this information well enough not to read it but I may have to confirm some facts. I will start with the United States and then proceed to the real problem."

Vladimir brought his chair back to the upright position and placed his hands flat on his desk at this comment. "What do you mean the real problem General?"

"Sir, the United States is no longer our immediate concern. If you would allow me just a moment to explain."

Vladimir sat back again and motioned with his hands for Stanski to continue.

"Sir, the Americans latest effort was an all-out effort to make us stand down from future aggression. Economically they spent several billion dollars to put these operations into action. They have overextended their resources and have little hope of putting together any type of major operation for at least six months or more. They have been able to push the Islamic forces out of their country but there are several hundred cells left behind that will harass the Americans as they attempt to reestablish complete control. Currently the U.S. is in firm control in the western and southwestern areas or their country but are only tentatively in control of much of the rest of the nation. There is indications that the Mexican president has alerted the Americans in reference to our proposed operation next week. The Americans have sent two submarines and a missile equipped destroyer to the Gulf of Mexico. They have also moved reserve troops and tactical fighter aircraft into the southwest theater of operations. An artillery division appears to be moving from the New York area toward the south. All of these indicate that the invasion we have currently planned may experience much greater difficulty than we originally expected."

Vladimir leaned forward and replied, "You have confirmed this information how?"

"Sir, we have satellite pictures and we have two agents in high ranking positions within their military."

"Fine, now what was the real problem as you described it?"

"Sir, the Islamic forces were a poor ally due to incompetence and now our Chinese ally appear to be branching out on their own. I believe that they have looked at our recent setbacks and decided to take advantage of them to change the picture so to speak."

Vladimir still starring straight into the general's eyes replied, "What leads you to this conclusion, general?"

"In the last three days there have been many unusual troop movements within the People's Republic of China. The Western Military Region has suddenly changed their headquarters location from Chengdu to the southwest border of Kazakhstan in a rural area south of Sumbe. Satellite surveillance indicates as many as 35,000 troops from the Chinese 54th Army are being transported to that area. We also know that the 2nd Artillery Corp has suddenly started to move from the coast area west toward this region as well. We have also determined that as many as 12 mobile missile launchers equipped with Dong-Feng 26 missiles have been loaded on board rail cars and are moving west. The DF-26 missiles can reach 3000 to 5000 miles. Finally, sir we have agents in the area that confirm that General Fan Chang, Commander of the Western Military Region, and General Wei Lei, Commander of the Chinese Army Rocket Force have both been seen at the new makeshift headquarters."

Vladimir sat silently for more than a minute and then said, "So what is your conclusion, general?"

"It is our belief, sir, that the Chinese Army is preparing to invade Kazakhstan with the intent to move across the state and seize the Baikonor Cosmodrome. The repairs on the complex are well underway and it can be operational again on a limited basis within three months and we believe that the Chinese wish to seize it as a possible launch facility for their rockets against us."

Vladimir clenched his teeth and the anger was visible on his face. He looked down at the maps and information that had been placed on his desk by the general. He then stood up and walked across the room to the windows and simply stared outside. He was hoping to see some fresh snow but this was June and even in Moscow that was unusual. When he turned back toward the desk Vladimir said, "Well, it would appear that your Emperor has a fault when he is picking allies. Maybe I should have played nice with the Americans since they seem to be the only ones outside of Russia with heart and courage. So what course of action would you suggest?"

General Stanski spoke up. "Sir, if it meets with your approval of course, the military council believes that we can attack America in a few months but our immediate concern should be stopping the Chinese and eliminating them as a threat. We would suggest that the forces preparing in Kiev should be taken to Baikonor at once to defend that location and we should begin bombing runs of the Chinese positions along the Kazakhstan border."

Vladimir wrote some notes on a pad of paper on his desk then looked up. "General, proceed with your plans. Do not lose sight of my ultimate goals of bringing the world to a status of peace with our empire ruling the world. The Americans will have to be dealt with sooner or later so also keep that in mind."

"Thank you, sir. We will prepare the troops and begin our activity against the Chinese as soon as possible, most likely by the twelfth. In addition, the bombing runs will begin within seventy-two hours. We will never lose sight of the ultimate goals sir and we will have additional troops enter training so that we will be ready to take the U.S. when the time is right."

Dmitry and General Stanski stood up and left the room quickly. There was much to accomplish and little time to accomplish it in.

JUNE 8, 2018

1:00 PM
WASHINGTON D.C.

The new Marine One was comfortable and somewhat quieter than the previous flights that TJ had made. Still the headphones and microphone were necessary to hold any type of conversation. TJ had been advised to return to the White House in a low key and quiet manner but he believed it was necessary to show the press his arrival in a way that displayed complete confidence in the situation.

The sky was a beautiful shade of blue this afternoon and the temperature was nearly 80 degrees. TJ could see the stress on General Hickman's face and the secret service personnel on board. All of which were keeping careful watch on the buildings and areas below. As TJ looked out of the window what he saw was most certainly a war zone. Overturned cars and pickup trucks blocking roadways, buildings that had burned, and numerous craters where explosives had been detonated and lives have been lost. A tear came to TJ's eye when he first observed the Capital which had been considerably damaged and burned. He could see bodies still strewn on the ground along the National Mall, TJ wondered if they were the good guys or the bad guys, more likely a mixture of both.

The helicopter began to slow and descend and TJ could see the White House just ahead. The military and police had the grounds completely surrounded. The damage to the building was significant but the structure appeared, at least from this vantage point, to be secured and stable. TJ looked over to General Hickman and asked, "Have you located Don yet?"

General Hickman looked a little distressed at the question. "Sir, we know that a few months ago he was in Baltimore but he apparently left the area and headed to D.C. for some unknown reason. We believe that he was captured and taken to some location for interrogation. Even though police service has been restored to nearly all of D.C. there are still areas where searches are underway building to building. We also have not searched any of the embassy compounds in the area because we didn't want to cause any diplomatic problems."

TJ replied, "General, start with the embassies of those nations that we have broken diplomatic ties with and search them carefully. You have permission to seize any records that are found in those structures as well. Then you can search the compounds of any other nation but don't seize records unless you have additional information that would cause you to believe that they were working with the enemy."

"Yes, sir. As soon as we land I will get those searches under way."

As Marine One was just passing 200 feet from the ground it suddenly began to move forward and gain altitude. There was a great deal of chatter and the secret service personnel were gathered close to and around the president.

TJ shouted, "What is going on?"

General Hickman answered, "Someone fired a rocket propelled grenade from the road but it never got close to us. There will be a quick search of the grounds and traffic will be stopped before we make another approach. The press was moved back toward the White House for their own protection. I guess you will definitely get the coverage you were looking for when we planned this event."

TJ didn't smile but simply nodded his head.

After about twenty minutes of circling around the area, Marine One landed. As the steps came down the president and General Hickman stepped off the aircraft and were immediately surrounded by secret service and military guards. Everyone jogged toward the White House and then disappeared from view. No questions were answered and no comments made.

TJ was glad to be back in the White House and as he walked down the familiar halls he listened as aides were barking out instructions and information about what was working and what was not. As he reached the Oval Office he walked inside and found that the exterior doors and windows were all gone and in their place were boards and plywood. Much of the office was suffering fire and smoke damage so he would have to find a new location to work until repairs could be made. The Resolute Desk, however, was still standing with no damage at all. It did smell like smoke but amazingly it was the one piece of furniture that had come through this trial unscathed. An aide touched TJ on the shoulder and as the president turned around he began to explain.

"Mr. President, if you will accompany me, sir, I will take you to your temporary office. It is down one level and has been prepared for your arrival. Your secretary has a schedule of phone calls for you today so the foreign leaders will be reassured that the United States is back in business."

As TJ was moving down the hall he stopped short and snapped around. "General Hickman, are the preparations in the south ready?"

Hickman had been a few yards away and behind the president but reassured the president's concern. "Yes, sir, we are on schedule. We now have reason to believe however that after the fifth we might not have to worry about that particular operation."

The President nodded and turned back around to continue to his new office.

It was 8:30 PM when three SWAT vehicles pulled into the courtyard of the Embassy of Oman. Ten soldiers jumped out of the first vehicle while twenty-six police officers from the D.C. Police and the Maryland State Police emptied out of the other two vehicles. As they spread out across the grounds they searched for any explosives or booby traps that might had been left behind. Finding none they attempted to make contact with anyone inside but no one came to the door and the building had no visible lights on inside. Four police officers carried a battering ram to the front door and as the remaining officers took defensive positions they broke the door down.

As soon as they searched the first few rooms it was obvious that this facility had been used for interrogations and holding prisoners. As they finished the second floor and the main floor a team of four moved to the steps leading downstairs to the basement. As they entered the basement it was dark and none of the lights seemed to work. The hall they entered had doors on each side and each door was locked. They called for the battering ram to be brought downstairs and forced open the first room's door. Inside they found a bed and a desk but nothing else.

As the team started toward the next room they heard a moan and someone weakly call for help. Sgt. Kennedy motioned to the third room down and he and Officer Snider grabbed the battering ram and moved to the door. The second time they hit the door it came open and as soon as they entered they saw a man on the floor who appeared to be beaten and only semiconscious. They gave the man some water as he sat up and became more alert.

"Sir, we are with the Metropolitan Police. Who are you?"

"Officer, I am Don Ladner and I was being held as a prisoner here. I am the White House Chief of Staff. Can you help me?"

"Yes, we can. Are you able to get up the stairs on your own or should we carry you?"

"I'll make it. Are the Islamists still in this area?"

"Sir, the entire country is free again and the last of the Islamist faction has fled. The White House is again occupied by the President."

"Help me get to a location where I can get cleaned up and then I need to get to the White House."

"Understood, sir."

JUNE 9, 2018

SATURDAY—9:00 AM
SITUATION ROOM

The new situation room was half the size of the one that had been used when this group last met. No flat screen televisions hanging on the wall or computers streaming the most up to date information along the walls. Instead there was simply a rectangular table with very plain chairs spaced around the table.

In the past each member of the cabinet would have several aids accompanying them and the room would be crowded with people hanging on every word spoken. Today was much different. The individuals waiting for the president included: Secretary of State Stephen Lambert, National Security Agency Director Jacob Owens, Central Intelligence Agency Director Lawrence Williams, Homeland Security Secretary Patrick Simmons, Attorney General Deborah O'Connor, and the Chairman of the Joint Chiefs General William Hickman. There were some quiet friendly greetings and then everyone sat at the table going over their presentations and notes while waiting for the arrival of the president.

As the door began to open everyone in the room immediately rose to their feet. President Samuels entered the room and immediately said, "Take your seats everyone."

It was then that everyone realized that he was accompanied by his Chief of Staff Don Ladner. As the president sat down Don grabbed a chair from against the wall and sat at the corner of the table to the right of TJ.

"I want to thank you all for being here today and for your service over this last very trying year that we have all survived. I especially want to thank Don for being here. For those who don't know Don spent much of the past year hiding from the Islamic forces and most recently as a prisoner of that same group. I have not had an opportunity to speak at length with Don about his experience but I appreciate the fact he made it here today after only being rescued from a cell last night."

"Now ladies and gentlemen, we have a war being fought all around us and we are fortunate to have secured our nation but that does not end the conflict in the world nor does it end the danger to our homeland. This is why I have called this meeting so we can begin to take whatever steps are necessary to secure our liberty."

"I am sorry that no one from the Treasury is here but we will have to assume that the funds needed for this effort will be found. Let's start with Larry from CIA."

CIA Director Larry Williams opened his portfolio on the table and stood up to make his presentation to the group. "As we meet this morning the world is much different than it was the last time we met in the White House. There are currently three villain states and those are obviously Russia, China, and the Islamic State. So here is the breakdown as how the world's status is as of this moment." He then reached down on the desk and picked up a stack of papers that he began to pass around the table. The top piece of paper was a world map.

The sheet underneath the map showed how most of the countries of the world were now aligned. No one was overly surprised but it still took a few moments for the full weight of the new world order to sink in to each of the people viewing the material.

The following countries are annexed, occupied, and/or controlled by:

Russia	China	Islamic State
Venezuela	North Korea	Spain/Portugal
France	South Korea	All North Africa
Germany/Austria	Thailand	Turkey
Italy	Cambodia	Arabian Pen. Except Israel
Poland/Czech/ Slovakia	Myanmar	Iran/Pakistan/ Afghanistan
Hungary/Romania	Vietnam	Malaysia/Indonesia
Greece/Bulgaria/ Balkan States		Philippines
Baltic States		

Director Williams continued, "As you can see while we have been attempting to regain control of our nation the aggressor nations have been very busy expanding their hold on the world. India has been fighting off both the Islamic State and China while we have been busy. Australia has been taking on China and the Islamists as well. It seems that Russia has been pulling the strings but the bulk of the fighting has been done by others in the group. Russia has been leading the charge but is not our only foe."

345

"We have finally received a bit of luck. We now have intelligence that indicates that this group may be coming apart at the seams. China is massing troops on the border of Kazakhstan and it would appear they are within days of an invasion into this Russian state. You will all recall that we struck the Baikonur Space Center with a nuclear strike that destroyed the facility. Well since that time the Russians made it a top priority to repair and restore this facility to make sure that they could service the space station and have strike capability to the west coast. The Chinese have apparently watched these repairs with great interest as well. Now we believe that they are preparing to seize this facility for their own use. We have also developed sources inside the Kremlin who indicate the Russians are aware of this and are taking measures to stop China. We know that the invasion force that Russia was going to use to enter the southern U. S. is currently awaiting deployment at Kiev. They will be flown into Mexico and we currently have forces prepared to destroy the aircraft as they are arriving. It now appears however if our source is correct that those forces will be deployed to Baikonur instead to fight the Chinese. It is the recommendation of the CIA to allow the fight between Russia and China to go on without any interference. We should instead concentrate on eliminating their stronghold on Venezuela and in assisting India, South Africa, Japan and other countries who are still free but in danger of falling."

Secretary Lambert then spoke up, "It looks to me like we should concentrate on keeping our country safe and it may be time to write off Europe and Asia for the time being. The Russians are spread thin so why not take steps to kick them out of the Western Hemisphere and keep the west safe from these who only know hate and violence."

For several minutes the discussion continued about the best course of action for the United States to take in order to end the threat to the country. Everyone thought they knew what was best but there were several different solutions being kicked around. Lambert and Deborah O'Connor argued for securing the country and the hemisphere while the intelligence chiefs and Patrick Simmons argued to strike Russia while they were spread so thin and fighting to protect their own country. TJ allowed the discussion to continue for over ten minutes without interruption and then stopped it to consider his decision on the course of action. Only two people remained silent during the discussion, Don and General Hickman.

"Before I make my decision I would like to ask you General Hickman for your feelings toward this situation."

"Sir, it is my opinion that we should not pursue the attack of Russia at this time. It is true they are spread thin and have sustained large losses but they are still a formidable force and we have sustained numerous losses as well. We have lost more than 22,000 personnel, billions of dollars of aircraft and naval vessels as well as the expenditure of much of our other weapons systems. We could also use some time to replenish our supplies and train additional personnel. We need to plan the defense of Japan as there is little doubt it will be attacked by China in the near future. We also need to work with Great Britain to assist South Africa and India in their positions. We also have 15,000 troops in Israel assisting with security and they may need to be reassigned unless Israel requests we maintain security in and around the north. Of course sir your decision will be accomplished regardless."

TJ turned to Don and asked the same question regarding the situation. "I have to agree with General Hickman, sir. We pay him to run the military command and I feel he knows his situation better than any of the rest of us."

At this point Patrick Simmons interrupted. "You know that sounds good but I got to tell you all this is a world war and we have to take the advantage while we can or we could be in serious trouble. I want to point out a fact that no one has mentioned thus far. Since this conflict started, when you consider the small pox crisis, the terror attacks in New York, Washington, and the other major cities, the deaths as a result of the power crisis, and last but not least the Islamic invasion and subsequent occupation do any of you know the estimated losses of American citizens?" No one said a word. "The latest estimate of total deaths of American citizens since the beginning of this conflict is 4.2 million. The Islamic State has attacked Russia in Turkey and Syria and now China is attacking them along the Kazakhstan border. We need to drive it home before that egomaniac in Moscow can catch his breath."

Looking at TJ, I could see the facts regarding the enormous number of deaths of Americans had touched him deeply. TJ acknowledged the information and then turned to the Attorney General.

"Deborah, I realize the justices of the Supreme Court have all been executed, but is the rest of the courts still intact and is the Justice Department able to operate as normal?"

O'Connor took a few moments to consider her answer but replied, "We will get by but I have to tell you that we have some serious problems and justice will function at a very slow pace for some time to come."

TJ leaned back in his chair and turned toward Don Ladner. He stared for nearly a minute before turning back to the rest of the group and leaning forward in his chair again.

"I am confused. I see both points of view and I agree that both perspectives have merit. I also am aware that we have used a great deal of ordinance in getting to the point we are at today. Our munitions plants are behind in turning out additional munitions and I believe it is more dangerous to go into battle without sufficient weapons and ammunition. We need to make manufacturing weapons and weapons systems a priority. We also need to establish immediate transportation of aid to the eastern areas of the country that have been most devastated by the recent occupation of the Islamic forces. I want to begin partial martial law in the areas that are in the worse condition. That should include military units searching and keeping a close watch on all Muslim property."

Immediately Deborah O'Connor stood up and said, "Mr. President, I am sorry but you can't do that. You realize or should that we cannot violate their freedom of religion and this will certainly violate the Posse Comitatus Act."

The President looked over to her and replied, "Madam Attorney General, I believe I have violated that a long time ago with the military operations all over the country and I do not believe the act is valid at a time of war. The troops won't keep them from practicing their religion but we will keep them from

349

practicing illegal activities that could be considered hostile acts against our nation."

"Sir, I still respectfully object to these actions because these acts will not bring peace but could lead to greater protests and disturbances,"

"I will take your objection in consideration and if you feel you can't live with my decision then I will consider your resignation as well. I am sorry to be harsh but it was the hands off attitude which greatly contributed to the situation we found ourselves in to begin with. We are at war and when we are at war we need to protect the rights of our citizens but we also need to protect the sovereignty of our country. It was easy in the 1980's to look back at Franklin Roosevelt's internment camps for the Japanese and say he was wrong. But I consider now if I had done the same thing with the Muslim population as soon as this all began it might have been much more difficult for their take-over of half of our country. There is no doubt that the majority of the enemy fighters responsible for the occupation of our country recently were either citizens converted to the radical Muslim effort or were immigrants who were legally allowed into our country in the past ten years. Sometimes the rights we enjoy need to be enforced with responsibility and it doesn't hurt if the population has a healthy respect and yes maybe a little fear of the government."

Everyone in the room sat stunned at this statement. Don looked at the President like he was a stranger because these statements were very different from anything he has said in the past. Don wondered if this was shock, fear or a combination because TJ's attitude was definitely changing and Don feared where he was headed.

As the group stood up and started for the door the president suddenly said, "Wait a minute everyone. You know I just remembered something from Revolutionary War history. Some of the greatest damage to the British came at the hands of a group of guerrilla fighters striking with a small group in surprise situations. We may not defeat our enemies with this style of warfare but I think we can inflict a lot of damage and harassment. So General Hickman can you arrange for our Special Forces, Rangers, Seals, and Raiders to conduct a series of raids at various places that will cause our enemies some distress? I would also like for you to arrange several submarines with missile capability to report to locations where they will be able to fire missiles at Baikonur and to wait for instructions."

As the meeting broke up everyone in the room was assigned tasks to be completed before they met again. As the others left the room Don and the president sat silently facing each other. Both seemed to be carefully studying the other. After several minutes President Samuels was the first to speak.

"Do you want to talk about it?"

"Now is not the right time, sir. If you would permit me, sir, can I ask you a personal question?"

"You have never needed my permission before, that's why I keep you around."

"Well, Mr. President, we have only been back together now a couple of hours but it has been long enough for me to see you have changed. Your attitude toward all of this evil going on seems to have become more harsh and aggressive and I don't believe it is something that I like in the leader of my country."

TJ leaned back in his chair and gazed at Don with a stare that seemed to penetrate right through him. TJ noted that Don's face was bruised and his face had become drawn. Don appeared to have lost a great deal of weight and the clothes he was wearing that at one time were snug now hung on him like they were several sizes too large. At the same time Don was considering the changes in the President's appearance. His dark hair had become nearly completely white. His face appeared rough and a number of wrinkles had appeared. TJ had aged considerably in the short time the pair had been separated.

TJ placed his hands on the table in front of him and cleared his throat. "Don, we have both been through a lot in the past year. Yes, you are right I have changed and I imagine you have as well. I don't know what you experienced but I am sure you experienced terror first hand and I can see you were beaten and mistreated. I wasn't living a life of parties and travel over the same period though I am sure it was quite different than your experience. I was sending people out to die. Loyal soldiers, sailors, airmen, and Marines were handling missions that I authorized and that left some of them dead, others injured and all of them emotionally changed. I also failed to protect some of our citizens because I didn't act quickly enough or made the wrong decision. Believe me I lay awake some nights reconsidering the decisions I have made. So if I am more harsh and aggressive it is a result of these experiences. Politics and world opinion are not as important as saving the citizens of this country and keeping our country free and sovereign. Far too often over the last several decades we have all put too much time into politics and power and not enough in what is really important."

The two men sat silently for several minutes. No one was now left in the room as the secret service agents waited just outside the door. TJ then continued, "I don't know if anyone has told you yet but I had the Madison County Sheriff check on your family and they are safe and well. Your wife is eager to come back to DC but she was told it would still be a little while before it was safe to return. They were also advised of your rescue and we can arrange for you to speak to them in about an hour. Phone service is a little sketchy so we are having some special arrangements made so you can speak to them whenever you like but a crew is still working on completing the task."

"Thank you, sir. I appreciate that and I am ashamed to think that I wasn't being insistent about that right away but I could only think about getting to the White House to contribute to helping the country."

"I know that and that is one of the things I appreciate most about you. I want you to know that over the next months, possibly years, this country will do some things that I never imaged that we would ever be part of when I took the oath of office. While you were out of touch, we have used tactical nuclear weapons against Russia and China and Russia has used them against us. You heard during the briefing that more than 4 million of our citizens have died in the year and a half we have been in office. I am ashamed of that information. Yet, I don't know if I would have reacted differently if it would have been better or worse. The Iranians sent those nuclear explosions that caused the EMP. The real reason so many perished as a result though was the fact that over the years so many have become dependent on the government. People who relied on government welfare instead of working to provide for their family. I am not talking about those who were unable to work but those who simply didn't want to work. People who have forgotten how to make a meal from scratch because it is too easy to heat and serve or pick up fast food. Many could not provide for their families because they have forgotten how to provide. That is because the government got too involved in people's lives and provided too much. We should have been more worried about the nation's defense and less about stuffing everyone's pockets."

"I don't know about that TJ, while I was hiding in Baltimore I saw a lot of people doing as well as they could to provide. You have to remember the sharia police were terrorists on patrol in the neighborhoods and everyday survival was tough without worrying about bringing home the bacon."

TJ smiled and shook his head. Don was very serious but he was obviously very fatigued and TJ could only imagine what he had been through over the past year. "Don if you would like to take some time off or leave the administration I will certainly understand and there will be no hard feelings."

Don looked at him with a slight smile on his face and shook his head. "No, sir. I signed on to this what seems to have been a long time ago now and I am not running just because things get bad. I will consider what you have said and try to get up to date on what has been happening but I am going to give you the guidance I think is appropriate, like always."

As the two men stood up TJ stepped in front of Don and gave him a hug. "Don, you can remain on my staff as long as you want.

I respect your judgment even though I might disagree with you a little more now since my experience this past year has really changed my state of mind on many things. We have a great deal of work to do now. We have paid with the blood of many patriots for our country's liberty and now it is time to gain some justice. Let's go put an end to this war. I think it might be a real sign of goodwill to get the emperor a new suit, maybe something in an orange jumpsuit."

BOOK SUMMARY

This is the continuation of the story of President T J Samuels and his Chief of Staff Don Ladner as their administration struggles with perils that threaten the very existence of the United States. In *The Cost of Freedom* the duo had to deal with epidemics, terrorism, military and economic aggression, and an assassination attempt while still attempting to establish their office. In the end of *The Cost of Freedom* Iran detonates nuclear weapons over the eastern portion of the U.S. causing massive power failures. In *The Cost of Liberty* TJ and Don are separated as Russia, China, Iran, and the Islamic Caliphate have now teamed up and have started an all-out attack on the United States and her allies. The story follows as President Samuels leads the military to defeat the invaders and to restore liberty to our country.